I DREAM OF
DRAGONS

ASHLYN CHASE

sourcebooks
casablanca

Published by Sourcebooks Casablanca, an imprint of Sourcebooks, Inc.
P.O. Box 4410, Naperville, Illinois 60567-4410
(630) 961-3900
Fax: (630) 961-2168
www.sourcebooks.com

Printed and bound in Canada.
MBP 10 9 8 7 6 5 4 3 2 1

To my loving family

I know, I know. That's boring.
Everybody thanks their family and I usually
try to be more creative than that.
Oh well.

This is dedicated to my loving family.

So there.

Chapter 1

THUNK.

"What the hell?" Rory picked himself up off the floor beside his bed, rubbing his sore hip. Three little men dressed in green stood by his bedroom door. One of them looked angry, and one of them was trying not to snigger. The other seemed like a neutral party with his hands in his pockets.

"Rory Arish, you're being charged with theft," the angry one said.

Rory blinked and stared at the little men. "Theft, is it? What is it I'm accused of stealin'?"

"Me gold. All of it."

Rory scratched his head. "Lucky, is it?" he asked, trying to put names to their faces.

"If you're talkin' about me name, it's Clancy. Lucky is me brother." The man with his hands in his pockets withdrew one and waved at Rory. "If you're talkin' about your day, I'd say this is the unluckiest of your whole long life."

The red-haired man who'd been trying not to laugh moved his hand, uncovering his short, red beard. "Nobody steals from leprechauns and gets away with it—no matter how big you are."

Rory sighed. "There's been some kind of misunderstandin'. I haven't stolen anyone's gold—or anythin' else for that matter. Do you see anythin' worth stealin' here?" He spread his arms wide and swiveled, indicating the whole sparsely furnished room.

He and his sisters had moved from the crumbling castle on the cliffs to the caretakers' cottage a few years ago. The Arishes hadn't changed much, leaving the cottage about the same as when the caretakers had lived and died there.

"Move your arse, dragon," the angry one said. "March me to my gold!"

"I will not march anywhere," Rory said. "Especially when I don't know where your feckin' gold is."

Clancy balled his fists.

The gleeful one muttered, "Oh, *that* did it."

"Be quiet, Shamus," Clancy snapped. Then he focused his attention on Rory again. "Mr. Arish, I'm trying to be reasonable, but I'm not a patient man. Now, admit what you did and rectify the situation, or we'll be forced to end the treaty between our people."

Clad only in their nightgowns, Rory's sisters appeared in the doorway behind the little people. Well…behind and over them. Even at five foot five or six, the girls were easily twice the size of a leprechaun.

"What's goin' on here?" his sister Chloe mumbled as she rubbed the sleep out of her green eyes.

"Apparently I'm bein' accused of a crime I did not commit," Rory said.

His youngest sister, Shannon, piped up. "Crime? What crime?"

Clancy whirled on the girls. "Mayhaps one of you took me gold. We don't know if it was your brother or not, but it had to be the work of a dragon. Who else would have the strength to move it?"

Rory rubbed his forehead. "Now wait a minute. Me sisters didn't steal anythin' either."

Clancy pointed a finger at Rory. "Then you admit it! It was you!"

"I admit nothin'." Rory's annoyance was growing now. *Fine, wake me up. Accuse me of something I didn't do. But don't go pointin' fingers at me sisters!*

"It could have been any one of you…or all of you colludin' together. The punishment will be meted out to each and every one until somebody confesses."

"Punishment?" Chloe laughed. "I'd like to see you try."

Oh shite. That was probably the worst thing she could have said, but leave it to Chloe to poke the beast. Even though they came in pint-sized packages, leprechauns possessed powerful magic. Either Chloe didn't remember the treaty because it was signed when she was so young, or she didn't believe the leprechauns held the power to protect or expose her and her family. But how else could their castle in the cliffs have remained hidden from humans for all these centuries?

It's true that the bulk of it was built underground with entrances in the cliff's caves, but there was one turret, like a large rook on a chess board, in plain view. It was for the few humans brave enough to live near dragons, plus the royals had posted a sentry there to see anyone coming by land.

Clancy narrowed his eyes at the three of them. Finally he said, "You leave me no choice! You will march to the cliffs—now. If one of you doesn't confess to the crime before you get there, I will cast you into the ocean and ban you from ever setting foot in Ireland again! In fact, you'll be banned from all of the United Kingdom!"

"Ha!" Chloe said. "Nobody's goin' anywhere."

Moments later, dragons Rory, Shannon, and Chloe Arish bobbed on a raft just off the western shore of County Kerry, Ireland. They had been marched, against their will, to the edge of the cliff, and then magically transported to the raft. Rory, head of his clan, shook his fist at the little bastards dancing and laughing on the cliff above them, right next to his clan's, now fully exposed, ancient castle.

"You can't do this! Our people have coexisted for centuries. You're violatin' the treaty signed by our ancestors," he roared.

Shamus, the most gleeful of the three redheaded leprechauns, yelled back, "We don't know who signed it. We weren't there. Maybe the dragons forged our ancestors' signatures."

"Why would they do that?" Chloe yelled. "We were protectin' each other. Your people with your magic and our clan with our might."

"Ha! Look who's high and mighty now," Shamus called back.

"This is the same as murder!" Chloe yelled. "You know damn well this raft won't make it across the ocean. And look what you're doin' to me poor sister." She pointed to Shannon, who was lying prostrate on the lashed logs, sobbing. The bastards hadn't even let her say good-bye to Finn, her intended.

Lucky elbowed Shamus. "She has a point."

"About a cryin' sister? Who cares?"

"Not that. About the murder part."

Clancy stroked his red and gray beard. "We should give them a worthy craft and enough food so they don't starve."

Shamus's delight faded fast. "You're not goin' soft on these thieves, are you? They took your gold!"

Clancy leaned in close, but Rory's superior hearing picked up what he thought was an admission of doubt.

"We didn't take your damn gold!" he shouted at the leprechauns.

"You did," Shamus insisted. "Who else but a dragon would covet our treasure?"

Rory set his hands on his hips. "Oh, I don't know… Everyone?"

Clancy finally addressed his brothers. "They should be kept alive. If we don't find the gold in their keep, we may have to question them some more."

Lucky nodded. "I agree."

Suddenly the dragons found themselves on a fishing trawler, probably large enough to make it across the sea *if* the weather was perfect the whole way.

"There. Now they have safe transport and all the fish they can catch," Clancy said.

Shamus let out a defeated sigh. "All right. I guess that covers our arses."

"Speaking of arses," Rory yelled. "What do you little shites expect us to do for money *if* we land somewhere? Are we to sleep on the docks and starve while we look for work?"

Lucky said, "Certainly not." He turned to Shamus. "There are women aboard."

Shamus rolled his eyes. "Fine."

A dozen plastic cards rained down on the dragons, bouncing off their heads.

"Ow," Chloe said. "You bastards did that on purpose." Then she picked up one of the credit cards and yelled, "Who the hell is Molly McGuire?"

Shamus shrugged. "Does it matter? She probably won't miss it for a bit."

"Surely we can have the treasure that you know belongs to us," Shannon pleaded. "All you're missin' is gold. We have jewels, antiques, silver…"

Clancy nodded and a jewelry box, a harp, and a silver tea set appeared on the deck. Suddenly the ship dropped a little lower in the water.

"There's more below," Lucky yelled.

"And what about our clothes?" Chloe called out. "Our instruments!"

Clancy tossed his hands in the air and said, "Do I have to do everythin'?"

"I'll get them," Lucky said. A moment later three small suitcases and their only means of income, the family's musical instruments, landed on the deck.

Suddenly Shannon shimmered off her nightgown, shifted into her dragon form, and flew at the cliff. Before either Rory or Chloe could scold her for changing in broad daylight, she bounced off an invisible barrier and landed in the sea, stunned.

Chloe gasped. "Shannon! Are you all right?"

A curl of steam escaped Shannon's nostril. She righted herself and flew at the cliff a second time—faster, as if speed could break through whatever magic barrier the leprechauns had created. Again she bounced off and landed in the ocean. This time her eyes were closed and her wings were limp as she floated on her back.

"You killed our sister," Rory yelled. He shimmered

off his sweat pants, shifted into dragon form, and swooped down to grab his precious baby sister's limp body. After he'd returned her to the deck of the boat, he shifted back to human form and put his ear to the soft part of Shannon's scaly chest, listening for one of her two heartbeats. Rory always suspected her softer nature was a result of those two hearts. He sometimes wondered if she'd also gotten Chloe's, because his middle sister could seem a bit heartless at times.

He heard a few faint beats. *Ah, she's alive. Damn good thing too, or I'd have found some way around that barrier to toast every one of the little bastards and serve them as s'mores.*

Lucky and Clancy leaned over the cliff and appeared somewhat concerned. Shamus folded his arms and said, "If she's dead, she killed herself."

Clancy whirled on Shamus. "Shut your trap."

Shamus's back stiffened, but he didn't argue with his brother.

Shannon groaned and her eyes fluttered open. She shifted back to human form and touched her head. "Ow."

"What were you thinkin', Sister?" Chloe demanded as she rushed over with a tarp. "I get the first time, but the second? Did the first bump on the head knock the sense right out of you?"

"Finn… I need to see Finn. How will he know what happened? He'll think I've just run off and left him."

"No, he won't," Chloe said. "You two have been joined at the hip since you were sixteen. He'll know somethin' is drastically wrong."

"And that's supposed to comfort me?" Shannon moaned.

Chloe just held up the tarp while her sister shimmered back into her nightgown. Soon Shannon was bawling again.

Rory began fiddling with the controls in hopes of getting the boat started. He couldn't stand it when his sister cried. "Try to buck up, Shannon. I'll do whatever I can to get this vessel to a safe haven. From there you can call or text or whatever you want to do to him."

Chloe smirked. "I'm sure she wants to do more than that to him."

Shannon let out another wail, and Rory narrowed his eyes at his middle sibling. "You're not helpin', Chloe."

At last the engine caught and he pushed the throttle forward. They sped west. Eventually he'd figure out all the controls and possibly even hit Iceland.

Amber, along with the other flight attendants, boarded the plane from Iceland back to Boston.

She noticed a young red-haired woman with her adorable daughter—the resemblance couldn't be missed—seated in her first class section. She thought she heard the woman explaining to the little girl that she could have snapped her fingers and they would have been home instantly, but she didn't want the girl to think that was the normal way to get around. The little girl nodded and her big, blue eyes didn't blink, as if the explanation made perfect sense to her. It made no sense to Amber. She must have misheard.

All was going well until a bit of turbulence ruffled the plane's smooth path. Amber happened to be standing next to the mother's and daughter's seats.

The captain announced over the intercom, "Sorry, folks. We seem to be experiencing a bit of rough air."

At that moment the plane bounced dramatically, and Amber braced herself against the passenger's seat and the overhead bin. "No shit," she muttered under her breath.

The woman giggled as if she had superior senses and had heard the inappropriate comment over the engine noise.

"Please be sure your seat belts are fastened," the captain continued. "Flight attendants, return to your seats and buckle up. It's going to be a bit bumpy."

The woman seemed to be glancing at Amber a little more frequently than she'd expect—almost sizing her up.

Oh well… If she's going to lodge a complaint against me, it will take the decision to quit or not to quit out of my hands.

Amber had been flying the skies ambivalently for several years. After high school, she didn't have the money for college and didn't know what her major would be, so rather than waste her mother's hard-earned money, she'd decided to go to work. She figured as soon as she discovered her passion, she could go to college and by then she'd have a bunch of money saved up for school. Maybe it was time…

A few hours later they made a safe landing in Boston, and Amber waited to deplane after everyone else.

The redheaded woman and the adorable mini-version waited until they were the very last passengers.

Amber couldn't help being a little nervous. Did the woman want to confront her on her language? Chastise her privately? She wouldn't blame her. The little girl didn't act as if she'd heard Amber swear, but using such language was inappropriate nonetheless. Yup, it was definitely time to think about finding another job. This had to be a sign of burnout.

Ah, good. The woman walked past her and disappeared into the crowd. Amber headed for the airport bathroom.

When she entered the restroom, the redhead was washing her hands.

Damn it. She hadn't seen the woman enter, but here she was. It must be a sign. Amber would have to stop trying to avoid her and just face the consequences of her stupid remark. Or maybe the woman wasn't upset at all. Better to keep it casual and see.

"What a beautiful little girl," Amber said.

"Thank you," the woman responded, beaming. "She really is a great kid."

The little one giggled and nodded.

"Awww… What's her name?"

"Nikki," the mom said. "And I'm Brandee." She extended her clean and now dry hand to shake Amber's, so she grasped Brandee's hand for a firm handshake. Brandee held it a little longer than necessary and a smile spread slowly across her face.

What was that about?

A woman in a crisp business suit joined them and stood next to Brandee. She seemed happy to see her. It wasn't unusual for travelers to bump into people they knew at the airport, so Amber didn't think anything of it until…

"I might have a candidate for you," Brandee whispered to the businesswoman, who gave Brandee a smile.

"Do you now?"

Brandee tipped her head in Amber's direction, but

she was already on her way to a stall. When she turned to close the door, she saw the woman pat Brandee on the head and say, "Good girl. I'll take it from here."

Brandee didn't seem to mind the businesswoman's condescending behavior. She simply smiled and then addressed her child. "Is it time for a diaper change, honey?" The toddler nodded.

When Amber exited the stall, Brandee and Nikki were gone and the businesswoman was washing her hands...again. *Must be a germophobe.*

She observed the flight attendant until Amber glanced at her and smiled. She was about to tell the woman to have a good day when suddenly she wasn't there. The whole restroom wasn't there! *She* wasn't there. She was surrounded by fog and couldn't see a thing. *Where the hell am I?* Suddenly the fog cleared and she was alone. What. Just. Happened?

———

By some miracle, Rory and his sisters made it to Iceland. They stood on the shore, shivering.

"I need a coat and a place to get out of this wind," Shannon said.

"We're *all* freezin' our arses off," Chloe snapped.

"At least the leprechauns gave us our clothes," Rory said. "Jeans and sweaters are better than your nighties."

Chloe snorted. "To be sure. That was so feckin' nice of them."

Rory's teeth chattered. "I spotted a cave off the south coast. We have our own source of heat. If the place is private, we'll be safe. But as far as coats are concerned, if either of you have a suggestion, let me know."

Chloe withdrew a credit card from her pocket. "I think Molly wants to go shopping."

"You can't!" Shannon said. "That doesn't belong to you."

"These are desperate times, Shannon," Chloe hissed out between her teeth.

"Look," Rory said. "The credit card company will reimburse Molly. I'll take Shannon to the cave I saw, and we'll get a fire going. Then I'll come looking for you. Where do you think you'll be, Chloe?"

Chloe bit out some kind of oath. "Sure. Baby our baby sister some more. That'll really help her get along in the real world."

Rory set his hands on his hips. "If we split the chores, we'll be comfortable that much sooner. We can stand here and freeze to death while we argue, or you can give me a direction so I can come find you in an hour or so."

"Fine," Chloe said. "I'm headin' northwest." She pointed a long, un-manicured finger at a building right off the dock. The place looked like a clothing store with all sorts of outerwear in the window. "What size do you wear?"

Rory rolled his eyes. "Just buy me somethin' extra large and extra warm."

"You can send Molly whatever-her-surname-is a check to cover it later," Shannon said.

Chloe laughed. "Yeah, I'll do that. I'll be sure to give the police our return address too."

Rory grabbed Shannon's wrist before he started swearing and marched off in the opposite direction.

"You don't have to drag me, Brother. I'll come willin'ly."

He sighed and let go. "Thank the gods. At least one of you can be reasoned with."

Although she had to run to keep up with his long-legged strides, she caught him. "Chloe's not really upset. It's just her way."

"Well, I'm glad you're not that way. Otherwise I'd probably be an only child by now."

Shannon laughed.

It was the first smile he'd seen from her since they'd left Ireland. He knew she hadn't accepted their lot. It was just a tiny truce until the next hissy fit. He also knew better than to bring up the name Finn Kelley or she'd begin to weep again.

How had he wound up in these circumstances? They hadn't done a thing. The leprechauns had hidden their castle from humans for centuries, and for the last several years, while the castle crumbled, they'd lived quietly in a cottage on the property far down the dead-end road, away from prying eyes. Suddenly they had been dragged from their beds and marched against their will to the castle, which was no longer hidden but standing—albeit crumbling—on the cliffs in plain sight of the ocean.

When the leprechauns demanded that the Arishes produce the gold that was missing from their coffers, Rory had thought they were daft. Apparently Clancy had discovered the loss and had convinced his cronies that the dragons' love of treasure had finally gotten the better of them.

When Rory and Shannon reached a deserted part of the coast, they found a large cave in which they could make a temporary home. Dragons weren't seafaring creatures, and he was glad to be on solid ground.

Shannon's face screwed up and tears glistened in her eyes.

Oh no. Here we go again.

"What it is, luv?" he asked, dreading the answer.

"Is this what we've come to? Livin' in some hard, dank cave? I miss our peat fire and our lovely flowered sofa. There's not a comfortable spot anywhere."

Rory patted her shoulder. "I need you to make it as homey as you can. Just start a small fire and keep it goin'. I have to fetch Chloe and show her where we are. The three of us will put our heads together and come up with a better plan soon."

Shannon's gaze dropped to her feet. Not long after, he saw shivers rack her body and a fat teardrop fall from her chin. "I hope Chloe gets us some warm boots—I mean Molly."

He thought he'd pull out every last hair on his head if he had to put up with his soggy sister much longer. "Come now. How can you start a fire if you're just goin' to put it out with tears?"

She took a few deep breaths, and he could see her trying to wrestle herself under control.

"That's a good lass. I'm sure you can warm the place a bit while I'm gone. Just don't move so Chloe and I can find you again."

"What am I supposed to keep burnin', Brother? Rock?"

Do I have to think of everything? "We'll bring some newspapers and branches back as fuel and give you a break. For now, just heat the rocks with your breath. That may produce a bit of steam, but it'll warm the air."

Shannon sighed, then took a deep breath and blew out a stream of fire aimed at the cave walls.

"Perfect. Thank you, luv. I'm off to fetch our surly sister." Before Shannon could think of anything else to complain about, he rushed out the cave's entrance and picked his way over the rocks toward town.

―⁓―

When Amber finally reappeared in the airport bathroom, she mumbled, "I need a vacation," and went straight home to her apartment building. She thought she must be losing her mind and just wanted to lie down—after having a much-needed drink. She ignored the sign on the elevator door. It was in small print and official look-ing. Probably a notice that the landlord would be spray-ing for bugs or something. She spied the same notice on each tenant's door as she fumbled with her keys. At last she let herself into her apartment and grabbed the notice, intending to look at it later.

Dropping her flight bags outside the kitchen, she took a mini wine bottle out of the fridge. She glanced at the notice on her way to the living room and almost dropped the bottle of Chardonnay. *An eviction notice?*

"Holy mother!"

"I'm right behind you," a woman said.

That caused Amber to whirl around and repeat her-self loudly.

"I said, I'm right here!" The white-robed woman slapped her hands over her ears. She had long, thick, white hair. Her robe was belted with a vine of ivy.

"Hey, aren't you the woman from the bathroom? Brandee's friend?"

"Sheesh. Have a seat, girlie. We need to talk."

Amber hesitated. The woman wasn't carrying a

weapon, although something about her seemed ulti-
mately threatening. As if to affirm the feeling, thunder
rolled and the sky outside the window darkened. Amber
stumbled backward and sat down hard on her beige
linen sofa.

"That's better," the woman said. "I'm aware you
don't know who I am, so I'll introduce myself. I don't
have time for your disbelief, so save me the trouble and
just go with it. Okay?"

Amber nodded woodenly.

"Good. The truth is, I'm Mother Nature. Those who
know me call me either Goddess or Gaia. That's my title
and my name. You should begin by calling me Mother
Nature just to drive the point home."

Amber heard herself say, "Okaaay," in a little girl's
voice.

"Here's the good news. You won't have to worry
about that eviction notice. I have a job for you, and it
won't matter where you live. I know you're getting dis-
enchanted with your job as a flight attendant."

"How do you know that?"

The woman smirked. "Really? I'm Mother freakin'
Nature. I know just about everything. If people were
meant to fly, I'd have given them wings." She cocked her
head. "Why did you become a flight attendant anyway?"

"I—uh. I wanted to see the world."

"You mean you wanted to meet a rich businessman
and do a little traveling before you settled down. How's
that working out for you?"

Her back went up. "He doesn't have to be rich."

"But relationships with men in general aren't working out. Right?"

She sighed. "Not so much. Every guy I get close to assumes I'm cheating when I'm out of the country and eventually finds a 'backup,' or he's just pissed because I'm not around much. And don't even get me started on the pilots."

"So, how much of the world have you actually seen?"

Amber grimaced. "Pretty much the same routes over and over again."

"So...nothing but the same foreign airports and hotels."

"You may have a point."

"Of course I have a point. I always have a point. I don't chat with mortals for my health. Speaking of my health, spreading all that noxious jet fuel so close to my ozone layer is the most harmful thing you can possibly do to me. Did you know that?"

"Um...not really. Is it?"

"Sheesh. How dumb can you be? You blow a hole in my sunscreen, and you think I won't get burned?"

"I...I don't really make those decisions."

Mother Nature—or whoever she was—rolled her eyes and sat down on the chair across from Amber. "Well, you may be able to make those decisions in the future. I want you to be my muse of air travel."

Amber's brows shot up. "Huh? You're offering me a job? As a...what?"

Mother Nature sighed. "I knew you'd have a hard time believing all of this. I gave you a trusting nature but also let you develop some healthy skepticism. Look, I don't have time for a lot of chitchat. I'm in desperate need of some modern muses. You've met one of them. Brandee is my muse of photography."

"I thought muses took care of poetry, dance, and other ancient arts."

The woman let out a groan. "Exactly. The original nine are useless in this modern age. I tried to get them to reeducate themselves in new areas, but it's been a disaster. I can't even get the muse of epic poetry to rap—or the muse of dance to crunk. And forget music videos! Technology is way beyond them, and I can't wait any longer for my muses to catch up. Your world is growing too fast. Therefore, I've begun the task of finding a few modern muses. Any questions so far?"

"Um, yeah. A few hundred…"

"Well, hold your questions for the end. I'll pair you with someone who'll have the patience to answer them. In other words, not me."

Amber wanted to throw her hands in the air and say something sarcastic, but she still wasn't sure how crazy this woman was—or *she* was, so she just waited.

"Good. Let's see now…" Gaia tapped her chin as if deep in thought. "I know. I'll pair you with Brandee since you've already met and she's the one who recommended you. That way if she doesn't answer your questions thoroughly and you screw up, it'll be all her fault."

This insulting woman was trying Amber's patience. How could she get the woman out of her apartment? Playing along with her was getting old.

"Why don't you give me Brandee's phone number? I'll give her a call sometime."

Mother Nature frowned. "You still doubt me, glitter tits?"

"What did you call me?"

"Look down."

Amber was bare to the midriff and indeed her breasts were covered in glitter. She gasped and tried to cover herself with her hands.

"Relax. I've seen them before. Heck, I made them."

Amber was struck dumb. If she protested, who knew what the woman…or goddess would do. "I—I…"

"Mother Nature" waved her hand and Amber was wearing her uniform blouse again. Then the self-proclaimed deity shouted at the ceiling. "Brandee, I need you."

To Amber's shock, the redheaded passenger from her latest flight appeared in her living room.

"Yes, Gaia. How may I be of service?"

"This is the woman you recommended for the muse of air travel, correct?"

Brandee turned to Amber and offered a friendly smile. "Yes. I liked her immediately and thought she'd fit in with the others. As you know, I can sense people's innate goodness and I'm a very good judge of character."

"Well, she needs to talk to someone like you or Bliss. One of my modern muses. She has questions, and I don't have the time or patience to answer them."

"Understood," was all Brandee said.

The woman looked relieved and smiled. "Thank you. As a reward for your help, I'll send an influential customer to visit your gallery tomorrow."

Brandee grinned. "Thanks! We're doing quite well, but I can always use more—"

"Yeah, yeah." Mother Nature disappeared into thin air and Amber let out the breath she'd been holding in a whoosh.

"Where did she go?"

Brandee shrugged. "Who knows? She likes to hang out in her office building on State Street, but she could be creating natural disasters like floods or earthquakes. You just never know with her."

"Is she really…"

"Mother freakin' Nature? Yeah, she is." Brandee chuckled. "You probably pictured someone wearing rainbows as a halo and patting kittens, didn't you?"

"Well, no, but I didn't think…"

Brandee sat next to her and lowered her voice. "You didn't expect a sarcastic crone with the patience of a gnat, am I right?"

Amber chuckled. "Well, no."

"You'll get used to her. You should meet my friend Bliss."

"She mentioned something about a person named Bliss."

"Yeah. She's rather famous among us muses, having been the only one gutsy enough to refuse Mother Nature's generous offer."

"Generous offer? I never received any offer sounding remotely generous."

"Really? Huh. I guess you didn't get that far. Gaia never expects her muses to work for nothing. She rewards us handsomely—usually with our greatest desire. But Bliss…" Brandee shook her head and sighed. "She stood up to Gaia and said no, even with a money tree growing right in the middle of her man's living room."

"Her man, huh?" Amber mumbled.

"Ah!" Brandee said. "Could that be what you want? A boyfriend?"

Amber snorted. "No. I've had plenty of boyfriends. What I'd like is a stable guy who won't cheat on me. I don't seem to be having much luck finding one of those."

Brandee set a sympathetic hand on Amber's shoulder. "We've all had our share of failed romances. If it isn't one thing, it's another, but both Bliss and I are now 'blissfully' happy, if you'll pardon the pun. So, if what you want is a wonderful, faithful man to love, marry, or live with, I'll mention that to the goddess."

"No! Oh no. Don't do that yet. I think I'm leaning more toward Bliss's reaction than yours."

Brandee raised her eyebrows. Then she smiled and seemed to relax. "You know what might be a good idea? If we include Bliss in this conversation."

"Ugh. Please don't. I can't stand any more people popping into my living room. I'm quite convinced I'm losing my mind as it is."

"Oh. Sorry. I forgot what it was like in the beginning. Of course your head is probably spinning. It's natural to doubt your own eyes and sanity. Why don't I give you my address on Beacon Hill? Let the dust settle and meet me there tomorrow. I'll ask Bliss to stop by, *if* you actually show."

"If I say I'll be there, I'll be there. Unlike some people, I can be counted on to keep my word."

Brandee winked. "I knew I liked you for a reason. Here's my gallery." She held out an empty hand, and then a business card appeared.

"Whoa. Neat trick."

"I'm not a magician. I'm a minor goddess. Take the card and turn it over."

Amber did as she was told. Brandee pointed to the card and a different address appeared on the blank side. "That's my home address and phone number on Mount Vernon Street."

"Fancy."

"We like it. Come by at noon. I take a lunch hour at home to feed the baby. Although I'll be meeting an important client tomorrow, and I don't know the time yet." She waved away the thought. "If I'm late, my husband will let you in."

"Are you sure? I mean, Mother Nature mentioned someone influential kind of offhandedly. Do you think it'll really happen?"

"She keeps her word too. Well, except when she's bellowing empty threats. Then we're just as happy she doesn't." Brandee smirked. "Well, toodles. I'm going to meet my family for lunch and will leave you to doubt your sanity for another twenty-four hours."

And with that, she disappeared.

Amber *was* doubting her sanity. Just out of curiosity, she peaked down the front of her blouse. "Yup. Covered in glitter. I'll be dammed."

Chapter 2

HOURS LATER RORY AND CHLOE FINALLY RETURNED TO the cave, wearing warm, puffy coats. They were chatting and chuckling as if nothing in the world was bothering them. Chloe carried a big tote bag filled with purchases, and Rory held newspapers and kindling.

Shannon's face was red and her expression livid. Then, as if she flicked a switch, she greeted them with a toothy smile. "Oh, did you have a nice time out there?" she asked with syrupy sweetness.

"It wasn't too bad," Rory said, carefully.

His youngest sister marched over to him, ripped the newspaper and logs out of his hands, and tossed them into the fire pit she had made with lava rocks.

Just as she ignited the paper with her breath, Chloe yelled, "Stop! That was our newspaper. We needed that to find jobs and such."

Shannon's jaw dropped. "Why didn't you say something?"

Rory started laughing. Chloe had been leaning forward, probably to look menacing, then she reared back and burst out laughing too.

Shannon glared at them. "What's gotten into you? You're laughin' like hyenas."

Rory wiped the tears forming at the corners of his eyes and wrestled his mirth under control. "The newspaper was useless. It's in Icelandic and every word is at least eleven letters long. We can't read any of it."

Shannon glared at her sister again. "Then why did you get upset?"

Now Chloe was wiping her eyes and trying to quit laughing—unsuccessfully.

"Oh, very funny." Shannon folded her arms and mocked the two of them. "Let's make our dear sister, who's been keepin' this bloody cave warm all day, think she's done somethin' terribly wrong when she hasn't a'tall. How entertainin' would that be?"

Chloe nodded. "Pretty entertainin'." Then the two older siblings burst out laughing again.

Shannon strode outside the cave before she lost it and pummeled the two of them into kindling.

Rory came after her, carrying her parka and still chuckling. "We're sorry, Shannon."

"No, you're not."

Chloe followed. "Okay, we're not *terribly* sorry, but you should have seen your face."

Shannon shrugged into her new coat. "I've had about enough of you two. How can you laugh when we're stuck in a land where we don't know a soul and can't even speak the language? Just how are we supposed to survive?"

Rory tugged on his jacket pocket. "Not to worry. I traded our boat for some magic beans."

Chloe cracked up all over again.

"Knock it off!" Shannon yelled.

"Relax, Shannon." Rory took his sister by the shoulders and turned her back toward the cave. As they walked together, he explained. "We were late gettin' back because we sold some of the priceless antiquities that were on the boat. We found someone who spoke English, and he helped us. We were very fortunate. He gave us the name of a visiting billionaire whose appetite for rare antiques might turn our treasures into quite a pile of cash."

"Then all we need to do is convert it into American dollars," Chloe said. "The best part is that the man has a yacht and will have his crew take us to Boston."

"Boston? What's in Boston?" she asked.

"Apparently, a large Irish population," Chloe said. "We can blend in. Plus we can speak, read, and write English. If we can't get back to Ireland, it's not a bad place to be."

"But we *must* get back home," Shannon insisted.

Rory balled his fists. "We will someday—when the leprechauns discover their mistake."

"Since when have you known leprechauns to admit they made a mistake?" Shannon pointed out.

"One thing at a time," Chloe said. "First we need a decent place to live. Then we can worry about gettin' back into the little shites' good graces."

"Before that, I need to call Finn."

"Uh. We tried callin' the pub for you," Rory said. "Somehow we've been blocked from even making phone calls to Ireland."

"But we'll keep tryin'," Chloe said. "Let's go check into a hotel, and we can try to email from there."

Shannon fell silent.

There really wasn't anything more to say. With magic keeping them out of Ireland, the dragons' best hope was to find a decent place to operate from and to change the minds of those who cast the spells. If that place was

Boston, then they needed to reach their temporary home quickly. Rory and his sister would come up with plans for revenge on the way. He was already thinking of a few ideas.

———∿∿∿———

"I must be out of my mind," Amber muttered.

A second before she rang Brandee's doorbell, a tall, good-looking blond man opened the door. "You must be Amber," he said in a whisper.

"Uh, yeah."

"Sorry. I'm trying not to wake the baby." He stuck his hand out. "Nick Wolfensen, Brandee's other half."

She shook his hand. "Is Brandee around?"

"She asked me to give you a message. She said the client she told you about just arrived and she won't be able to leave the gallery for a while, but Bliss is expecting you at the Boston Uncommon Tearoom on Charles Street."

"Oh. Bliss is there now?"

"Yes. Her best friend owns the place. They're probably gabbing away."

"I see. So if I walk back down the hill to Charles Street, is it a left or…"

"Go right. There's a big teapot hanging from the sign. You can't miss it. Oh! But before you go…" He retrieved a business card and handed it to her. "She wanted you to have this."

Amber stared at the Beacon Street address on the card. "What's this?"

"I understand you need an apartment. You have an appointment with the manager, Morgaine, at two o'clock."

"Wait. How did you know?"

"Brandee didn't say. Just trust me. If she's sending you, there's a good reason. She seems to know the future sometimes."

As unsettling as that was, Amber said, "Okay. Great."

"Have fun," he said and smiled as he closed the door.

Uh, yeah. Fun. Crazy fun.

Amber headed down the hill, appreciating the gorgeous historic buildings and tree-lined cobblestone sidewalks. She wondered what it would be like to live in a pretty neighborhood like this. Her apartment building was situated among businesses and lacked any neighborhood feel at all.

When she reached Charles Street and traffic whizzed by, she felt as if she were reentering the city. The general vibe accelerated to its usual frantic pace. She had spent the previous evening scanning the real estate pages and getting depressed. Rents in this city were outrageous.

If the place on Beacon Street was as nice as most of the addresses in the area and reasonably priced, she'd snap it up. She checked her watch. Twelve thirty. Good. By keeping her schedule tight, she was allowing herself enough time to meet the modern muse, but she also had an excuse to leave if the muse tried to give her the hard sell.

She found the tearoom easily. Just as Nick had promised, a teapot dangled above the door. When she stepped in, the atmosphere was homey and lowered her stress level—slightly. She smelled baked goods and honey. The large front room held several tables with white linen tablecloths and happy diners. Mismatched bone china was set on the tables, but everything meshed in a cohesive design. Flickering candles helped illuminate the room, which added to the relaxing ambience.

A young woman with blond-highlighted hair greeted her. "Will you be having lunch?"

"I'm supposed to be meeting someone, but I'd love to order tea and a scone while I'm waiting."

The hostess swiveled back toward the cash register where a very pregnant brunette was standing. "Is this the lady you're looking for, Bliss?" she asked.

"Oh!" Amber said. "I probably should have asked for her by name since I was told… Never mind. Yes, I'm looking for her. I'm Amber," she babbled.

The brunette's smile and graceful walk, despite her advanced pregnancy, should have put Amber at ease, but knowing she was meeting a minor goddess had her more on edge than she'd realized. She mentally rolled her eyes at herself. She had met Mother freakin' Nature. Why should a minor goddess scare her?

Bliss surprised her with a warm hug…or as close as she could get to one.

"Nice to meet you, Amber. It's funny…"

"What's funny?"

"Your hair matches your name. It's Amber."

"Oh." She chuckled. "Yes, I guess it does."

"Let's sit in the back." Bliss hooked a hand around Amber's elbow and swept her over to an empty table in an out-of-the-way back corner.

Now Amber was nervous again.

"There's no need to be nervous," Bliss said.

"How did you know… Oh, never mind. You probably know everything about me."

Bliss raised her pretty, perfectly matched brows. "I

know almost nothing about you. Here. Sit and make yourself comfortable. I heard you wanted tea and a scone. I'll get us some. Any kind in particular?"

"Oh, you don't have to do that. I can wait."

"I can't. I'm starving," Bliss said. "Besides, I used to work here. They think nothing of me going to the kitchen and serving myself."

"Oh. Well, then, I'm not picky."

"Okay. I'll be back in a jiff."

While the minor goddess was gone, Amber tried to mentally shake herself. A muse giving her a hug and waiting on her wasn't at all what she'd expected, but how would she know what to expect? *Try to relax, Amber.* She felt like a pile of nerve endings, all crackling and snapping at the same time.

A few moments later, Bliss returned with a tray. She set two plates of blueberry scones and a pot of fragrant tea on the table between them.

Amber tried to appear nonchalant, which was sort of the opposite of how she felt. "So…"

Bliss smiled. "So I imagine you have some questions."

Amber laughed nervously. "I do, but I don't even know what they are yet. Thank you for taking the time to see me though."

Bliss waved away the polite nonsense. "I was excited to hear that Brandee had someone to recommend for the job. Gaia has been nagging the… Well," She lowered her voice and leaned closer. "I shouldn't speak out of turn, but the Goddess of All isn't very patient."

Amber snorted. *You think?* "I'm glad I'm meeting you, because I was told you refused the muse job at first.

Mother Nature said I'd regret it if I refused. Why is that? Did she do something awful to you?"

"Oh, heck no. She might sound threatening, but she's a pussycat, not the monster she wants you to believe she is. But just FYI, you probably shouldn't piss her off. She might whip up a blizzard just to prove a point."

"But winter is over."

"Exactly."

"She can do that?"

"She's Mother Nature. She can do pretty much anything she wants."

"That's frightening."

"Tell me about it."

Amber tried to get her heart rate under control again. "So is that why you refused?"

Bliss cringed sheepishly. "No. She doesn't scare me—anymore. I guess I'm not the most forward-thinking person sometimes. My husband is a firefighter, and there's a whole bunch more I can't tell you about him. I'll just say he had a bit of supernatural protection that kept him safe. When I was approached about the job, Gaia wanted me to be muse of the Internet."

"The whole Internet?"

"Exactly. I told her it was impossible. Rather than do a half-assed job, I just flat-out refused."

Amber took a sip of tea. "I can't say I blame you."

"Well, I hadn't anticipated my husband giving up his immortality, but he begged Mother Nature to take it away. He refused to go on living for centuries after my death. While he was human, I had to worry about everything! His job fighting fires. His commute. Heck, he could have gotten the flu or slipped in the bathtub and drowned. It was intolerable, especially knowing I could change it.

"Finally, Gaia and I were able to come to a compromise. I would become the muse of email only. Drake took back his immortality when I received mine." She looked down at her baby bump. "At least we were able to conceive while we were both human, so that much was worth the stress."

Amber tried to sort it out. "So, it was more stressful being human?"

"Absolutely," Bliss said.

"And your job?"

"I'm a greeting card designer," Bliss said. "I still enjoy that, but when I get a psychic 911 that someone is about to send an obnoxious email, I can just excuse myself for a moment if there are humans around—run to the bathroom, then pop in behind the idiot and whisper, 'You don't want to send that yet.' As soon as he or she decides to reword or just hit Delete, my job is done and I can go home."

"But with all the email and all the, pardon me, *idiots* in the world, aren't you flat-out busy all the time?"

Bliss laughed. "Brandee said I'd like you." She shook her head and sipped her tea. "It's not as bad as you'd think."

"What about those who hit the Send button before you can stop them, or do it despite your best efforts?"

Bliss shrugged. "It happens. Then they learn from the consequences of their own actions. If a person is determined to self-destruct, they'll find a way. No one can save *everyone*, especially from themselves."

"Hmmm…" Amber had been thinking that failure

wasn't an option. But all that seemed to be required was her best effort. If that weren't enough, it wouldn't be her fault.

At that moment Gaia appeared in a chair that had been vacant a moment before. Everyone in the restaurant was frozen and silent.

Bliss muttered, "Uh-oh…"

Gaia rose and didn't stop until she hovered a few inches above the floor. "Muse of email, are you out of your mind?"

"Uh…no. I may have made a tiny mistake, but I'm not insa—"

"Oh?" Gaia roared. "Tiny? Is that what you call it when you violate my number one edict?"

Amber hadn't seen this side of the goddess, and her hand shook as she raised it. "Um… May I ask a question?"

Gaia paused, then said, "You're right. You need to know what that rule is so you don't accidentally screw up—unlike this one who knows better." She pointed to Bliss with her thumb.

Can she read my mind? Now Amber was shaking visibly.

Gaia glared at Bliss. "Paranormals are *not* to reveal the paranormal world to humans without my permission. That means discussing supernatural business in public places. Conclude your business immediately and find a more appropriate place to meet."

The goddess disappeared, and normal conversation resumed among the relaxed tearoom patrons.

"Let's go." Bliss rose.

"Don't we have to pay for our order?"

"My best friend is the manager. She says my money is no good here." Bliss grinned.

Amber couldn't believe Bliss was grinning so soon after being chewed out by the most powerful being on earth. She herself was still reeling from the encounter.

"I think I know all I need to at this point," Amber said as they wound their way to the front door. *I like the idea of saying no, and I don't have a husband to worry about.*

Bliss waved to the blond behind the cash register.

"Are you sure? We can go to my house and talk. My husband is home today, but he knows all about us."

Married to a minor goddess… What must that be like?

They stepped out onto the sidewalk. "No, I'm good. Actually, I have an appointment."

Bliss looked askance at her. "Really? Or are you just scared?"

"No. I really do have an appoint—"

She felt a thump and turned around to see that a big man had bumped into her…a big, *gorgeous* man.

"Beggin' your pardon," he said. "I was payin' more attention to me map than your lovely self."

Amber adored accents and had heard quite a few in her travels. This one was decidedly Irish. But the sparkle in his blue eyes and his dark auburn hair would have given a hint about his lineage anyway. A red streak coming out of his widow's peak flopped over his forehead. Quite a unique look.

Then she noticed the two women who were with him. There was a definite family resemblance, and that red streak didn't appear as unique to him as she had thought. They all had one.

"Are you all right?" one of the women asked.

"Oh. Yes, I'm fine," Amber said when she finally realized she'd been standing there mute and staring at the hot guy. "I'm sorry. My name is Amber. Are you lost? Maybe I can help."

"Ah," the man said with a smile. "Amber is a beautiful name for a jewel such as yourself."

She grinned, completely captivated by his Irish charm. *Get hold of yourself, Amber. It's probably as much a load of blarney as any pick-up line. It just sounds better with the accent.*

"And I'm Rory. These are me sisters, Chloe and Shannon. Actually, we are a bit confused," he said. "From what we were told, Boston Uncommon is supposed to be a bar."

"A *special* bar," his sister said, implying…something.

"Let me see your map," Amber said. When she reached for it, her hand touched his and a sizzle of warmth radiated through her.

Bliss jumped in. "I think I know what you're looking for, but this isn't it—anymore. As you can see, it's now a tearoom."

"That's right," Amber said. "You used to work here. Was it a bar at one time?"

"Oh yeah. And a *special* bar for sure." Bliss winked at the guy.

Amber was a bit put out. Wasn't Bliss married? She reminded herself that it was none of her business, but flirting could lead to… *Oh, get it together, Amber. You just met these people.*

Just then, Bliss whipped out her cell phone and brought up a picture on the screen. "I think you might like to meet my husband," she said as she showed the photo to the Irish trio.

They all exclaimed about what a wonderful photo it was. What a cute couple they were. And how, yes, they'd love to meet him. Maybe they were just being polite.

"He happens to be off today, so if you'd like to come to my place, I can introduce you."

They all seemed excited about the idea. Weirdly so. *A five-way?* Amber wasn't sure what was happening, but it didn't really concern her. "I—uh… I have an appointment and should get going. It looks like Bliss has your situation in hand."

"Oh." Rory looked disappointed. "You'll not be joinin' us then?"

"Sorry." She checked her watch. "Oh dear. If I don't go right now, I'll be late." *Damn. That apartment won't be available long.* If only she had time to do both—but the place was in her favorite part of town. And considering her luck with men, this one would just disappoint her too.

She sighed. "It was nice to meet you. Welcome to America," she said lamely.

―――

"Drake!" Someone was shaking him awake. "I found more dragons," Bliss exclaimed.

Drake sat up and rubbed the sleep from his eyes. "I must still be dreaming. I thought you said something about more dragons."

"I did. Get up. They're in the living room."

"Our living room?"

She stuck a hand on her hip. "Who else's living room would I put them in?"

"I don't know. The Wolfensens'? Last I heard you were going to Brandee's house."

"I did. A lot has happened since then."

"Jeez. How long have I been asleep?" Suddenly he felt like Rip Van Winkle.

"C'mon. Hurry and get dressed. They can't wait to meet you."

"I'll be right there."

Bliss hurried out of the room as he hopped into his jeans and pulled a Boston Fire Department T-shirt over his head. He didn't think his wife was asking him to put on his Sunday best…just get decent.

Striding out into the hall, he heard some accented voices coming from their spacious living room.

The minute he walked in, he knew Bliss was right. A large man with a solid build rose, and two young women remained seated. A red streak grew from their widow's peaks, subtly marking them as dragons from the same clan. Drake sported a similar yellow streak, but unfortunately, he was the last of the Cameron clan. He had thought he was one of the last dragons on earth.

"I'll be damned," he muttered.

"Hopefully not from simply layin' eyes on the likes of us," said the stranger. He stuck out his hand and Drake shook it.

"Irish?" he asked.

"From Ballyhoo. County Kerry. I'm Rory Arish. These are me sisters, Chloe and Shannon."

"I'm sorry. I should have made proper introductions," Bliss said.

Drake smirked. "When have you ever been proper?"

She rolled her eyes. "This is my husband, Drake

Cameron, in all his sarcastic glory. Drake, meet Rory, Chloe, and Shannon Arish."

"Arish." Drake rubbed his chin. "That's an ancient Gaelic name."

"I'm surprised you know that."

"I'm originally from Scotland." Drake sat beside Bliss on the love seat.

"Ah…now that you mention it, I do detect a *wee* Scottish accent," Chloe said.

"Very wee." Drake grinned. "I've been in this part of the world for…well, a long, long time."

Rory smiled. "It was quite a stroke of luck, running into your lovely wife. We were lookin' for Boston Uncommon but expected it to be a bar. We used the word 'special.'" He winked. "And she knew what we were about. She showed us your picture, and we knew we had found a fellow dragon."

Drake let out a deep sigh of relief. "Whew. I wasn't going to say it first. We have strict rules here. We're not allowed to talk about the paranormal with humans around."

All three of them stared at Bliss.

"Oh," she said. "I'm not exactly human either. I used to be."

Chloe looked her up and down. "What are you now?"

"I'm a muse. A minor goddess. The muse of email, to be exact."

Chloe's eyes rounded. After a brief pause, she reared back and burst out laughing. "Ah, that's a good one. Muse of email indeed."

"It's true," Drake said. "The um…powers-that-be really don't like a dragon and a human as a couple.

Fortunately, a few modern muses were needed to help the original nine handle all the technological advances, so Bliss was offered the job."

Chloe squinted. "By whom?"

Bliss elbowed Drake. "We're not supposed to talk about *her* with anyone."

"Sorry. I know. It's really hard to explain without referring to—you know who."

Shannon seemed shy but spoke up at last. "That's amazing. The gods themselves must have recognized how strong your love was and made it possible for you to be together."

Bliss sighed. "We've said too much. Please don't press it further."

"But…the babe." She nodded at Bliss's huge belly. "I thought dragons and humans couldn't conceive."

Drake nodded. "I gave up my immortality for her. I couldn't picture living forever without Bliss by my side." He slipped an arm behind her and rubbed circles on her back. "That's when it happened."

She rested her head on his shoulder and crooned, "That feels so good."

"Oh. So you run into burnin' buildings, knowin' you could die?" Chloe looked stunned.

"Yes and no." He turned toward Bliss and they exchanged a meaningful gaze. "I did that for a short time."

"I had no idea he'd keep fighting fires without being fireproof, as dragons are. Then I couldn't stand worrying about him."

"Being mortal was actually a good experience," Drake said. "I realized I had been taking stupid chances and could put my fellow firefighters, who *aren't* fireproof, in danger if they followed my lead. I have a renewed respect for what they do now."

Chloe straightened her back. "I'd like to become a fire-fighter. We're goin' to need jobs soon. I can do anythin' a man can do…and probably better. As you know, I'm stronger than a human and fireproof to boot. It's a brilliant idea." She coughed. "O' course, you thought of it first."

"I can look into it for you. Do you have a believable birth certificate?"

"I don't," she answered honestly.

"A work visa?"

"Nor that either."

He sighed. "I'm afraid you can't get a paying job with the fire department without certain papers."

"Blast." Her eyes narrowed, and a curl of smoke exited her nostrils.

Bliss bailed him out, thank goodness. "What did you do in Ireland?"

"Ah," Rory said with a grin. "We sang at the local pub. Shannon and I composed most of our songs."

Bliss sat up straight. "So you're Irish folk singers? That's wonderful! I could probably ask Claudia to give you a gig at the tearoom."

"Who's Claudia?" Chloe asked.

"Oh, she's my best friend. She's part owner and man-ages the place."

The three of them glanced at each other. Rory said, "That sounds grand. Would we need to fill out an appli-cation to work there?"

"I'll ask if she can pay you under the counter."

Drake recognized the twinkle in her eye. It meant she would find a way to make it happen.

"Now you're talkin'," Rory said. "We may not be here long enough to get regular jobs. I just need to clear up a few things and we'll be returnin'."

"Oh." Drake was somewhat disappointed, but he tamped it down. After all, he had Bliss and his old friends, and soon he'd have a new baby. Then he thought about how the dragons probably needed new friends more than he did.

"Do you have a place to stay?" he asked.

"Not yet. We had hoped to talk to the locals at the bar and get some recommendations."

Drake smiled. "I can help you. Bliss, why don't I take the Arish clan to the paranormal club? You can stay here and get some rest."

"Great idea!"

Chapter 3

IT WAS A BEAUTIFUL SPRING DAY—SUNNY BUT WITH a breeze off the river, still cool enough for a brisk stride—and the paranormal club was within walking distance. As Rory, his sisters, and their new dragon friend walked the few blocks, Drake explained the philosophy of the place and how it started.

"As you probably know, there are many different paranormal factions. For some reason, they all seem to like Boston, but not always each other."

Rory glanced at Chloe, who shrugged. The only other paranormals they had met were the leprechauns. Drake was still speaking, so Rory didn't interrupt.

"Boston Uncommon used to be a bar, and the bar's owner believed that if the different species of paranormals got to know each other, they'd find commonalities and learn to respect one another's differences. 'To know me is to love me,' so to speak."

"And did it work?" Shannon asked.

"Indeed it did. Although not right away. But when faced with a common enemy, they were able to work together and neutralize the problem."

Neutralize. That word had a host of different meanings. Would Rory have to fight for his family's place here if they couldn't return home? He was hoping that this club might hold an answer to their supernatural problem. Perhaps one of these other species would have a suggestion.

Chloe cleared her throat. "Just what kind of species are we apt to find there?"

Drake shrugged. "Shapeshifters mostly. Some of them live in the building. There are several apartments, all rented to paranormals or the paranormal-friendly. One of the apartments has been converted to a club space. As long as you're inside the club, you're safe to ask any of the members what special powers they have."

At the mention of shifters, Rory had to ask… "I guess we could be considered shifters, since we shift from human form to dragons and back again. Is that what you're talkin' about?"

"Yes, although as far as I know, the three of you and I are the only dragons in the city."

"Really?" Chloe asked. "I knew we were rare, but I figured in a big city like Boston there might be more."

"Boston isn't all that big. It's smaller than New York, and I only know one dragon there."

"Gettin' back to the other species…" Rory said. "What else are there besides shifters?"

"Oh, you know…witches, wizards, vampires—"

Shannon gasped. "Vampires! What? How? Bollocks!"

"Watch your language, lass," Rory said.

"They don't *all* belong to the club. Only those paranormals who want to keep the peace with each other will be there. As long as you believe you can do that, you'll be welcome."

"I see no reason why we couldn't," Rory said. He shot a pointed look at Chloe.

"What?" she asked. "You don't think I can hold me temper when I need to?"

He leveled his eyes with hers. "You'd better."

Fortunately Shannon distracted them with another question. "Are there leprechauns here? We're used to them."

Drake's eyes widened. "They're real? We have the occasional house brownie, but leprechauns?"

"Sure'n they're the reason we got kicked out of Ireland," Chloe said.

Drake stopped walking and stared at them. "How bad do you have to be to get kicked out of Ireland?" Then he caught himself. "Oh. Sorry. I didn't mean that the way it sounded."

"No offense taken," Rory said.

Chloe chuckled. Shannon just shook her head.

"Actually, we didn't do a damn thing," Chloe said. "The little bastards accused us of takin' their gold, but we didn't."

Rory added, "They thought because we're dragons and like our treasure as much as they value their gold that we stole it."

Drake nodded in understanding.

"We had all we needed and then some," Chloe said.

Rory sighed. "We knew that livin' high and mighty would call attention to us, so years ago we moved to a caretaker's cottage and had our castle hidden by magic."

"The magic of leprechauns," Shannon added.

"And now our castle is exposed and vulnerable," Rory said. "And they set up some kind of force field to keep us out of our own country. We need to find a way around that."

At last they stopped in front of a typical lovely brownstone.

"Here we are," Drake said.

"That's it?" Chloe asked. "It looks like a normal building."

Drake chuckled. "What did you expect? Bats in the belfry?"

"Well, no…"

"Come on. I'll show you the secret to getting in."

They followed him up the steps to the stoop. He bypassed the intercom buzzers and opened the outer door with no problem. Rory was about to ask what the big secret was when they entered a foyer and stopped at the inner door, and another intercom materialized on the wall.

"This is the one we use," Drake said.

"Holy mother," Chloe muttered. "Whose magic is that?"

"One of the managers is a witch. Actually, she's a witch *and* a vampire."

Shannon started to tremble. "I-I don't know about this, Rory…"

"Please, don't worry," Drake said. "I wouldn't have brought you here if you were in any danger. She's a real pussycat."

"Wait." Shannon folded her arms. "She's a cat-shifter *and* a vampire and a witch?"

Drake chuckled. "No, not a real pussycat. It's an expression, meaning she's sweet and harmless."

"As long as she doesn't swipe us with claws, we should be all right," Chloe said.

Rory set a reassuring hand on Shannon's shoulder. "I imagine they'll be asleep now anyway."

"Actually, these particular vampires aren't nocturnal. They've found a cure for most of the negative aspects of vampirism—including the bloodlust. Trust me. They won't snack on you. They won't even be tempted."

Shannon blew out a deep breath.

"Are you ready to meet them?" Drake asked.

All three Arish dragons exchanged a look and nodded.

———

The Arish siblings stood in the lobby of the beautiful brownstone on Beacon Street. Marble floors and gleaming dark wood stairs greeted them. Gazing up, Rory noticed a huge crystal chandelier. *If we* were *into stealing treasure...* He quickly squashed that thought. Sly, the building manager standing before them, was a vampire, Rory reminded himself. Hopefully Sly couldn't read minds.

They were just getting to know each other when Drake got a phone call.

"I'm sorry, I need to leave. It's Bliss, and it sounds like she's in labor."

Everyone exclaimed their congratulations, mostly in Irish, and added wishes for good luck.

Sly asked Drake to call when he had good news and details that could be shared with the other members. "They'll all want to know. You two have a lot of friends here."

Drake glanced at the Arish clan, especially focusing on Shannon. "Will you be all right if I leave you here?"

She glanced at Rory. "I feel safe enough."

"Go." Rory slapped Drake on the back. "Give Bliss our very best."

"I'll bet you wish you could use your wings now," Chloe added.

"Yup. But Brandee is with her, and a run will do me good." With that he waved and bolted out of the building.

Sly smiled at the trio. "Would you like to see the club?"

They seemed to have passed the initial test, and Rory was relieved. "We'd love to."

Sly led the way up the grand staircase and opened an unlocked door on the second floor. A buxom blond in a slinky red dress and a guy with a buzz cut were playing pool. Rory noticed a dartboard on the opposite wall. Floor-to-ceiling bookshelves were filled with volumes of all sizes, some paperbacks and some hardcovers. A rolling ladder allowed access to the higher shelves.

Shannon wandered over to peruse the titles.

"There's a quieter room for reading down the hall, as well as a bathroom," Sly said.

The two pool players had just finished their game with a cheer and a groan. Obviously the woman had won.

Sly said, "Let me introduce you to a couple of our regulars, Ruxandra"—he pointed to the woman scooping up the stack of bills from the edge of the pool table—"and Kurt"—he indicated the solidly built guy with a tattoo on his bicep that read "Semper Fi."

"Be careful if you play this one," Ruxandra said. "You can never be sure if he's using wizard magic to win."

"I don't need to use it to win against anyone—even you, most of the time," Kurt said.

"Guys, I'd like you to meet the Arish family. Rory, Shannon, and Chloe. Drake recommended them," Sly said.

They both came over and shook hands with Rory and his sisters—as if it didn't matter *what* they were. According to Drake, it really didn't.

Dare he ask? Apparently one was a wizard, but the other wasn't.

"So, are you shapeshifters? Vampires? Something new and exotic?" Kurt asked.

Rory chuckled. "We're shapeshifters, I guess."

Ruxandra laughed. "You guess?"

"Well, we're dragons."

"Nice. I'm a vampire," she said.

Rory tried to act cool as if they'd known dozens of them, but Shannon squashed that impression. "Really? I've ne'er known any until today, and now we've met two of you."

Ruxandra smiled. "There aren't a lot of us."

That was welcome information.

"And you?" Chloe asked Kurt. "Are you a wizard only, or somethin' else?"

Ruxandra smirked. "Oh, he's something else all right."

"She means that metaphorically. I'm one hundred percent human. I just happen to have a talent for magic and became a wizard with a lot of study and practice."

I wonder if he knows enough about magic to outsmart the leprechauns, Rory thought.

"Well, we have to get going. We promised to help a friend move some heavy furniture," Ruxandra said. "She's always redecorating."

She and Kurt waved as they left.

Damn. There went our chance to get to know the wizard. There seemed to be a lot of kinds of people—er, creatures—he still hadn't met. Maybe if they stuck close to the club, somewhere along the line he and the wizard would run into each other again. Or perhaps he'd meet someone else skilled in magic. Someone had mentioned a witch…

"So, are you up for a game of darts, Sly?" Rory asked.

"Sure. My wife is showing a potential tenant one of the vacant apartments, but when she's finished I'll introduce you to her." He gathered the darts from the board and returned to the group.

"You have flats to rent?" Chloe asked. "In this buildin'?"

"Yes. We have two available at the moment."

The siblings glanced at each other and seemed to be thinking the same thing.

Rory accepted the yellow-tipped darts and at the same time asked, "Would you be open to a small clan of displaced dragons?"

Sly smiled. "Each unit is only a one-bedroom apartment. Do you need a place to stay long-term?"

"Yes."

"My sister and I can share," Chloe said. She shot Shannon a look so fierce that it could have impaled her on a spit.

Shannon took a step back. "We've shared a room all our lives, and even a bed when friends came to visit. But we were young then."

"Great! My wife and her cousin used to share the one-bedroom apartment we live in now. Would you like to have a look at the vacant ones?"

"We'd love to," Rory said. His sisters nodded their heads enthusiastically.

"We can have our game first, if you like."

Rory chuckled. "No need. If we live here, there will be plenty of time for games."

Sly set his darts on the bar-height table that must have been for observers. Then he dug a key ring out of his pocket. The dozens of keys clattered together as he found the right one.

"The first place is right across the hall," he said. "We've done some soundproofing, so you shouldn't be bothered by noise from the club—not that it's all that busy."

"Oh? Not many members then?" Chloe asked as she followed him.

"About a dozen total."

Sly opened the door to a spacious, open-concept living room, kitchen, and dining area. To the right stood the big bay window Rory had seen from the outside. Without furniture or rugs to hide them, the beautiful hardwood floors gleamed. A fireplace with a majestic mantel stood out as the room's focal point.

Shannon took in a deep breath and wandered toward the kitchen as if in awe. Chloe nodded and said, "I'll take a look at the bedroom." Rory inspected the bathroom. A large glass shower took up the entire back wall. A small window let in some natural light, but the glass was frosted so no one would be putting on a show for the neighbors across the alley. The other necessary parts were there, including a claw-foot tub, and everything looked sparkling clean.

When the three of them converged again in the living room, Sly said, "The place downstairs has exactly the same layout and decor, but it's a bit smaller—allowing room for the foyer."

Chloe sighed. "You should see the size of that walk-in closet. If Shannon and I needed some separation from each other, she could just move in there."

Sly and Rory laughed. Shannon huffed and raised

herself to her full height. "Just because I'm the youngest doesn't mean I'm the smallest anymore."

"I'm kiddin', Shan. But think of the fun we could have fillin' that closet with new clothes."

Shannon glanced down at her rugged jeans and favorite sweater, knowing she'd been wearing them too long. "'Tis true," she said. Then she turned to Rory. "Can we afford this place?"

"That depends. How much is the rent for both flats?"

Sly stroked his chin. "I've never rented two at once before. I suppose we could strike a deal if you're willing to sign a year's lease."

Both Rory and Chloe stared at Shannon. At last, she nodded.

"You won't find a better deal anywhere in Back Bay. We take care of our own. I just need to know one other thing…"

"Ask us anythin' you wish," Rory said.

"Can you control your powers? And I mean one hundred percent of the time. We had an Asian dragon a couple of years ago who had allergies. She sneezed fire and scorched the floors in her apartment. They had to be replaced. We hate to evict a good tenant, but for everyone's safety, she had to go."

They all expressed appropriate horror. Chloe shook her head emphatically. "We have no such problems."

"Sneezing fire! Imagine!" Shannon said.

"Okay. I'm glad to hear that."

"So…the rent?" Rory reminded him.

"Ah, yes. We could let you have both places for twenty-five hundred per month. Fifteen hundred for this one and a thousand for the smaller one downstairs."

Rory almost swallowed an audible gulp, but he managed to keep his poker face on. He knew rents were high in Boston, but he hadn't realized how high. And that was the best deal in the city?

"Ordinarily the larger one goes for that amount all by itself. You'd be getting a two-for-one deal," Sly added.

"Then we'll take it," Rory said. He asked Chloe for his wallet. It was so fat that he couldn't fit it in his back pocket anymore and had to keep it in her purse, along with two large envelopes of cash. They'd planned to find a nearby bank after they had an address.

Rory counted off five thousand, feeling like a millionaire. If it weren't for having to sell off priceless artifacts at a tenth of their worth, he might have been a billionaire. "That should take care of two months up front."

"Actually," Sly said with an apologetic expression, "that will take care of the first month and the security deposit." He shrugged. "It will serve as your last month's rent if there are no damages."

Were they being lied to? Was Sly really *sly?* They weren't in a position to argue.

Rory stuck out his hand and they shook on it. In Ireland, the deal would have been done at that point, but Sly said, "Okay. Let's go upstairs and fill out the paperwork. Hopefully my wife is finished showing the place downstairs, and you can meet her."

~~~

Amber had just signed the contract when the door to the managers' apartment opened. Along with the manager's husband, in traipsed Rory, the unbelievably hot guy she'd met on the sidewalk, and his Irish sisters.

"Wow, small world," she said.

Sly glanced back and forth between his little group and Amber. "You know each other?"

"We've met briefly," Rory said and smiled. Amber's heart fluttered.

Blond, willowy Morgaine rose. "I haven't met your friends, Sly."

"I was just bringing them up to introduce them to you. Morgaine, these fine folks are our new tenants, Rory, Chloe, and Shannon Arish. They're taking *both* apartments 2B and 1B. So, we're full up," he said, glancing at his wife and Amber. "No more vacancies."

Morgaine's mouth dropped open. When she didn't speak right away, Amber gestured to the papers in front of her. "I rented 1B. I think the ink just dried on my signed lease."

"Drake recommended the Arishes," Sly said.

"And Brandee recommended Amber," Morgaine added.

Sly stared at his wife. The two managers did the oddest thing. First Morgaine folded her arms. Then Sly placed his hands on his hips. Then Morgaine began tapping her foot. It was as if they were having a completely silent argument.

What the…

Rory and his sisters glanced at each other, looking equally confused.

"But we paid…in cash," Chloe said. She rubbed her fingers together, then glared at the check Amber had sitting on the table like it wasn't worth the paper it was printed on.

Amber returned her gaze to the stalemate between

the managers. Were they able to argue with their eyes? Did they solve all their problems with a staring contest?

Rory whispered to his sisters, "Do you think they're telepathic?"

Chloe and Shannon shrugged.

That would be one explanation, Amber thought. *One very* weird *explanation.*

"Look. I'm sorry, but I got here first, and I can't lose this apartment," Amber said to Rory. "My whole building is being renovated and turned into condos. Everyone has been evicted."

He cocked his head. "Well, I'm very sorry for your troubles, but I believe we have the right of it. We already paid first and last month's rents on both apartments—in cash, as my sister mentioned."

At that point, Sly withdrew quite a wad of hundred-dollar bills from his pocket and held it out to Morgaine. She took a step back and shook her head as if the money were on fire.

"This is the oddest spat I've ever witnessed," Shannon muttered.

Chloe chuckled. "We've seen some outrageous disputes, but you're right. This one's downright peculiar."

Morgaine leaned forward with her hands on her hips and stamped her foot.

Finally, Sly rose to his full height and said, "In this country, possession is nine-tenths of the law."

Amber and Rory exchanged a look, and telepathy wasn't needed to interpret what they were thinking. They both took off and charged down the stairs. Chloe and Shannon were right behind them.

"Grab 2B, Sisters. I'll get the first floor," Rory called over his shoulder.

Chloe almost knocked Amber over, then pushed her way into the partially open door of apartment 2B. Amber lost some precious time righting herself, and Rory almost passed her. She elbowed him in the ribs and regained her lead.

As she was rounding the bottom of the stairs, he vaulted over the railing and they both tried to charge into the vacant first-floor apartment at the same time. Getting stuck in the doorjamb for a moment, Amber and Rory were squashed into each other. At last, as if something went "pop," they unceremoniously tumbled inside.

Righting themselves, they faced off and stared at each other. "I was here first," Rory said, panting.

"Ha! You wish. I got my foot in first."

A thin guy who must have been one of the other tenants rolled his bike through the inside door at that moment. "What's going on?"

"Oh, nothin'…" Rory said.

"We're trying to decide which of us got here first. We both want to be your neighbor, and apparently the managers rented to the two of us separately but at the same time."

The guy leaned back and laughed. "Perfect. I'm Nathan, by the way."

Rory didn't take his eyes off Amber, but addressed the bicyclist. "I hear that possession is nine-tenths of the law here. Is that true?"

The guy was still chuckling. "Uh, yeah. I guess so. At least that's what I've heard."

"The manager said it aloud," Amber said. "I figured whichever one of us got here first would be allowed to stay…even though *I* signed the lease."

"But *I paid* in cash, and we shook on it," Rory said. "Did you see which one of us entered the place first?"

"Nope," Nathan said. "But there's still a way you can let that rule work it out for you."

"How?" they both asked at once.

"Well, since you both possess it now, whoever leaves first is giving up possession."

They glared at each other, and then a smirk stole across Rory's lips.

"Oh, you think you've got it, don't you? Just because you have sisters who can go get you food and whatever else you need, huh?"

He grinned. "I imagine so, since they live just upstairs—and there are two of them."

She was furious and felt her cheeks heat. Her purse was upstairs. Her cell phone was in her purse. If she could get someone to bring it to her, she could arrange to have her furniture moved in—and then let him try to prove the place was his. Ha!

Suddenly the bizarre offer from Mother Nature smacked her upside the head. That could be her secret weapon! *If I were a muse, I could go to the bathroom, pop over to the store, and come back with groceries.*

Oh, right… She'd have a hard time explaining how she managed to buy groceries in the bathroom, and Mother Nature had that pesky law about not revealing the paranormal world. *Damn.*

Still, something about having the powers of a muse sounded like it might work in her favor. But how could she contact Mother Nature? Maybe through Brandee or Bliss? How long would it be before one of them came to the paranormal club?

She might starve to death by then.

The important thing was not to let this arrogant Irishman think he'd won. She strolled off toward the bedroom. At least she could claim that and have her privacy…or maybe she should claim the bathroom. She almost burst out laughing. *Yup. Not having a place to pee would drive him out pretty quickly.*

Amber made a sharp right turn and hurtled into the little room. "I claim the bathroom. Gotcha!" She quickly slammed and locked the door.

She heard Nathan the bicyclist laugh loudly and say, "Oh yes. You guys are going to be wicked fun neighbors."

"Finn…Finn! Get off the floor," Mrs. O'Malley yelled.

Finn Kelley felt a couple of strong hands grab him. It must have been the Burke brothers. They were farmers and smelled of cow dung. One on either side, they lifted Finn enough to drag his deadweight out the door of the pub and deposit him on the lush, green grass. Standing over him, they summed up his condition.

"He's fluthered, all right," one said.

"Twisted and sozzeled," added the other.

"You'd be scuttered too, if your fiancée suddenly went missin'." Finn's best friend, Patrick, must have felt the need to defend his friend, although he had cautioned him about drinking a fourth glass of whiskey in so short a time—or was it his fifth?

"That Arish girl? The young one?" Mr. O'Malley asked. He must have followed them outside.

"That's the one," Pat said. "Shannon. They've been pre-engaged forever. Rather, they were."

Finn rolled over and mumbled, "Shannon…Shannon, where are you?"

"She isn't here," the village doctor snapped. He must have followed them outside too. "And you won't find her by passin' out at O'Malley's."

Finn's arm flopped over his eyes as if to block out the sun—but the sun wasn't shining. More likely he wanted to block out the doctor's logic.

"I wish the Irish had never invented whiskey," Pat said.

Mr. O'Malley smirked. "The Irish didn't invent it. God did. It was his way of keepin' the Irish from takin' over the world."

"I'll be headin' back to me office," the doctor said. "Tell Mr. Kelley here to take two aspirin and not to call me unless he really is dead—not just dead drunk."

One of the farmers asked, "How can he call anyone if he's dead?"

"I don't think he much cares," the other one said. "We should be gettin' back. It looks like rain is comin'."

"But a rainy day is the perfect day to spend at the pub."

Finn briefly opened one eye to check for dark clouds.

"Right you are," Mr. O'Malley said. He wrapped his arms around the brothers' broad shoulders, and all three ambled back into the pub.

Patrick squatted beside Finn and pried his eyes open again. "Get up."

"Leave me be."

Patrick rose and leaned against the rustic building. "I

hope you'll be soberin' up soon. I can't keep the garda from tossin' you in jail if they've a mind to."

Finn pushed himself up to a sitting position, then slumped over. "Why?" he asked for the hundredth time. "Why would she leave me without a word? If they went on holiday, she'd have told me in advance."

And for the hundredth time, Patrick answered, "I don't know, Finn. It's a mystery."

Finn took a deep breath and leaned back on his hands. "Somethin's not right." Focused on the heavens, he called out, "I've been prayin' for a sign." Then more quietly, he added, "If God knows where she is, he ain't talkin'."

"I'm sure wherever she is, she'll be callin' you when she can."

"*If* she can." Finn put his head in his hands and began to shake. Tears burned the back of his eyes.

"None of that, now. C'mon. The Irish ignore everything they can't drink or punch."

"I wish I knew who to punch," Finn said. "Lord knows the drink ain't workin'."

Chapter 4

Rory leaned against the bathroom door of apartment 1B and crossed his arms. "You can stay in there as long as you want, darlin'. I'm not goin' anywhere."

"You will when you need the facilities," she called out.

She didn't need to raise her voice. His dragon senses were a little sharper than a human's—even when he was in human form.

She thinks she has me beat. Well, let's see if I can have a little fun with her first. "I have a nice sink here in the kitchen. Don't think I won't use it."

She gasped. "You wouldn't!"

"Oh, but I would. You see, this apartment belongs to me, and I can do anythin' I darn well please in it."

"Gross," she exclaimed.

The lock clicked and the door opened, but only a crack. "I can't let you ruin *my* apartment. Why don't we call the bathroom neutral territory?"

"I guess we could do that." He smiled and winked at her. "For now."

She opened the door slowly. "Let's add the kitchen to that list."

"Why not? I don't suppose either of us likes our food raw." His breath could whip up a nice barbecue, but he couldn't tell her that.

She slipped out of the bathroom, then made a quick

right turn and dashed into the bedroom. She shot him a grin of satisfaction. "I claim the *only* bedroom."

He shrugged. "Fine by me. I have the whole living room, which appears to be the bigger area."

Her lush lips compressed into a hard line, and her pretty hazel-green eyes narrowed.

A knock sounded at the apartment door, followed by Morgaine's voice. "Amber…are you in there?"

"Damn," Amber muttered under her breath. Without leaving the bedroom, she yelled, "Yes. I'm here. Come on in."

The front door opened slowly. Both managers walked in. Sly strode over and stood by Rory. Morgaine carried a handbag to Amber.

"Are you two talking this out?" Morgaine asked as she handed Amber her purse.

Amber looked relieved. "Thanks." She reached into it and withdrew her cell phone.

Now she can call in reinforcements. Speaking of which, where were his siblings?

Rory tried to appear nonchalant. "We're workin' on it. You wouldn't happen to know where me sisters are, would you?"

"Chloe signed their lease, then said they were going shopping," Morgaine replied.

"They said they'd get a few things for you," Sly added. "I told them where the grocery store is, as well as where to buy a futon. Since they're on foot, I imagine they'll have to have that delivered. If you two don't work this out, you could spend an uncomfortable night or two on the floor."

"So let me get this straight," Amber said. "My

signature on the lease means nothing? You're going to let this big oaf stay in my apartment until one of us gives up and leaves?"

"Or until your check clears," Morgaine said. "Neither of us are lawyers, and we were hoping you'd have resolved this on your own."

Amber stared at Rory. "Oh, it'll clear. Are you sure you want your sisters buying furniture for this place?"

"I'm a man of simple tastes. A futon and small milk crate are all I need to sit, eat, and sleep."

Amber sighed. "Well, at least you won't have much to carry when you move *out*."

"I'm not movin'. And from the looks of it, you'll be the one sleepin' on the floor. Unless…"

"Unless what?"

"Unless you want to share me futon." He waggled his eyebrows.

She slammed the bedroom door, and a click said she'd locked it.

Sly and Morgaine faced each other and began another staring contest. Rory stepped a few feet away, cleared his throat, and waited to get their attention…and waited some more while they continued to stare at each other.

At last he cleared his throat loudly, and they finally looked at him. He waved them over.

They glanced at each other, then followed him.

"Are you two telepathic?" he whispered.

Sly smiled. "You picked up on that, huh?"

"I didn't know if you had some weird nonverbal way to settle an argument. Maybe if you let me in on your concerns, I can shed some light on me and mine."

Morgaine's posture relaxed. "I suppose we should

hear you out. *Both* of you. An informed decision usually results in a better outcome, and right now I'm not happy with the outcome we're getting."

Sly put his arm around her waist. "That makes two of us. We never fight."

She smiled at him, and eventually they kissed. Just a peck.

"So, what are your concerns, Morgaine?"

She lowered her voice. "I know you're dragons, and we want to help our fellow paranormals, but we had a bad experience with a dragon living here before."

Rory nodded. "Sly mentioned that. We don't sneeze fire. We have no allergies that I know of, and we have complete control over our powers."

"Are you sure? I was told that if a dragon didn't 'blow off steam' sexually from time to time, he or she could shift inadvertently."

Rory laughed. "Sounds like a pickup line. No. Me sisters and I have powerful dragon magic. It allows us to shift quickly, but only when necessary. We prefer our human forms anyway."

"Why do you want to live here?" Sly asked.

"Drake and Bliss seemed to think it was perfect for us. I believe they're right. It's para-friendly, and the neighborhood is safe for me sisters."

"Can you afford it?" Morgaine asked point-blank.

Rory laughed. "For as long as we live, and that's a long, long time."

"How do you get along with others?"

"Quite well, ordinarily. We Irish tend to be charmin' and friendly."

She nodded. "Good."

"Then you're satisfied? I can stay here?"

She held up her palm to halt his assumption. "Not yet. We need to talk to the other party. Remember?"

His hope faded. "Of course." He gestured toward the bedroom with a sweep of his hand.

Both of the managers approached the door and knocked.

"Who is it?" Amber called out.

"The managers," Sly answered.

She opened the door a crack. "Have you come to a decision?"

Ah! She can't hear through doors. That means she's probably not supernatural, which is a point in me favor.

"We have not. May we come in and talk to you?" Morgaine said.

"Does a certain stubborn Irishman have to come in with you?"

"Not yet," Morgaine said. "We'd like to talk to you both individually first."

Amber stepped back and opened the door wider.

As soon as the managers were inside, she gave Rory an arrogant smile and closed the door in his face.

He was tempted to shift. His hearing was even better in his dragon form. He chuckled to himself as he pictured her expression when she came nose to snout with a full-sized dragon in her living room. She'd probably run, screaming.

Sly was speaking, but Rory could tell the vampire was trying to keep his voice low. Still, Rory was able to pick up the gist of the conversation. Why did she want to live here? Would her references check out? Had she ever been late with her rent? And, *if* she wound up with the apartment, could she get along with other tenants? All the normal questions a landlord with two potential renters would ask.

There was no question hinting about her being paranormal, which meant they didn't know if she was.

Finally the managers emerged and Amber closed the door, but she didn't lock it this time. That could be an oversight or a sign of confidence. Either way, he was sure he could convince her to leave.

Before either Sly or Morgaine spoke, a knock at the door indicated visitors. Rory strode to the door and opened it to reveal his grinning sisters. They held a futon laden with grocery bags and they hadn't even broken a sweat.

"Ah," he said. "How lucky am I to have such a *strong* and loyal family?"

Sly smiled. "Let me help you with that."

"No need. We've got it," Chloe said. "Where do you want this, Brother?"

"Me thinks right in front of the fireplace would be nice. Don't you?" he asked Morgaine.

She nodded. "You can only burn candles in the fireplace though."

"A pity. But I always abide by the rules." He turned to his sisters. "You didn't happen to purchase any candles, did you?"

They set down the futon in front of the fireplace and Shannon grunted. "We were thinkin' you might like to eat and sleep, so we got you a bed, food, and cutlery."

Chloe snorted. "I suppose you wanted a complete set of silver and bone china for twelve, but we didn't get those either."

He held up his hands. "You've got the right of it. I only need the basics for now."

"I can bring you a few candles," Morgaine said and smiled.

"Thank you!" Rory didn't mean to sound so surprised.

The bedroom door opened. Amber glanced at the cozy setup and the girls carrying bags of groceries to the kitchen.

"Oh. You're moving in? Well, don't get too comfortable, because I just called a moving company to pack my apartment and bring *all* my things here."

"And how are they supposed to get into your old apartment?" Chloe asked. "It's not like we're about to help you turn out our brother so you can leave."

"I called my neighbor, Candy. She has an emergency key to my apartment and said she'd let the movers in."

Everyone focused on the managers, who'd been silently observing the whole time.

At last, Morgaine said, "Since we can't seem to come to a decision, we're going to let the other tenants weigh in. Are you both agreeable to meeting them?"

"Absolutely," Rory said. He hoped there were a lot of female tenants he could use his Irish charisma on… even though the only woman he wanted to charm at the moment was the one least interested in his existence.

─◇◇◇─

Finn Kelley sat at a card table across from a gypsy inside a colorful tent.

I must be mad. Truth be told, he'd consult the devil himself to get a clue to Shannon's whereabouts. The doctor was right, drinking didn't solve the problem. As soon as Finn had sobered up, he'd known that.

"You're missing someone," the gypsy woman said. "A young woman, I see."

Finn leaned forward, hoping to get a glimpse of whatever was in the seer's crystal ball. "Where is she?"

The gypsy stared into the crystal and her brows furrowed. "Hmmm..."

She leaned forward and seemed to be straining to see something. A full minute passed. At last she shut her eyes, leaned back, and rubbed her temples.

"What's wrong?"

"That knowledge is blocked."

"Blocked? What do you mean?"

"I mean that bit of information is shrouded—being kept secret by someone or some*thing*. An entity... And trying to get to it is hurting my head."

Finn narrowed his eyes. "Is this a ploy for more money? Will another dozen euros find a way through that block?"

Her back stiffened. "As much as I'd like more money to offset the pain I just suffered, I am not a fraud. I am telling you that someone or something is not allowing me to see more."

"I don't understand."

She sighed. "It must be powerful magic. Now, don't roll your eyes..."

He hadn't.

"I don't know what you've heard of the ancient little people, but I'd say the block must come from someone or something like that."

Finn rolled his eyes—he couldn't help it this time.

"I'm Irish. Of course I've heard the legends of lepre-chauns, fairies, and the like."

"They are not legends. Or as my people say, 'Legends come from somewhere.' They tend to be ancient truths."

If this woman wasn't a fraud, he'd eat his hat, but on the off chance she wasn't full of shite… "Fine. Let's say the little people are hidin' her somewhere. How do I find them?"

"Ah, now that's the trick. You'll have to find some-one who doesn't want to be found."

Here it is… I'll need to pay her a hundred euros and go to some far-off location while she conve-niently disappears.

"Fortunately, I know a bit of magic has upset the area recently. I'd say they're a lot closer than you might think."

"Close, huh? How close?"

"Right here in Ballyhoo. An ancient castle has appeared out of nowhere. It's built into the cliffs off Braydon Road."

Now she had his attention. Shannon's cottage was on Braydon Road's dead end. It was too much of a coincidence. Perhaps magic was responsible for her disappearance—*if* magic of that kind existed.

"I'm surprised I haven't heard about an ancient castle appearin'. It seems like the kind of news that would spread through a small village in minutes."

"That's what the villagers get for shutting out us trav-elers. We see things, yet you turn us away from your pubs. If we're not welcome, why should we tell the 'good' people of Ballyhoo what's happening right under their noses?" She emphasized the word "good" as if she were spitting it. "They'd never believe us anyway."

She had a point, but why hadn't he seen a castle when he went looking for Shannon at her home? He'd been riding his bike and looking down to be sure he didn't fall over a wagon wheel rut. He could have missed the castle—especially if it was tucked into a cliff.

He rose and reached into his back pocket. "How much do I owe you?"

"How much did I say it cost at the beginning?"

"Thirty euros. But I already paid it."

"Then our business is finished."

He was surprised but not unhappy. "Is there anythin' else you can tell me? Like, is she all right?"

"I've told you all I know."

Finn rode his bicycle along the familiar tire ruts in the dirt road. For once, the weather was agreeable, allowing him to wear short sleeves and no slicker. Perhaps the cloaked hood he'd worn to keep the rain off his face had prevented him from seeing a castle before. He shook his head. Unlikely.

If there was a full-size castle near the Arish cottage, and not one made out of sand, he'd eat his derby hat.

When he rode into view of the cottage, he caught sight of a projection rising from the side of the cliff. *Funny, I don't think I've seen that before.*

He hopped off his bike, abandoned it in the sod beside the road, and strode toward the ruin. As his view became clearer, he realized the projection resembled a turret and he quickened his pace. At last he ran toward the outcrop and halted in time to keep from tumbling off the grassy cliff.

Gazing down, he spotted a few openings in the cliff. Seeing such a thing wasn't unusual in Ireland, but for stone arches to be built right into the side of a cliff like this... The caves looked more like doorways. How did the ancient residents get into it? And why hadn't modern fishermen spotted it?

"What magic is this?" he muttered.

The sound of a throat clearing behind Finn startled him. He whirled around and came thighs to face with a small man. He was larger than a midget, but perfectly proportioned, unlike a dwarf. Wearing a green suit and a hat with red curls peeking out from under it, he looked like a...

"Top o' the mornin'," the little man said.

Hmmm... Nobody in Ireland says that anymore. Finn scrambled to remember all he'd ever heard about the little people, specifically leprechauns. They had gold and powerful magic to protect it. They liked to play tricks. His throat went dry. "Good mornin'," Finn croaked politely.

"Can I help you?" the little man asked.

"I—um..." He had to find Shannon, and if the little people weren't just a myth and had her, he had to find a way to ask. *Careful now, Finn*, he told himself. *Legend says the leprechauns are easily insulted. Don't accuse him of anythin'.*

"Does your tongue work?"

"Ah, it does. I was just wonderin' if in your travels you mayhaps have seen me friend. About yea high." He held his hand out straight, level with his nose. "Hair as red as your own, but long and wavy. Lips like a perfect cupid's bow, and eyes as blue as the sky this fine day."

The little man scratched the short beard on his chin. "I can't say as I've seen a lass like that."

Finn hadn't said she was a lass. The man was either lying or assuming her sex.

"I can see you love her," the mysterious gentleman added quickly. "I'm sorry if she deserted you."

Now Finn was insulted. He straightened his spine. "She would never desert me. Never. That's why I'm afraid somethin' terrible has happened."

"Oh. Somethin' terrible, is it? Let's hope that's not the case. Mayhaps you'll find her—eventually."

Finn was almost paralyzed with indecision. Should he grab the little man and, instead of demanding his pot of gold, insist that he return his ladylove? Not yet. Not until he knew who or what he was dealing with.

"We've not been properly introduced," he said at last. "My name is Finnegan Kelley, but everyone calls me Finn."

"Pleased to make your acquaintance, Finn Kelley. You can call me Lucky."

"A rare name. Does it apply?"

Lucky tittered. "Sometimes."

Finn kicked at a clod of earth in front of him. "I wish I had a bit of luck right now. I must find Shannon. She was to be me wife someday. I miss her somethin' fierce."

Lucky reached out and laid a hand on Finn's arm. "Close your eyes. See the lass in your mind," he said.

Finn did as he was told. After all, he pictured her several times a day. When the small man removed his hand, Finn had a sense of peace and calm. It was as if he just knew she was all right.

"Well, I must be on me way," Lucky said. "I have some business to conduct."

Finn nodded. "It was good to meet you, sir."

The leprechaun—or whatever he was—grinned. "No need for such formalities. I'm not a knight, after all. Not that you can tell from me appearance." He chuckled and strode away toward the road.

Finn gazed at the castle again. He only turned his head for a moment or two, but when he looked back, Lucky was gone.

———

"Brandee," Amber whispered as quietly as she could.

When no one appeared, she tried the other one. "Bliss? Bliss can you hear me?"

She figured if she could get someone to find Mother Nature for her, she'd gladly take the goddess up on her offer. Being the muse of air travel actually sounded interesting—depending on what the job entailed. And her actual job was getting so rote that she was thinking of switching to one of the bargain airlines just to have a little fun over the PA system.

When Bliss didn't show up either, Amber decided to try the goddess herself.

"Mother Nature?" she called out quietly.

Rory's voice answered her from the living room.

"If nature is callin', the bathroom is free."

"Crap."

"Don't stink it up," he called out.

She marched over to the bedroom door and opened it. "You are the most disgusting man!"

He had the nerve to laugh. "Aren't you glad we're roommates?"

As gorgeous as he was, she would not tolerate bad

behavior. This guy seemed to think he could do no wrong. "Arrogant Irish prick," she muttered.

"Oh! That's hardly ladylike language, me darlin'."

"I never said I was a lady."

He grinned and spread his arms across the back of the futon. "Is that so?"

She blushed and quickly added, "I don't usually talk like that, but you deserved it."

He laughed. "Perhaps you're right. I'll try to be less—what was it you said? Ah, *disgustin'*, I believe."

"Good. And while you're at it, maybe you could try to be less arrogant too."

He crossed his long legs at the ankles. "That's unlikely. Where I come from, a little arrogance is a positive trait. We call it self-confidence."

"Oh, is that what it is? I thought it was *over*confidence, conceit, and false pride."

His big hand pressed his broad chest. "You wound me, luv."

"I'm not your love or your darling. Let's get that straight right now." She crossed her arms and tried to look tough. The smattering of freckles across her turned-up nose made that a difficult task, and she knew it.

So did he, apparently. He just continued to grin at her, his green eyes twinkling mischievously.

"Why don't you come and sit next to me? We should get to know each other if we're to be livin' together." He patted an empty spot on the futon. He hadn't left much room on either side, and she suspected that was on purpose.

She made a noise of repulsion and stared to her left. With no retort coming to mind, she shuffled into the bathroom and locked the door. She *had to* get some of those muse powers—and soon. Sure, she could have groceries delivered, but she'd prefer to pick the freshest items herself. She was used to being trapped in small spaces, but off the clock, she loved the feeling of being in an open space all her own.

She could barely breathe in Rory's presence, but the enclosed space wasn't entirely responsible. The handsome, infuriating Irishman filled the room with his presence and took her breath away.

Then Amber remembered something. When she met Brandee's husband, he'd introduced himself by first and last name. *Maybe he's in the phone book.* But she'd left her phone in her purse in the bedroom.

Panic seized her. *Rory wouldn't invade my privacy by going into my purse, would he?*

She tore out of the bathroom and was relieved to see he was still on the futon. *Whew.* As soon as she grabbed her purse off a hook in the bedroom closet, she glanced through the contents. Everything seemed to be there.

Now, how would she explain needing her purse in the bathroom? *Aha! Two can play the gross-out game.*

Chuckling, she slung the purse over her shoulder and returned to the bathroom. "I needed something *important*. Something I use *on a monthly basis*."

He laughed. "You didn't even have to hint at it, me darlin'. I have sisters. You may think that'll put me off, but it won't a bit. Now, go take care of the responsibility Mother Nature gave you."

Hmmm…Mother Nature. Interesting that he referred to her, specifically. Amber hoped the deity wasn't too hard to reach. If she didn't take this job… Her posture sagged. *Nothing* was going to discourage this stubborn Irishman.

"Why do you want this place so badly?" she asked.

"Because it feels like the right fit for me and me family. What's your reason?"

She didn't answer him—just humphed and shut the door.

Why *did* she want it so badly? Sure, she'd always wanted to live in the beautiful, historic Back Bay area. She'd grown up in the suburbs, but they were meant for families. This area was full of young, urban professionals. Okay, so that could mean a yuppie, but she really didn't care. Someday she wanted to marry a well-paid guy and transition to being a *dink*—short for "dual income, no kids."

This was the perfect area to meet someone of that caliber—when she was ready to date again. At the moment, she was still smarting over the pilot she'd dated for about a year. They'd only flown together a few times, but on the last flight, she'd overheard his outrageous flirting with one of the other flight attendants. He hadn't realized she was listening, and when she confronted him, he admitted to having a little something on the side. Correction…*a lot* of little somethings.

Ouch.

With her luck, the hunk in her living room would be the same way—but probably not if the guy never left the apartment. She chuckled to herself. *That's one way to keep a man's eye from roving.*

Amber took a seat on the edge of the bathtub. It wasn't the most comfortable place, but all she wanted to do was look up the muse's family in the phone book. *What did he say his name was again?* "Nick Wolfensomething…" she muttered.

Her phone's automated voice answered her. "Nick

Wolfensen. Wolfensen Investigations. 555-4321. Do you want me to call the number for you?"

Stunned, Amber stammered, "Y-yes."

"Calling Nick," her phone said, and before long a male answered.

"Wolfensen Investigations. Wolfensen here."

"Hi, um…Nick?"

"Yeah. Who's this?"

"Oh, um. It's Amber. I met you earlier today. Is Brandee around? I really need to speak with her."

"Oh sure. She's not here right now, but I can get in touch with her. It sounds important."

"It is. Can you call her for me?"

"Sure. Brandee…" he yelled. Amber thought he was being a smart-ass.

"I'll give you my number and— Eep!"

Amber startled when red-haired Brandee joined her in the bathroom…seemingly out of thin air.

Nick chuckled. "I guess she found you."

When Amber could breathe, swallow, and make sounds again, she said, "Um, yeah. She's here. How did you do that?"

"It's our little secret. If you're all set, I'll let you go."

Brandee pried the phone from her hand and spoke into it. "I'm here, hon. Thanks for the message." After a couple of murmured endearments, she clicked off and handed the phone back to Amber.

Then Brandee sat on the opposite edge of the tub, facing Amber. "So, what's up?"

"I—um…I think I'd like to take Mother Nature up on her generous offer, but I can't seem to get in touch with her on my own."

"Oh. Sure." Brandee rose and said, "I'll take you to her."

"Wait." Amber held on to the lip of the tub as if she might be swept away against her will. "I can't leave yet."

"Oh?"

"It's hard to explain, but here goes…" She took a deep breath and launched into her view of the situation at hand.

Brandee nodded, but the crease in her forehead made it look like she either wasn't getting it or didn't approve.

At the end of Amber's long-winded explanation, Brandee held up one finger. "Stay here. I'll be back in a flash."

A moment later, Mother Nature took Brandee's place, sitting on the edge of the tub. Her expression seemed grim.

Huh? I thought she'd be happy to know I want to be a muse.

"Amber," the Goddess of All said.

"Yes, Mother Nature?"

"Call me Gaia. If we're going to be working together, you may as well use my name, not my title."

Whew. At least it sounds like I've got the job. "All right. Thank you for coming, Gaia. I imagine Brandee didn't have time to fill you in on my situation…"

"Actually, she did. We discussed it at length."

"You did? But I only told her a few seconds ago."

"Yeah. We're good at cutting out the baloney and getting right to the point."

"Oh. I guess I'll have to learn how to do that."

"You'll have to learn a lot of things. I have Brandee on another assignment, and Bliss is busy with a new baby. That's why I'm assigning you to Euterpe for training."

"You-what-e? Who is she?"

Mother Nature rolled her eyes. "Yoo-*tur*-pee. You weren't paying attention during your class on Greek mythology, were you?"

Amber shrugged and grinned sheepishly. "I guess not."

"Well, according to my horny son Zeus, he *bemused* young Mnemosyne and slept with her for nine consecutive nights. The nine muses were the result of their encounter. When the muses grew up, they showed their tendency toward the arts and were taught by Apollo. Ever since, the muses have supported and encouraged creativity, enhancing imagination and inspiring artists."

"Okay. So Euterpe is one of the nine?"

Mother Nature snapped her fingers and a beautiful brunette woman appeared, wearing a white off-the-shoulder maxi-dress that barely covered her boobs. She was holding a small flute.

"This is Euterpe. She discovered several musical instruments and dialectic."

"What's a dialectic?"

"It's like a debate… Considering the situation you've gotten yourself into, I thought she'd be the best possible fit."

Amber had to admit that Euterpe seemed like the perfect muse to help—or hinder—her goal of being the sole occupant of the apartment. She simply had to persuade the muse to see it her way.

"And don't think that because she's training you, she'll be partial to your side of the argument."

Damn. I hate it when she knows what I'm thinking.

"Get used to it, muse of air travel."

"Oh. I'm already a muse? But I have questions…"

"And Euterpe has answers."

"I guess there's no formal ceremony or papers to fill out?"

Mother Nature smirked. "You wanted a ceremony and paperwork?"

"No! No, I really don't. I just never thought it would be this easy."

"Well, it isn't. You'll need to learn a lot from Euterpe. If you screw up—and please don't…but if you do, there's a nice family in Atlanta looking for a child to adopt."

"But I'm not a child."

One finger snap later, Amber was lying on the floor, waving her baby-sized fists and feet in the air. Fortunately, the goddess snapped her fingers again and returned Amber to her adult size. She was still lying on the floor though.

"Oh! You mean…"

"Yes. I can be very mean. That's why they tell you not to mess with Mother Nature."

Amber pushed herself up to a standing position and said, "Well, um…thank you, I guess. I'll try not to screw it up."

"Good." Gaia smiled at the other muse. "She's all yours, Euterpe. Good luck."

The muse bowed and the all-powerful one disappeared.

"So, that's it? You're my teacher? I'm a muse now?"

"Yes. Let's leave this tiny room and meet your unintentional roommate." Euterpe started toward the bathroom door.

"Wait!" Amber grabbed the muse's arm. "He'll wonder how you got in here. You have to pop out to the street and come in through the front door."

"Hmmm…" Euterpe tapped her lower lip. "I could do that, but supernaturals aren't supposed to expose their powers to humans. There are people on the sidewalk. On the other hand, I could go out to the back alley. My senses aren't picking up any large life forms, only the tiniest—probably birds and insects."

"Okay. As soon as you're gone, I'll go out to the living room and wait for you to ring the bell."

"Agreed," Euterpe said and disappeared.

Amber opened the door slowly and peeked out. She was startled when Rory appeared. Apparently he'd been hiding on the other side of the doorjamb.

"Nervous?" he asked.

"No." Amber crossed her arms. "And why were you skulking about?"

He raised his brows. "There was no skulkin'. I was merely waitin' me turn."

"Yeah, right."

They traded places, but before he shut the door, he asked, "And who were you talkin' to?"

Her jaw dropped. "Uh, nobody. I was…um… rehearsing."

"Rehearsin'? Are you in a play?"

"Not exactly. I—um…I read books to the blind. I mean, I make audiobooks. I was just testing the acoustics in the bathroom."

"And are they acceptable for your purposes?"

"Yes. It should do nicely. I may have to tie it up for a few hours at a time…"

A sly smile stole across his face. "No matter," he said. "There's always the sink."

She wrinkled her nose. "Ewww… Don't you dare. Just tell me when you need the privacy, and I'll pause the recorder."

He shrugged. "That seems fair. By the way, where is your recorder?"

"Um. It's…well…"

"Still at the store?"

She gritted her teeth and couldn't think of a retort. Damn this man. One look at him and she forgot everything but her name. *Wait. What's my name again?* Disgusted with herself, she just bit out, "Ugh. You frustrating, arrogant—"

"Now, now. I must use the facilities. Perhaps you can finish your insult later."

He shut the door in her face, and it was all she could do not to scream.

Chapter 5

"I TELL YOU, THERE'S A CASTLE THERE THAT DIDN'T USED TO be," Finn insisted from his perch at O'Malley's Tavern.

Mr. O'Malley laughed. "You must have hit your noggin pretty hard when you fell off my bar stool the other day."

The villagers who overheard crowded closer.

Pat grabbed Finn's shoulder. "What did I tell you? People will think you're crazy. Keep that foolishness to yerself."

One of the local farmers piped up. "A castle, you say? Whereabouts might that be?"

"Near the Arish cottage, but it's built into the cliff beyond."

One of the local fishermen turned to his mate and said, "And you thought I was daft."

"You *are* daft, but that's beside the point."

Finn focused his attention on the first fisherman. "Did you see it? From the ocean?"

"I did."

The other fisherman said, "It looked more like rocks crumbling into the sea."

"That was down below. I saw something that looked like a castle at the top of the cliffs."

One of the elderly female shopkeepers spoke up. "Maybe the legends are true."

Her friend elbowed her in the side. "You can't be

serious, Margaret. The legend of ancient dragons livin' in the cliff caves is just a story our mothers told us to keep us in line. Is that the one you're talkin' about?"

"To be sure," Margaret answered.

"I admit it sounds far-fetched," Mrs. O'Malley said. "But the lad could have seen what started the legends in the first place."

"There's only one way to know for certain." One of the farmers gestured toward Finn with his beer mug. "You could take us there."

Finn shot a panicked look at Pat.

"Now you've gone and done it," Pat said. "The whole village will follow you to the cliffs, and now that it's dark and everyone's had a few pints, we could lose a few over the edge."

"We'll go in the mornin'," the first farmer said. "Right after the milkin'."

"Ha. We'll beat you to it," said one of the fishermen. "We'll cast our nets out there and have a better view to boot."

"'Tis not a good fishin' spot," his mate said.

"I wonder why not? Perhaps the fish have all been eaten by dragons," one of the farmers quipped.

The whole pub erupted in laughter.

Pat leaned in and whispered to Finn, "Perhaps you can laugh and pretend you were jokin'. All this talk of people fallin' over the cliff is makin' me nervous. If it happens, it will be blamed on you."

Finn shook his head. "I can't lie."

"Then you should learn to shut up when liquor loosens your tongue."

"'Tis not the liquor, Pat. I need answers. I need

to know what happened. Maybe they moved into the caves."

"And were eaten by a dragon?" his friend asked without saying the rest of what he was probably thinking... something like, "you love-besotted fool who can't or won't believe your lady up and left you." Patrick sighed. "Whatever the reason, she's gone. You may never know why. You must accept that."

"I'll accept nuthin' of the kind. She *will* find a way to contact me." He lowered his voice. "Or I'll find her, by God."

"Meanwhile, gettin' the whole village lookin' for a castle on the side of a cliff? Think, Finn. It's an accident waitin' to happen. Tell everyone you were jokin'. Please."

Finn stubbornly shook his head. "I'll not take back the truth."

"Then whatever happens is on you."

Pat stormed out of the pub, leaving Finn to listen to the entire village debate the possibility of dragons, ancient castles, and his own loss of sanity.

———

Rory exited the bathroom wiping his hands on a paper towel. "This was all me sisters could find at the grocer. We need to pick out terry-cloth towels together." He shot Amber a wicked grin as he tossed the towel in the trash under the kitchen sink.

"We? As in you and them, right? You want a female point of view to decorate *my* place, I imagine."

"I do not. Me sisters would just confuse matters. Shannon would pick ruffles and Chloe would talk me into camouflage." He reclaimed his spot in the middle of his futon and patted the empty space beside him. "I meant you and me. After all, we're the ones who are to be livin' together." The more he thought about sharing his intimate space with the sexy, honey-haired flight attendant, the more he liked the idea. And the less he was just teasing.

A pretty blush colored her cheeks and she stuttered, but Rory was saved from another poor attempt at an insult when the intercom buzzed.

"Ah, we have company." He rose and strode to the buzzer before she could get there, then punched the Answer button. "Who might you be, and who are you callin' for?"

The female voice announced, "I am Euterpe, and I'm here to see Amber."

"Euterpe, is it? Like the muse?"

He heard a giggle on the other side of the intercom.

"She's my…my funny friend," Amber said quickly. "Let her in."

Rory pushed the Enter button, and a few moments later there was a knock. Amber was ready for it. She opened the door, clamped her hand around her friend's arm, and practically dragged her to the bedroom with no further explanation.

"Wait," Euterpe said. Amber paused but didn't let go.

"Who is your handsome friend?"

Rory straightened to his full six-foot-two height and sent her his most charming smile.

Amber rolled her eyes. "That's Rory. Pay no attention to him. He'll be gone before you know it."

"No, I think you should introduce us," Euterpe said. She lowered her voice. "I have the feeling we have something in common."

Amber hissed, "How could you possibly think you have anything in common with my unwanted roommate?"

Rory, with his acute sense of hearing, caught every word. He strode over to the women and extended his hand.

"Pleased to meet you, Euterpe. If you be named after the muse I'm thinkin' of, we may well have somethin' in common."

"Like what?" Amber asked.

Euterpe took his hand and they both said, "Music," at the same time.

Rory grinned and lifted the woman's hand to his lips, where he placed a kiss on her knuckles.

Euterpe seemed perfectly comfortable with the gesture. "Do you play?"

Amber snorted. "He plays with my patience."

Rory ignored her. "I play the fiddle, squeeze box, guitar, and bodhran. I sing and compose a bit too."

"Really?" Euterpe sighed. "I'd love to hear some of your songs—"

"Not. Now," Amber bit out. She tugged on the muse's arm until it was clear she'd rather dislocate it than let her talk to Rory.

Ah. She must be threatened by me Irish charm. That's well and good.

"A private concert it is then. Me sisters make up the rest of our trio. I'll call them down."

"Don't bother." Amber marched her friend to her bedroom, shoved her inside, then closed the door behind them.

Rory chuckled. *Ah, I'm gettin' to her.* He needed to speak to his sisters anyway, so he removed his shirt and shimmered, allowing his dragon form and wings to magically appear.

He flew up to the ceiling and rapped on it. He probably didn't need to use the secret knock he and his sisters had developed, but he did anyway.

Chloe was the first to come downstairs. She let herself into the apartment, and as soon as she spotted Rory's dragon form, she slammed the door behind her. "Stop feckin' around," she hissed. "You've a human in the next room."

He transformed quickly and stood with arms folded as Shannon opened the door and walked in.

"Why did you slam the door in me face, Sister?"

"This foolish idjit had his dragon out." Chloe glared at him. "Next time, bang on the ceiling with a broom handle—like a human would."

"I guess you'll have to buy me a broom. Don't worry. Amber is fully occupied with a friend right now," he said. "A friend we may be able to sway to our side. She loves music. Her name is even Euterpe."

Shannon's jaw dropped. "Euterpe? The muse of music? *Our* muse?"

Rory lowered his voice. "I don't know if she's supernatural or not, but this building must be a safe place for muses. Bliss comes here."

Chloe pulled a crumpled piece of paper from her jeans pocket. "I was makin' a list of things we need. Which is more important? Puttin' on a show or movin' in fully?"

"I may not have a place to move into if a muse is against me livin' here. I'll probably end up in a cardboard box," he said. *And I need to protect my sisters—not that*

they'll admit it. Plus, seein' that wizard again is vital.
Three pairs of eyes on two floors will be better for spot-
ting him.

Chloe and Shannon glanced at each other. "We'll get the instruments."

"I was hopin' you'd say that." Rory dug a key out of his pocket. "Do you remember the way back to the storage locker we rented before going to the tearoom?" he asked.

"I do." Chloe snagged the key and slipped it into her front pocket.

"Never fear, Brother," Shannon added. "We're here for you."

Chloe smirked. "We may fight amongst ourselves, but when outsiders attack an Arish, they take on the whole clan and rue the day."

Rory chuckled. "I'll compose a special song. Something that will irritate Amber and entertain her friend."

Shannon moved closer and touched his arm. "You might not want to anger her overmuch. Did you not notice her eyes? They're hazel green. Grandmother gave you a magic gem at birth. I can't remember if the color was gold or green, but it was amber, which comes in both colors. Heavens, even her hair and her name are Amber."

He'd noticed all right. Perhaps his sister was giving him good advice, and it was best to tread lightly. Their gifted gems were said to match their true love's eyes.

Chloe reared back. "I know his magical gem is amber, but surely you don't think she's the one for Rory?"

Shannon sighed. "My gem is sapphire, and Finn's eyes are as blue as the princess's ring."

Chloe muttered, "Bollocks. At least me gem is an impossible color for eyes. One more bit of proof there's no lover meant for me. I can't think of anyone with diamond eyes."

Shannon smiled. "You never know. Mayhap a supernatural has diamond eyes."

"Ha. I'll believe it when I see it."

One side of Rory's lips rose. "Or maybe he just has the hardest head on earth. In that way, she'd have met her match."

"I should let you get your own feckin' instruments, food, and furniture."

"All right. All right." He held up his hands in surrender but couldn't help chuckling all the same. "Don't rush. I'll probably need the night to compose something, and it's late already."

"Do you think her friend will be here tomorrow?" Shannon asked.

"I think if we invite her to a session, she'll arrive at any time we agree upon."

"I want to know more about the actual duties of being the muse of air travel. Can you tell me what I'd be expected to do?" Amber asked her trainer.

"Um…I can show you, although I may need your help."

"But how can I help if I don't even know what I'm doing? I'm a flight attendant, not a pilot. Am I supposed to tell the pilot or copilot how to fly a plane?"

"Of course not." Euterpe laughed. "One would suppose they're in the pilot or copilot's seat because they already know how to fly. All their muse would do is encourage them to stay calm and focused on a safe flight or landing—or whatever. I think. I don't know."

"Okaaaay…" Amber said, still confused.

"Let's start at the beginning. Why do you want to be the muse of air travel?" Euterpe asked and began pacing.

"I'm not sure I do. I know I want this apartment, and if being a muse gives me an edge…"

Euterpe snapped her focus back to Amber. "That's it? You just want the muse power to throw your weight around? Why, I should report you!"

Amber jumped up. "No! Please don't do that."

Euterpe continued pacing and kept right on talking as if she'd heard nothing. "On the other hand, since I haven't even trained her yet, that might not be fair."

"Yes. That's the right idea." Amber nodded emphatically. "I need to be trained."

Euterpe continued to ignore her and spoke as if carrying on a conversation with herself, alone. "I suppose I could give her a warning."

"Absolutely. I'd appreciate that. Consider me warned."

She whirled on Amber and folded her arms. "You must concentrate on your muse duties first and foremost. Your personal wishes come second."

"Agreed." Amber would have agreed that the sky was yellow and the grass was blue at that point.

Euterpe looked down her nose at her. "That is your first lesson. Now, sit."

Amber almost fell to the floor, as if a giant invisible hand had pressed down on her shoulder.

Euterpe remained standing with her arms crossed. "I

know nothing about air travel. You will have to teach me as well."

Amber gulped. How much was she expected to know? Flight attendant training had taught her about safety, how to put out fires, keep passengers calm, and respond to medical emergencies, but *not* how to actually fly a plane. Flight attendants might pull off a miracle and land a plane in the movies, but it wasn't part of their certification.

Amber didn't feel particularly confident at the moment. In her bedroom, she had a goddess who spoke in riddles and couldn't make a decision without a long monologue with herself. In her living room was a drop-dead gorgeous guy who acted like he owned the place. And nowhere could she find a piece of furniture that she could call her own and sink into for a good cry.

The intercom buzzed. *Maybe it's the movers.*

"If you'll excuse me, I need to see who that is," Amber said as she escaped the bedroom.

Rory was already speaking over the intercom. "She's here. Please come in." He hit the buzzer that opened the outside door.

Well, at least he's polite to strangers.

She strode to the door, asking, "Is it the movers?"

"No. Some woman. She said she was a friend of yours."

She opened the apartment door and in strode Mother Nature herself. She was wearing perfectly fitting jeans and a clingy green sweater that could have been made for her by a famous designer. *Why couldn't I have become the muse of fashion?*

The goddess's white hair was bound in a trendy chignon at the nape of her neck.

Oh, crap. Did Euterpe decide to tattle on me after all?

To Amber's surprise, the Goddess of All grabbed her shoulders and kissed the air on either side of her cheeks. "Amber, my dear. I hope you don't mind me showing up without calling. I need to speak to you." She glanced at Rory over Amber's shoulder. "In private."

"Certainly. You can join me in my bedroom." She lowered her voice and whispered, "Our mutual friend is already there."

"Lovely! We'll have a party," the goddess said.

Amber doubted that. She led Gaia to her bedroom, and upon opening the door, was shocked to find a white folding table and chairs that looked as if they had come from a wedding or a garden party. A basket of fruit graced the middle, and small plates and saucers were spread around on three sides.

The goddess took a seat as Amber closed the door. Euterpe sat next to her.

"What kind of tea do you like?" Gaia asked Amber.

"Oh, anything. As long as it has no caffeine. My nerves are kind of shot."

Mother Nature pointed at the table and said, "Herbal it is." A teapot appeared on the table. "You'll pour," she told Amber.

That said, the goddess launched right into it. "Euterpe, I'm afraid you didn't understand what I wanted you to do when I asked you to train the new muse."

"Oh? I'm sorry, Gaia. What did I do wrong?"

"Well, just about everything, but I'm here now, so we can straighten this out."

Amber let out a sigh of relief, then realized Euterpe could interpret that as an insult and tried to cover it with a cough.

"I see," Euterpe said. "Please tell me what to do and I'll comply."

"Simply teach her the basics of being a muse. What her powers are and how to use them."

"I thought that was what I was doing."

Amber had finished pouring the tea and finally sat down. "Actually, you were teaching me what *not* to do."

"But both sides are necessary," Euterpe insisted. "She needs to know what to do as well as what *not* to do. Don't you agree, Goddess?"

Gaia took a long sip of tea and Amber did too.

"Actually, we don't have a lot of time. I think it would be better if I gave her the quick version and you can be excused to do"—she twirled her hand in the air a couple of times—"whatever it is that you do."

"Yes, Goddess. I understand." She rose and left the room.

Amber gazed at Mother Nature and wondered what she'd meant when she said they didn't have much time.

"Amber, as a muse you'd be able to listen for Mayday calls. Did you know that?" Gaia asked.

"No, I didn't. How would I do that?"

"Simply tune your frequency to pick up those words. You might want to specify that you only hear them when spoken above one thousand feet. Otherwise Beltane will drive you crazy."

"What's Beltane?"

Gaia rolled her eyes. "The springtime festival held on May first. May Day. With a May pole. Sound familiar?"

"Oh, yeah." Amber tipped her head. "But how do I 'tune a frequency'?"

Mother Nature closed her eyes and pinched the bridge of her nose. "She really taught you nothing." She focused her gaze on Amber again. "I'm sorry. Simply ask for whatever you need. Be as specific as possible, and I'll give you the ability."

"I see. So if I say, 'Mother Nature, I'd like the ability to hear the term "Mayday" when spoken above one thousand feet,' you will grant me that ability?"

"Correct."

"What about mountain climbers? They might be calling for help at above one thousand feet."

Gaia leaned back and stared at Amber. "You're a smart little shit."

"I'm sorry. I wasn't being a smart-ass. Do I need to take care of them too?"

"No, I really meant it. You're smart to think of that. I want you to concentrate on air travel. I'll find someone else to look after fools who insist on going where they don't belong. Or not. Maybe I'll let them learn from their own stupid actions."

She took a deep breath and stared at Amber. "Since I know what you meant, I'll grant you the ability to hear 'Mayday' limited to air travel, but understand that you must be as specific as possible in the future. I can't be held responsible for misinterpretations."

Amber didn't point out that Mother Nature herself had not been specific enough. Somehow she knew the powerful goddess wouldn't take it well.

Before either of them could go on, Amber heard a Mayday call. It sounded far away, but she heard it plainly.

"There it is," she cried. "I heard a Mayday!"

"Drat, I'd hoped they could keep that piece of junk in the air," Gaia muttered. Then she grasped Amber's hand. "Here we go."

Suddenly Amber was in the back of a cockpit, and the plane was losing altitude. She heard one engine sputter and go silent.

"Lean over the pilot's shoulder and tell him what to do."

Amber's throat almost closed in panic. *Tell the pilot what do?* All she could think of to say was, "Tighten your seat belt, and the sick bag is in the pocket in front of you."

But suddenly she just knew—and she directed him toward a long, straight, deserted field in Polynesia. The pilot managed to lower the landing gear and steer. At last, he landed the plane safely.

She heard a cheer rise up behind her. Gaia tapped her on the shoulder and gave her a thumbs-up.

Then she was back in her bedroom—alone. She collapsed on the folding chair and mumbled, "Holy fuck."

All the furniture disappeared and she landed on her butt on the floor. "Oww!"

A moment later, Rory knocked and opened her door. "Are you all right, lass?"

"I will be when the movers get here." She rose and rubbed her backside.

"I have a fine futon."

"How nice for you."

Finn leaned on the bar and wondered if Shannon could

be trapped in that cave that seemed to be part of the castle built into the cliff on her property. If so, how would he get down there to save her? Just then, a man with an English accent swiveled his stool toward his partner and leaned in to speak in a low voice.

"So, how did the town of Ballyhoo get its name? Do you know?"

"Nobody remembers how the town got its name, or if the term *ballyhoo*—meaning 'uproar, commotion, or hullabaloo'—came after the township. The place is ancient, with relics and weaponry carbon-dated to 300 BC. The bogs were lousy with them before they all got carted off to the national museum. The ancient Irish kings must have had quite a ballyhoo here."

His partner chuckled. "I remember hearing that. They may have hidden some of their treasure in the bogs, knowing a war was coming."

"All of it is now in the Dublin Archeological Museum and National Museum of Ireland, but if a newly discovered ancient castle exists in Ballyhoo…" The first man gazed over his shoulder at a dejected Finn.

"I'm way ahead of you, mate."

Finn turned toward the gentlemen. "Are you archeologists?"

They looked startled at first. Then sly smiles stole across their faces. "Why, yes. We didn't know you were listening. Are you interested in the castle and caves?"

Finn straightened. "Very."

—~~~—

Minutes later, Finn was rappelling down the cliff. They had already searched the ruins of the castle that were visible above the section that seemed to be built into the cliff below. Any treasure that might be found had to be hidden in the caves. There didn't appear to be any steps connecting the upper and lower parts. *How did the ancient kings get into the caves? They must have had wings...*

The portly English guys might be archeologists, but neither one was Indiana Jones. At least they rented the equipment and showed him how to use it. If he weren't so worried about what or *who* he might find in the caves, he'd admit this was a lot of fun.

At last he came close enough to one of the caves to peek inside. Nothing seemed to bar the entrance, but beyond that, it was just a hole of darkness. He grasped the flashlight they'd loaned him and shone the light inside the cave.

One of the gentlemen leaned over the cliff and called down, "What do you see?"

"Nothin' yet," Finn called up.

The guy above him snorted. "Well, perhaps you should go inside."

Go inside? "And how do you propose I do that when I'm hangin' from a string?"

The other bloke laughed. Then he leaned over far enough to see Finn. "It's a very strong cable. You should be able to push off from the cliff and swing inside the cave. Then it's just a matter of planting your feet and unhooking yourself."

"Oh, sure," Finn muttered. "Just swing back and forth and hope to land far enough inside to do that." Then he followed through on the thought. "How will I reach the cable again when it's time to come back?"

"Pull a little extra in with you. The weight of the harness should hold it in place, but if you're worried, you can put a rock on top."

That sounded reasonable. He didn't want too much slack however. Then he'd have to dive off the cliff and bounce when he came to the end of the cable. Trusting it to hold him was hard enough, even though he was slight of build. Tall and wiry, one might say.

But Shannon could be in there.

He had to try.

Finn lowered himself just enough to reach the bottom of the cave entrance, scrunched his knees, and pushed off the edge. His feet landed on the rough floor, but the cable dragged him back outside before he could stand.

"Oh, I have a bad feelin' about this," he called up. The guys ignored him and looked like they were having a heated discussion with each other. He could just make out what they were saying.

Apparently one of them wanted to take any artifacts they found to the Royal British Museum and the other thought they should stay in Ireland. Hmmm… Finn was a loyal countryman and didn't want any more treasures leaving his homeland. Therefore, he needed to keep whatever he found a secret. Unless he found Shannon, in which case he'd be unable to contain his joy.

He had to try again. This time he let out a little more cable. Just enough to send his bum over the threshold. Hopefully he could stand up quickly and have the slack he needed to prevent being dragged outside again.

He pushed off the cliff and swung inside. This time he stuck the landing. He took a couple more steps inside and let out a little more cable before he dared remove the harness.

Now he just needed something to weight down the equipment so it wouldn't leave him stranded even if a strong wind tried to take it.

He took his flashlight again and shone it farther into the cave. Something glinted. He couldn't quite make it out, but it appeared to be gold on top and black on the bottom. Best of all, it looked heavy enough to tether himself to. He inched forward.

Mother Mary! It's a feckin' pot of gold coins! There was no way he could tell the Englishmen about this and expect them to leave it all in Ireland.

Suddenly a short man dressed like Lucky rushed up to the black iron cauldron. It was almost as large as he was. He grasped the edges.

Appearing angry, the little man said, "You'll not be takin' me gold, so just forget it."

"Who are you?" Finn asked innocently.

"Me name is unimportant. Just go."

"I can't. I'm lookin' for me girl. She disappeared a while ago. If I have to turn over every rock in Ireland to find her, I will."

"You'll not find her in here."

"How do you know that?" Finn shone the flashlight farther into the tunnel. "This place looks like it could be quite large."

"It may be large, but I know every bit of it. There are no lasses here."

"Ha. Her sister is missin' too, and you said 'lasses.' You know somethin'. I caught you in a lie."

At that moment the little man tried to run but

couldn't. His feet were stuck firmly in place. He pushed against the cauldron, straining so hard his face turned red. "Shite! Why did you have to say you caught me?"

Could it be? Finn almost laughed. He'd caught a leprechaun, and according to legend, that pot of gold was now his.

But there was something he wanted more than gold. He prowled around the cauldron in case the little bugger managed to pull free. He'd catch him and sit on him to find out what he knew.

"So," Finn said confidently, "I've caught a leprechaun."

"No, you haven't. No, you haven't," the little man said as he struggled against the force holding his feet.

"And looky there. I've caught you in two more lies."

The leprechaun finally gave up the struggle and lay over the gold. "You can't have it. It's mine! I sto—"

His eyes widened and Finn realized what he'd been about to say.

"Ah. You stole it, did you? And who might you have stolen it from?"

"That's it. I'm not sayin' another word."

He had the little guy. Finn doubted even a leprechaun lawyer could get him out of this. He crossed his arms. "I'll make a bargain with you."

The little leprechaun straightened up and looked interested.

"I'll let you keep your gold if you help me find Shannon and her family," Finn said. "Oh. And I'll be needin' your name."

The little man's lips thinned. At last he ground out between clenched teeth, "It's Shamus."

"Shamus what?"

"Just Shamus. It's not like there's so many of us that we need last names."

Finn nodded. "All right. Now, tell me how to find Shannon Arish."

Shamus let out a deep sigh. "Last I saw, they were on a fishin' boat headin' west."

Finn narrowed his eyes. "And why would they suddenly decide to go fishin' and never come back?"

The little man looked away and shrugged.

"I wonder if you might remember more if I ground your foot under me heel."

Shamus didn't react.

"Hmmm. Don't value your foot much, do you? Mayhaps if I gouge out your eyes and toss them over the cliff so you can't see your gold."

The leprechaun winced. "You'd never..."

Finn tipped his chin up stubbornly. "Desperate men do things they'd never do otherwise. If you know somethin' you'd better start talkin' or prepare to say good-bye to your eyes."

"No. Don't do it. I'll tell you."

After a brief hesitation, Shamus confessed.

"We leprechauns set them on the boat and gave it a tiny push. I don't know where they be now."

Finn clenched his fists and tried to wrestle his temper under control. This leprechaun knew more than he was telling.

"Do you have some magic in you? Can't you see them if you close your eyes or somethin'?"

Shamus scratched his whiskered cheek. "First let me go, and I'll tell you what I see."

Finn laughed. "You'd like that, wouldn't you?" He was careful not to use the words 'I release you' in any way. Not even with the word 'if' in front. "Sure'n you'd disappear down that tunnel and take your gold with you."

Shamus looked as if he were trying to stomp his foot. Or maybe he was making one last desperate attempt to get free. "If I do as you wish, you must let me go."

Finn mulled it over. He figured it was a good bargain—if it led to finding Shannon. "Go ahead."

"How do I know you won't take me pot of gold and leave me here as soon as I tell you what I see?"

"First, I don't want your stinkin' gold. Second, I couldn't get it out of here without some help, and that would involve leavin' and comin' back. You'd be long gone by then. And third, I'm a man of my word, and I give you me word."

Shamus stroked his beard and stared off into the distance. At last, he said, "All right. I'm trustin' you, though you should know that if you try to take me gold, I'll come after you. And leprechauns can be mighty creative when it comes to playin' tricks on humans."

Finn didn't bother pointing out that if he'd lied and didn't release the leprechaun, there was little Shamus could do to "come after him." He wanted the little man to trust him completely, so he nodded.

The leprechaun took a few deep breaths and closed his eyes. He remained silent for so long that Finn worried he might have fallen asleep.

At last he opened his eyes. "I saw the young Arish women walkin' up to a brick building. A brownstone, I think they call it, though it wasn't brown. Trees lined the street, and many cars were drivin' down the road. I'd say she's in a city with her sister."

Finn wondered why their brother wasn't with them, but he'd have to find out later. Right now he needed the little bastard to narrow down the search. "They could be in any number of cities. I need more than that."

Shamus shrugged. "I didn't see much more."

"Tell me everythin' you saw. There must be a clue."

The little man sighed. "I saw a sign. It said 'Speed Limit,' and under that it said '30.'"

"That doesn't sound like kilometers."

"It isn't. I'm guessin' they made it all the way to America."

Finn snorted. "No thanks to you."

"I did as you said. You must release me now."

"Not yet. I need more to find her."

"Like what?"

"Like what city in America are you talkin' about?"

Shamus huffed in frustration. "I don't know. I didn't see much else."

"Think harder."

When no more information came, Finn strolled over to his harness. "Let's see. There are some pretty sharp hooks on this equipment."

Shamus held up both palms in a "Stop. I give up" gesture. "All right. All right! I saw two more things in the distance."

"And those were?"

"Street signs. One said 'Massachusetts Avenue,' and the other said 'Cambridge and MIT next right.'"

At last. Finn knew enough about American geography

to know that Boston, Massachusetts, was a northern city in America.

"Could it be Boston?"

Shamus looked hopeful. "I suppose it could."

"I need to be sure. Why don't you go back into your trance and take a walk around the town?"

"It hurts me head to do that, you know."

"More than it hurts your eyes to be gouged—"

"Fine!" Shamus spit in Finn's general direction. "I'll do it."

I wouldn't really gouge out his eyes, but I have to keep him believin' I could if he doesn't confess all.

Shamus closed his eyes and rattled off words as if reading every sign he saw. "Beacon Street, Cambridge, Massachusetts Institute of Technology…"

Finn would check the references later, but he was pretty darn sure the leprechaun was visualizing somewhere in Boston.

Chapter 6

RORY FINISHED TUNING HIS GUITAR AND SAID TO HIS sisters, "Thanks for gettin' me guitar here so quickly. I was beginnin' to feel naked." He waggled his eyebrows at Amber.

She rolled her eyes.

"Did you bring everythin'?" he asked.

"Don't worry," Shannon said. "Your precious squeeze box, bodhran, and tin whistles are upstairs."

He grinned. "Ah, I knew I could count on you."

He plays all those instruments? Amber couldn't help being a little impressed. "I imagine you had other belongings with you," she said, hoping the answer was no.

All three siblings stared at her.

Shannon blinked first. "These aren't belongin's, luv. Our music is part of us. To leave me harp behind would be like leavin' me arm or leg."

Euterpe nodded. "I understand completely." Sitting beside Amber on the futon, she elbowed her and rubbed her hands together like an excited teenager at a rock concert. "I can't wait to hear them play."

Amber sighed. *Why did I have to get the muse of music?* Amber was interested in hearing them play, of course, but she *could* wait until they were at the tearoom, playing for their supper. That would mean this stalemate was over.

"First, a ballad in honor of our home," Rory announced.

His sisters nodded solemnly.

Shannon sat on the window seat and pulled her harp close. Standing, Chloe put the flute to her lips. Sitting on the other side of the window seat like Chloe's bookend, Rory strummed the opening and his sisters joined in one by one. When all three instruments were harmonizing, the sound became so rich, it took on a life of its own. Amber had to admit the music they made together was amazing. It sounded like more than just three instruments. Then Rory added his deep bass voice to the mix.

> *"The Battle of Ballyhoo was a long and bloody thing,*
> *But the invaders were defeated, led by our mighty King.*
> *Nobody knows how long they fought. It lasted many days.*
> *But in the end 'twas all for naught, repellin' foreign ways.*
> *'Tis said that time, it heals all wounds, and it healed our*
> * sacred land.*
> *Yet time defeated what wars could not, and kingdoms did*
> * disband…"*

A knock sounded at the door. The music ceased. Amber rose and strode to answer it.

The managers were on the other side. "I'm sorry. Was the music too loud?" she asked hopefully.

Morgaine and Sly stood there with Nathan and a beautiful redhead behind them. All were wearing neutral expressions and didn't seem annoyed at all. *Darn it.*

"I'm sorry to interrupt you," Sly said. "We just wanted you to know that we're having a tenants' meeting to address who gets apartment 1B. We figured we'd let your neighbors decide who they'd like to live next to."

Chloe piped up. "When is it? Me and Shannon would want to be there."

Morgaine winced. "I'm sorry. You two are excluded for the obvious reason that you'd favor your brother."

Chloe opened her mouth to say something else, but Shannon clamped a hand over it.

"'Tis fair," Rory said. "Thank you for tellin' us in advance."

The redhead strode forward. "That music was beautiful. Are y'all part of a larger band?"

Rory aimed his charming, hundred-watt grin at her. "Thank you kindly, but no. This is it—the whole band." He stuck out his hand. "I'm Rory. I don't think we've met."

The gorgeous redhead shook his hand and said, "Gwyneth Wyatt. I live on the third floor."

Amber was afraid he'd turn her hand and place a kiss on Gwyneth's knuckles, just like he had with Euterpe, but he didn't. And why did that thought bother her so much? She didn't even know this woman, but she wanted to slam the door in her face.

Nathan strode forward and placed a possessive arm around the redhead's waist. Amber was relieved for some reason, and that annoyed her even more.

"How often do you practice?" Nathan asked.

"Not so often as to bother you," Chloe said. "We've been playin' together since we were children. Not much need to practice."

Shannon raised a finger. "But when me or me brother

write a new song, we may have a session or two, makin'
sure to get it right before we play in public."

Chloe focused on Nathan. "We can practice upstairs
in 2B and not bother you overly much since you live
across the hall."

"If the music is always that good, I'd love it if y'all
would practice upstairs. I live in 3A," Gwyneth said and
smiled up at Rory.

Nathan narrowed his eyes and pulled Gwyneth a
little closer.

Ah, jealousy. Good, Amber thought. *Maybe that's
another point in my favor.* And maybe this Nathan guy
will keep a leash on the redhead.

So far it looked like two against two.

"Are there any other neighbors?" Amber asked.

"Not really," Sly said. "The penthouse is occupied
by the owners; my daughter, her husband, and their
son. They value their privacy more than anything
else—particularly my son-in-law. He's rather famous.
That's why they appointed my wife and me to manage
the rest of the building. I'll certainly invite them to
the tenants' meeting, but there's no guarantee they'll
be available."

"By the way," Morgaine added, "if you happen to see
the owner and recognize him, *do not* tell anyone he lives
here. The place would be mobbed."

The Arishes glanced at each other. Finally, Chloe
spoke up. "That shouldn't be a problem for us, considerin' we wouldn't recognize anyone in your country—
save maybe the president, and only because we've seen
his picture in the local newspaper."

"We don't even have a movie theater nearby,"

Shannon said. "He could be a famous actor, and we wouldn't know him if we tripped over him."

Sly nodded. "That's good, but he's not an actor. Are any of you fond of sports?"

Rory folded his arms. "Everyone in my country loves football, but the United States plays it differently. We don't know any of your footballers."

Nathan smirked. "Yeah. What you call football, we call soccer." Then he glanced at Sly. "And the closest thing they have to baseball is cricket."

Ah, so he's a baseball player.

"How about you, Amber? Are you a sports fan?" Sly asked.

She chuckled. "The only sport I'm remotely interested in is hunting, and by that I mean *bargain* hunting."

Gwyneth smiled. "Now ya'll are speakin' my language."

Finally, I scored a point with the redhead.

Sly turned to Nathan and Gwyneth. "So, do you two have any more questions for the newcomers?"

"Just one," Nathan said. "How do you react to *odd* occurrences?"

Rory and Amber glanced at each other. Finally, Rory laughed.

Amber tried to keep her expression neutral. That question might have been a red flag under less desperate circumstances, but she wasn't about to let anything drive her out of her prime spot. "I'm quite open-minded, actually," she said. "I doubt I'd let anything *odd* bother me in the least."

"Well, me sisters can be a bit odd at times, but I haven't abandoned 'em yet," Rory said.

Shannon chuckled and Chloe gave him a good-natured poke with her flute.

"Do y'all get along?" Gwyneth asked, and she glanced at Morgaine. "Families can have some powerful rows."

Morgaine laughed.

Maybe they're speaking from experience. "Are you two related?" Amber asked.

"Gwyneth and I are cousins," Morgaine answered.

"And if it weren't for Konrad, one of us might not be here," Gwyneth added. "He had to pull us apart more than once."

"Who's Konrad?" Shannon and Chloe asked at once.

Gwyneth smiled. "A good friend. He used to live in the apartment upstairs that's now the para—" Nathan bumped her with his hip. "I mean, the place across from y'all."

Amber couldn't help wondering what Gwyneth had been about to say.

This place—and these people—had secrets.

———— ∾∾ ————

Chad the ghost eavesdropped during the tenants' meeting. After all, he had lived there longer than anyone—or, not lived, but still existed or… Oh hell. He haunted the place.

Morgaine and Sly were at one end of the large table in their living and dining area. Gwyneth and Nathan were on the opposite side. Sly's daughter, Merry, was at the head of the table with her toddler, but Jason Falco, her famous baseball player and falcon-shifter husband, was on the road at an away game.

Nathan was clairvoyant, so Chad positioned himself out of the raven-shifter's sight line. The witches, Morgaine and Gwyneth, were clairaudient and could hear Chad when he spoke, so he remained quiet. Truth be told, he loved being the proverbial "fly on the wall."

"Thanks for coming, everyone," Morgaine said. "This is your home too, and I know everyone wants to retain our peaceful atmosphere. That can't happen with the contentious situation in 1B."

Gwyneth raised her hand.

"Go ahead, Gwyneth," Sly said.

"Are the two sisters part of this, or do they keep 2B no matter what y'all decide happens to their brother?"

"Good question," Morgaine said. "I see no reason why we should ask them to leave unless they cause problems."

"They're all dragons, right?" Nathan asked.

Merry, the owner, gasped. "Dragons? You didn't tell me anything about dragons. Remember what happened last time we let a dragon move in? Fire sneezes! I had to evict her."

Sly held up his hand. "They assured me they have no allergies and never sneeze fire. They have complete control over their powers." He smiled at his daughter. "Don't worry. I made sure of that right away."

She let out a relieved-sounding breath.

"Except for Merry, you've all met them," Sly said. "What did you think?"

Nathan raised his hand. Sly nodded to let him know he had the floor.

"Before we get to that, I have another question. What about the girl? Is Amber a dragon too?"

"Great question," Sly said as he stared at Morgaine. "We don't know what she is. And on the off chance a human found her way to us, we can't ask her."

Chad almost laughed. *Another human? In this building? Now that 2A is the paranormal club, this could be very interesting.*

"Are you forgetting what it was like for me when I first moved in?" Merry asked.

Morgaine smiled. "I put a spell on that newspaper ad so only you would see it."

Merry raised her eyebrows. "You never told me that."

Sly shrugged. "I wanted to get to know the daughter I had to give up when I was turned. I asked Morgaine to cast the spell."

"Ah. Now it makes sense," Merry muttered. "So can we assume… No, that's the wrong word. Can we suppose that Amber might be some kind of paranormal?"

Nathan smirked. "Birds of a feather…"

Clever, coming from the raven-shifter to the wife of a falcon-shifter, Chad thought.

"I wish there was a surefire way to find out," Gwyneth said.

"Maybe there is." Chad couldn't contain himself any longer. He was in a unique position to spy—er, observe.

Gwyneth bopped herself upside the head. "Chad. I shoulda known you'd be here."

Morgaine chuckled. "Hey, Chad. I think I know what you're proposing, but go ahead. You have the floor."

The non-witch residents looked uncomfortable. "Be sure to tell us what he says, since no one else can hear him," Merry said.

"Of course." Morgaine nodded.

Nathan turned around. Chad had purposely stayed on the other side of the raven because he knew Nathan could see him, but now he could lip-read too.

"Why don't you give me a chance to observe her? If she wants that apartment so badly and has any powers or witchy ways, she'll use them and I should be able to let you know."

Gwyneth snorted. "Witchy ways?"

Morgaine raised her hand. Sly nodded to her.

"Chad reminded us that he's in the unique position to observe Amber for a while. If she wants the apartment and has some pertinent powers, she may use them."

Nathan and Merry remained quiet but appeared to be considering the idea.

"That's not a bad plan, depending on how long it takes," Sly said.

Gwyneth raised her hand and waited for Sly's nod.

"How long do y'all think you can give him to find out?"

Sly and Morgaine stared at each other. Unfortunately, Chad couldn't listen in on their telepathic conversation. That privilege was reserved for vampires and their fated mates.

Sly refocused on the group. "Amber's check hasn't cleared yet. It may take a few more days. Are any of you uncomfortable with postponing the decision that long?"

Everyone shook their heads.

Chad chuckled but kept his secret plan to himself. It had been a long time since he'd frightened a resident, and he missed watching the silly mortals dash out the door and down the street, screaming.

Amber needed to charge her cell phone before her battery ran down and all communication with the outside world was lost. She hoped her neighbor Candy was able to arrange a moving company to come with her things—including her charging cable—soon. She made one last phone call to her neighbor to see what the holdup was.

Candy answered the phone on the second ring.

"Candy! My battery is almost gone. Did you find a moving company?"

"Yes, but they're not cheap. I thought I'd call around—"

"No. Don't bother calling around for better deals. If they can get my stuff packed today and brought over no later than tomorrow, I'll pay whatever they ask."

"When I called, they said they could come Thursday."

"Thursday?" Amber cried. "That may be too late."

"Why?"

"Because I need my stuff. Especially my computer and charger cable. My phone is almost out of juice."

"Well, hang in there. Tomorrow is the best they can do, and it's going to cost to a fortune if—"

Amber winced. At that moment, her phone died.

"Dammit!"

She stormed over to the door, opened it, and called out, "Euterpe, get in here."

Euterpe strolled over to the bedroom door and said, "Hold on there. You don't get to tell me what to do. You can ask nicely or not at all."

Frustrated, Amber raked her fingers through her hair. "I'm sorry." She lowered her voice. "I need you to be on my side, Ms. Muse. I know you're into music and Rory is a musical genius or something, but I'm supposed to be learning from you. And here you are enjoying my nemesis."

"Point taken." Euterpe strolled into the room and closed the door behind her. "Have a seat. What do you want to learn?"

Amber scowled. "I need to learn how to leave this room undetected and then return with no one the wiser. I have shit to do."

"I don't think he's preventing you from using the bathroom…"

Amber whooshed out a deep breath, realizing the muse might be rather literal. "I meant to say, I have *things* to do."

The muse smirked. "I knew what you meant."

Oh, great. A muse with a literal sense of humor. Spare me.

"Let's take it slow," Euterpe was saying. "Think of where you want to be, but before you go, make sure no one else is there."

"My old apartment is where I need to go, and no one else will be there… I'm pretty sure."

"Until you know how to hover in the ether and check to make sure you're alone, you'll need to find a place where you're guaranteed not to be discovered."

"How about my walk-in closet?"

"Is anyone apt to be in there?"

Amber was tempted to make a smart remark until she realized that potentially the movers could have arrived, if her neighbor had managed to get them to come instantly. "Let's call it highly unlikely."

Euterpe nodded. "In that case I'll go with you and hold you in the ether until you can check the area without being seen. I can't stress enough how important it is not to be caught appearing and disappearing."

Amber nodded. "Okay. How do we do that?"

Euterpe took her hand. "Close your eyes and picture your closet."

Amber did.

A few moments later, Euterpe said, "Now open your eyes."

Amber found herself staring at the fluffy blue bathrobe she'd hung on the back of her closet door.

Euterpe dropped her hand. "We're here. I took a brief look around the place and didn't see anyone."

Amber's mouth had gone dry and she was barely able to speak. "How…how did we—"

"How did we find your tiny closet that you laughingly call a walk-in?"

"Hey, I'll have you know it's rare to have more than a tiny closet in Boston apartments."

"My sisters and I love clothes. We have several walk-in closets all over the world. They're called retail stores."

Amber's jaw dropped. "You steal your clothes?"

Euterpe frowned. "Certainly not. We merely borrow what we need for a few hours and then return them. Haven't you ever been shopping and had a clerk tell you she had the item you were looking for in your size, only to return from the back room confused, saying she must have been mistaken?"

"Huh. That's because one of you muses was wearing it?"

"Yes. At least you know you had good taste." Euterpe pulled out a navy-blue-and-white color-blocked designer dress. "Why did you buy this? It's the wrong color for you."

"No, it's not. It looks fine."

Euterpe swiveled the hanger so she could see the back. "It might be cute on the right person, but you're not that person."

Amber examined the garment. It's true she didn't wear that outfit often, but not because it looked bad on her. "Oh, I see. The dress is all right, but the person wearing it is all wrong."

"Exactly." Euterpe looked pleased that her charge had understood.

Amber sighed. "Well, if you don't mind, I'd rather get what I came for. We can dissect my closet another time."

Euterpe shrugged. "As you wish. I'll stay here and see if I can find something that will flatter you."

She'll see if *she can find something?* Amber pushed her way out of her closet in disgust.

Heading to her charging station in the kitchen, she unplugged and wrapped up the cord. Her stomach rumbled. "Christ, I'm starving," she muttered.

She found one of her reusable grocery bags and opened her fridge. *Let's see. Yogurt is something I can grab and eat in my room.* She loaded all the yogurts into the bag.

Ah, snacks. She didn't eat a lot of junk food, but she had a few packages of chips and pretzels. She wouldn't even have to leave her room for those.

"Wait a minute," she said aloud. "I'm supposed to

be learning how to travel in the blink of an eye. I ought to be able to pop into restaurants whenever I want to."

She tossed the snacks into the bag anyway. There was no telling when she might need a midnight snack and wouldn't want to get dressed and find a restaurant or a convenience store.

Euterpe breezed around the corner with an ivory blouse that Amber didn't recognize.

"Where did you find that?"

Euterpe held the item up against her. "Lord and Taylor," she said, then giggled. "See? Even the gods need a tailor."

Amber rolled her eyes. "Listen, I have a few things to get me by, but I still don't really know how to pull off that travel trick by myself."

"I know, and I'll teach you. I will. But right now we should get back before you're missed." She thrust the blouse at Amber. "Try this on."

"Why?" Amber glanced down at her serviceable gray sweater and blue jeans. "There's nothing wrong with what I'm wearing."

Euterpe shook her head. "There's nothing right with it either."

"Argh." Amber swiped the blouse out of Euterpe's hand and marched to her bathroom. She pulled the sweater over her head and tossed it onto the floor. Then she let the silky cream material float over her head. Her eyes shone in the mirror. She could tell in an instant that she looked better and suddenly felt a surge of confidence. She grabbed her brush and quickly ran it through her hair. Yup. As much as she hated to admit it, Euterpe was right. She looked much better.

Deciding to give the muse the thanks she was due, she strode back toward the bedroom and almost tripped over a suitcase. "Sheesh. Where did that come from?"

"I put it there. You needed a few other necessities, so I packed for you."

"But how would you know…"

Euterpe tipped her head and smiled at the blouse and its wearer.

Yeah, she probably did know what to pack. Still, there were a few items the muse might miss. "What about my toiletries?"

"I got you all new products. That bargain junk will dry out your hair, and the makeup was about a year old."

"Oh." Amber was torn. She didn't like people making decisions for her, but the muse was probably right—about everything.

"Okay. Well, I guess we can come back later if I need anything else."

"Sure." Euterpe looked put out.

"What?"

"You didn't even say thank you for the blouse. I bought that for you with my own money."

Amber slapped herself upside the head. "I'm so sorry. I was about to thank you but I got distracted. It's beautiful. You really do have wonderful taste."

The muse smiled. "I know, don't I? You look amazing in it."

"Thank you." Amber picked up the suitcase. "Well, let's get back."

"Put that down and we'll go." Euterpe nodded at the suitcase.

"Put it down? But I need these things. You said so yourself."

"And how would it look if you walked out of your bedroom with all these new things when fifteen minutes ago you had nothing but your purse and the clothes you were wearing?"

Amber dropped the suitcase on the hardwood floor with a plunk.

"So I should leave this for the movers?"

"No. I'll leave your apartment and come back with it and your bag of snacks in about three hours. Muse lesson number two…everything needs to look as normal as possible."

Amber didn't like it, but she certainly could see the wisdom in not angering the goddess or raising suspicion in others.

"Okay. Sounds like a plan."

Euterpe grabbed Amber's hand, and an eye blink later, they were in her empty bedroom.

"Wait! My charger. That's what I went there for."

"And you'll have it in three hours," Euterpe said.

Ballyhoo had disappointed the archeologists and they'd finally left the little town. Finn breathed a secret sigh of relief.

On a stool at O'Malley's, he sipped his Guinness and waited for his friend Patrick. He knew he'd have a hard time convincing Patrick to go to Boston with him, but having company would be so much better—and safer. From what he'd heard, American cities could be unfriendly places and some were downright dangerous.

The door opened and Pat strolled in.

"Paddy, me boy," Mr. O'Malley called. "Shall I pour you a pint?"

"Do you have to ask?"

"Actually, I do." He chuckled. "The missus doesn't want me drinkin' me mistakes anymore."

"Where is your lovely wife?"

"She's at home. Her cousin is visitin' from America."

Finn's ears perked up. "What part of America?"

"Some big city in the middle of the country. Chicago, they call it."

"Ah." *'Tis a shame it's not Boston.*

O'Malley dried one of the beer glasses as he talked. "The Yank is doin' some kind of genealogy trip. Wantin' to trace her roots and all that…"

As O'Malley droned on, Finn thought about how to propose a trip going the other way. He knew Patrick's family had been roughly split in two during the famine. Half went to America, and he thought he remembered Pat telling him that many wound up in Boston.

When O'Malley finished his monologue, Finn asked, "Pat, have you ever wondered what happened to your family that went to America?"

His friend considered the question as he took a long swallow of Guinness. "Never much thought about it. I didn't know 'em. They left a hundred and fifty years ago, give or take a decade."

"But you must have cousins over there. Perhaps many by now."

Pat shrugged.

"Well, wouldn't you like to meet 'em?"

Pat scrunched his forehead and studied his friend.

"What are you gettin' at? I know you well enough to believe you aren't merely passin' the time with idle chatter."

Finn draped an arm casually around Pat's shoulder. "Ah, it's probably nuthin'…"

"What's nuthin? You haven't said anythin' of importance yet."

"Well, I heard on the radio that some big, hotshot businessman from Boston was runnin' for president over there. I think he had your last name. People were makin' a big deal of it, sayin' he'd only be the second Irish Catholic American president, with John Fitzgerald Kennedy bein' the first."

"No kiddin'."

Pat seemed interested. Then he abruptly changed the subject. "Hey, did you find whatever the English bastards were after in those cliffs?"

"Ah, no. And if I had, I wouldn't have told 'em about it."

"Good lad," said a man about four stools down.

Finn peered at the stranger. He'd need to lower his voice. The bar wasn't busy enough to drown out a private conversation. But whispering would be considered suspicious.

"'Tis too nice a day to sit inside a pub," Finn said to Pat. "What do you say we find one of those picnic tables out front?" He hopped off his stool. "C'mon, Pat." He leaned in close. "I have somethin' to tell you in private."

Pat swiped his beer off the bar. "Sure'n we can talk to these idjits any time. Let's go be social with the sun."

Finn and Patrick settled onto the picnic table and

raised their faces to the perfectly blue sky. The warm rays on Finn's face comforted him and made him feel braver.

"So, you were going to tell me something," Patrick said.

Finn sighed. It was now or never. "Do you believe in the little people?"

Patrick stared at him. "Little people? What are you talkin' about? Dwarves?"

"No. I mean the *little* beings of *Ireland*. Leprechauns."

Patrick raised his brows and then burst out laughing. As his laughter died down, he shook his head at his friend. "Ah, you're playin' with me. What's this really about?"

Finn dropped his head into his hands. "I have to tell someone or I'll explode. You're my best mate, Patrick. If I tell you and you don't believe me, t'will be a shame, but not the end of the world."

"I'm beginnin' to worry about you. I think you'd better tell me. I promise, whatever it is, I won't breathe a word."

Lowering his voice, Finn leaned in and said, "The leprechauns, they exist! I've seen one…maybe two."

Patrick stared but didn't tell Finn he was daft. That was a good start.

"It was out by Shannon's place. I rode out there a few days ago and found the ruin on the cliffs that the traveler said might have been a castle."

Patrick nodded slowly. "I remember you sayin' that. Then the archeologists wanted you to go with them and investigate. You said you didn't find a thing. Just some caves."

"That's so they'd give up and go home, which is exactly what they did."

"What has this to do with leprechauns?"

"That's where I found one. In a cave with a bloody pot of gold. And I caught him in a lie, which was apparently as good as catchin' him with me bare hands. He was supposed to give me his gold, only I swapped the gold for information on where to find Shannon. She's in Boston, like some of your family."

Patrick groaned.

"Come on. You didn't expect me to want gold over me own fiancée, did you?"

Patrick clapped his big hand over Finn's shoulder. "I'll tell you what I think. I think you've been missin' that girl so much that you've finally gone 'round the bend."

"Feck. That's what I thought you'd say."

"Then I didn't disappoint."

Finn stewed quietly while Patrick leaned back and let the sun shine on his face.

"I suppose you'll want to go to Boston…"

"Yes." He had to convince his friend he wasn't dotty. "Patrick, I hadn't planned on tellin' you the whole of it, but I trust you. I hope that our friendship means enough that you'll give me the benefit of the doubt before pronouncin' me a lunatic."

Patrick sat up and looked Finn in the eye. "I believe *you* believe. Is that all right for a start?"

"It'll do." Finn nodded.

"Good. Then I'm goin' with you."

He heard snickers from the window.

"Shite. Apparently someone was eavesdroppin',"

Patrick said. "And it's a feckin' small town. In minutes, everyone will know whatever was heard and then some."

"Let's get a head start then," Finn said. "Come with me right now."

Chapter 7

Amber opened the bathroom door and almost barreled into Rory.

"Jeez! You startled me. Tell me when you need the bathroom, and I'll hurry up."

"I didn't need it, luv. I wanted to talk to you about invitin' your friend to our next session."

"Euterpe?" She almost said something snarky about the Goddess Benedict Arnold but stopped the comment in time.

"Yes. If you're talkin' to her, let her know me sisters will be down this evenin' after supper."

Oh damn. Supper. Maybe I'm just hungry. Amber's posture sagged. "I'm sorry. I'm not feeling well. I need to go to my room and lie down...on the floor."

"You could borrow me futon." He shot her a wolfish grin. "I could always lie next to you and make you feel better."

She waved, dismissing him, and returned to her room.

Euterpe popped in. "One of your lessons is that you cannot get sick—unless you want to. But who would want to? You're a minor goddess and have complete control over your body now." She tapped her lower lip and looked pensive.

"Then why have I felt queasy all afternoon?"

"That must be tied to your powers as muse of air travel."

"Seriously? Are you telling me I'm airsick?"

"Well, yes, in a manner of speaking. When someone needs your help flying, that may be how you'll know. You'll feel airsick."

"Oh lovely." Amber rolled her eyes. Then she suddenly snapped to attention. "Wait a minute. Does this mean someone needed my help and didn't say 'Mayday'?"

"Yes. I imagine so."

"You *imagine* so?"

"Well, *I'm* not the muse of air travel, *you* are!"

"But why didn't they call 'Mayday'? How would I know where the help was needed?"

"Close your eyes and feel the panic. Then follow that energy. It should lead you right to the source."

"And what do I do when I get there?"

"I don't know. *You're* the—"

"Yes, I know, I know. *I'm* the muse of air travel. Maybe you should get Brandee or Bliss to come over. Since they've already been through this learning curve, they might be able to help."

"Now that's a lovely idea. I'll pop in on them and see if they're free. Meanwhile, why don't you investigate the problem?"

"Okay." Amber closed her eyes and breathed deeply. Now that she knew how to interpret what she was feeling, she focused on the anxiety someone was putting out there. *And now I'm supposed to follow it?*

In her mind she saw an invisible thread floating toward her. She grasped it and followed where it led with her mind. A rush of noise and light met her, and when she opened her eyes, she was somewhere else.

She could see the scene before her. Pieces of a broken

seaplane bobbed on the water. One young girl—maybe six years old—wore a life preserver and clung to a floating object. She looked exhausted and waterlogged.

This must be the ether Euterpe was talking about. I can see her, but she can't see me. Amber felt her own panic now. *How do I get to her? And where is everyone else?* The little girl couldn't have been alone.

Then she saw what the girl was holding. A teddy bear.

Oh, dear Goddess! What do I do? Amber cried aloud.

Suddenly Euterpe appeared beside her. "Visualize a boat coming to her rescue."

Amber closed her eyes and conjured up a Coast Guard rescue boat speeding toward the little girl. It slowed and circled her. Shouting orders, a man in a white uniform urged the men to lower a lifeboat into the water.

Amber watched as two sailors leaped into the lifeboat and steered it over to the girl. One sailor looked like he was murmuring encouraging words to the little girl and held out his hand toward her as they came alongside. The girl nodded and bravely grabbed the sailor's hand. The other sailor waited with a blanket. As soon as they pulled her aboard, she was wrapped in the blanket and taken to the larger boat. They didn't even try to take the stuffed animal away from her.

"What about her parents? They must have been with her," Amber said.

Euterpe rested her hand on Amber's shoulder. "You did all you could do at this point."

At this point. "You mean to tell me that if I had gotten here sooner I'd have been able to help her whole family? Maybe the pilot too?"

Euterpe clasped Amber's shoulder tighter, and she

experienced a whooshing sound and light. Then she was in her bedroom again.

Amber stepped away from her teacher. "I-I failed, didn't I?"

"Not completely. You saved a little girl."

Amber's legs went out from under her and she burst into tears.

"Oh dear," Euterpe said, but she made no move to comfort her. "Try to understand that you can't win 'em all."

All Amber could focus on was, *I could have saved her family—and I didn't. I didn't know how.*

Euterpe patted her shoulder. "Please, try to think of something else."

"How am I supposed to do that?"

Euterpe crossed her arms. "You have a very handsome man in the next room."

Amber cried even harder.

"I-I'll go get your things," Euterpe said, and she disappeared.

Amber wondered why her muse trainer had just deserted her in her moment of need. Maybe she was going to Mother Nature to report that Amber had screwed up her first assignment. The goddess would be furious—probably with both of them. Amber let out a wail.

Rory came bursting through the bedroom door. He stopped and assessed the situation for a moment. It was too late to pretend nothing was wrong, so she remained on the floor and let herself cry.

He approached her cautiously. "Ah, me darlin'… I don't know what's got you so upset, but I'm not heartless. If you need the apartment so badly, I'll find another place to stay."

She shook her head and managed to eke out, "That's not it."

"Somethin' awful must have happened between you and your friend, then."

She shook her head again.

"Well, whatever it is…" He sat next to her and took her in his arms. She didn't even try to resist.

He stroked her back gently and began to croon softly in another language.

She buried her face in his shoulder and soaked his shirt with her tears. He didn't pry or ask her to cheer up. He simply held her for what seemed like an hour and let her cry herself out.

———

All three leprechauns sat on rocks in a circle. Without the usual preliminaries, Lucky got right to the point. "I think I know where your gold went, Clancy."

"Is that so?" Clancy asked.

"Well, not so much where the gold went, but I think I know where the dragons went. That's the next best thing, since we think they're the ones who took it."

"Ah," Shamus was quick to add. "The dragons must have hidden it well. We've looked all over for it. I haven't found your gold. Have you, Clancy?"

Clancy shook his head. "No. I thought you said you knew where it was, Lucky."

"Apologies. I didn't mean I could point right to it. I've been followin' a young lad from the village who seems quite determined to locate the Arish girl, Shannon."

"And does he know where the gold is?" Shamus asked quickly.

"I doubt he even knows about it…unless young Shannon told him something."

Shamus added, "I wonder if he's trying to find out where she is because she *did* tell him—and now he wants to share it with her."

"Like I said, I've been followin' him. I hid in the bushes by the pub this mornin'," Lucky said.

Shamus bit his lower lip. "The pub is where they all go, but you should be careful. If they catch you…"

"I know," Lucky said solemnly. "Me pot of gold would be gone too."

"So, tell us the rest of your story, Lucky." Shamus bounced up and down on his rock, which made him look like a toddler on a bouncy ball.

"The lad was confessin' to a friend that he had seen a leprechaun. That would be me. I became suspicious of him returnin' again and again to the area where the castle is now exposed."

Clancy reared back and stared at him. "You showed yerself?"

"I did. I counted on him not believin' in leprechauns and spoke to him as if I were a normal shortish man or dwarf. He was leanin' over the cliff, examinin' what's left of the entrance to the castle when I came to investigate."

"Shite," Shamus said. "And you didn't think to give him a tiny push?"

Both Lucky and Clancy stared at him open-mouthed, like land trout.

Shamus shrugged. "We can't let humans know about us, after all. They'd hunt us down like dogs hunting rabbits. 'Tis bad enough that what's left of the castle reappeared after the treaty was broken."

He was about to give Lucky a stern warning when the latter held up one palm. "I know what you're goin' to say."

"Do you now?"

"I do. That I shouldn't have exposed meself to the lad. That I may have put all your gold in peril by doin' so. But he'd already seen the castle and thought his lady-love might be hurt or tied up and hidden in there. He wouldn't have given up without explorin' it further—if I didn't put the idea in his head that young Shannon was all right. He calmed considerably after that."

Shamus narrowed his eyes. "But he didn't give up, did he?"

"No. Apparently he brought archeologists back to the cliffs and they lowered him into one of the caves."

Clancy's eyes rounded. "He's been in the castle's caves? Did he tell the archeologists anythin'?"

"No, thank goodness," Lucky said. "He said it was just some old, musty cave with nothin' in it. Apparently the archeologists left town after that."

Shamus wiped his brow dramatically. "Whew!" Then he glanced back and forth at his mates. "We'd have half of Ireland and archeologists from all over the world tryin' to get inside that castle. Thank heavens we sent the dragons away with their ancient treasure to pawn," Shamus added. "Or most of it."

"The archeologists are out of the way, but there's more." Lucky scratched his beard.

Clancy raised his palms in entreaty. "Then tell us what it is. Leave nothin' out."

"The lad told what he *really* saw to his best mate."

"And?" Clancy prompted.

"He said he'd caught a leprechaun in the cave. Caught him in a lie, he said. Then the lad gave up the pot of gold he'd won for information on where his lady-love might be."

"What?" Shamus laughed. "And you believe that? Obviously the lad is lyin'. He probably wants his friend to go into the caves for him. Probably thinks his lady is hidin' in there, and that maybe she'll show herself to his friend. Mayhaps he's thinkin' she's mad at him for some reason."

"And what about the gold?" Clancy asked.

"That's the part he made up, you dolt," Shamus said. "How else would he get his mate to lower himself into the caves and look around?"

Clancy scratched his head. "It's a mystery, all right."

"He thinks his Shannon is in Boston," Lucky said. "Why would he want his mate to go into the caves?"

"For the gold, o' course," Clancy said.

"There is no gold. I already looked," Lucky said.

"Did you? When?" Shamus asked.

"Weeks ago. When we began lookin' for it. That was the first place I checked. And just in case I missed it the first time, I looked again this mornin'."

"And you didn't find it anywhere, did you?" Shamus asked, more as a statement of fact than a question.

"That's what I said. Apparently the lad wasn't interested in gold at all. He was hopin' his mate would go to Boston with him."

"And made up an elaborate lie to get him to go?" Clancy asked, still puzzled. "It doesn't make sense."

Shamus shrugged. "I guess he had to come up with a story to explain how he knew she was in Boston. He probably guessed she could be there, but didn't want to sound unsure."

"That could be part of it," Lucky said. "He promised to show his friend the castle. Said if he saw that much, he'd know he wasn't losin' his mind."

Clancy rose and paced across the circle of stones. "Somethin' isn't right. Are you sure you didn't mishear, Lucky?"

"Nay, I was close enough."

"And shame on you again for doin' somethin' so dangerous," Shamus said, shaking his finger.

Watching Shamus, Clancy stroked his beard. "We need to go to Boston ourselves."

The other leprechaun stared at him mutely.

"Why?" Shamus asked.

"In case they know where Clancy's gold is," Lucky said. "If it's not in the caves or in the cottage, they must have hidden it somewhere else. If the lad thinks the dragons are in Boston, mayhaps they have family there."

"We know for a fact they're not in Ireland anymore," Clancy said. "And you assured the lad his Shannon was all right, Lucky. Do you know any more about them?"

"I do not. I took his hands and saw her sweet, sad face. If she were no longer alive, I'd have seen darkness."

With both hands on his hips, Clancy said, "We need to find modern clothes. And we should disguise ourselves so the dragons don't recognize us if they see us before we see them. We should spy on them before we confront them openly."

"If they think they can speak freely, we may hear where they've hidden the gold," Lucky added, following Clancy's logic.

"So we're goin' to Boston?" Clancy asked.

"We are," Lucky said. "And we'd better be ready soon, if we're to follow the lad to Shannon."

———

"Come," Rory said to Amber, who was still sitting on her bedroom floor an hour later. "I'll make supper."

"I'm not hungry."

"You must be. We've been here since late this mornin', and you haven't had a bite to eat. I'm famished."

She didn't answer.

Rory wondered what was making her so miserable. She must have received bad news over her cell phone. Or Euterpe could have said something cruel. That would explain why she didn't reach out to her friend. "What is it, lass?"

She remained mute and simply shook her head.

"All right. I'll be in the kitchen. If you want to talk, I'm willin' to listen."

He left her door open so that if she started to cry again, he could hear her. As he pulled ingredients out of the refrigerator and began cutting up vegetables, he thought, *This is crazy. I still want the apartment, but not if it means Amber's wretched mood fails to improve.* Even after her insults, he still liked the girl.

A knock at the apartment door interrupted his thoughts. Amber made no move to answer it, so Rory turned off the gas burner and went to see who it was.

He opened the door to Euterpe, who stood there holding a suitcase.

"I hope you're not movin' in too."

She smirked. "I can't think of anything I'd like less.

No. I went to Amber's apartment and brought her some of the things she needed."

He reached for the case. "I'll take it to her."

"No need. I've brought it this far." Euterpe started to enter the apartment, but Rory stepped in front of her, blocking her way.

"I don't think she's in the mood for company."

Amber drifted out of her bedroom. "Who's here?" she asked him.

Euterpe leaned in enough to show Amber her face. "It's me. I have your things. You know…the clothes and toiletries you wanted?"

"Oh. Yeah," Amber said in an unexcited monotone. She waved her friend in.

Rory stepped aside, and Euterpe gave him an odd look as she passed by. She took the suitcase to Amber's room.

"I guess I could eat a little bit after all," Amber said to him.

He smiled. "Good. Is your friend goin' to stay? We can always stretch the meal with bread and a few more vegetables."

Euterpe emerged from the bedroom. "Stay for dinner? No, thank you. I'd rather not interfere."

"Suit yerself."

He returned to the kitchen and stirred the pot of stew he had made. It smelled as good as his sister Shannon's, and she was the best cook in the family.

Without a ladle, he did his best to spoon plenty of meat and potatoes into Amber's bowl along with the broth. Then his own. He had already set the milk crate for two and placed a half loaf of bread and a tub of butter between them.

Euterpe turned before leaving. "Are you and your sisters still having that session you spoke of earlier?"

Rory paused. The song he had composed was meant to make Amber uncomfortable at first, but then maybe she'd laugh after the punch line…unless she misinterpreted it. He was torn. She could certainly use a good laugh—but would she see the song as good-natured fun?

"I…don't know."

Euterpe clasped her hands and begged, "Oh, pleeease. I really want to hear that new piece you said you were working on."

Oh shite. If she was indeed his family's muse, he didn't want to upset her. They might never be able to play again. But Amber…

"I suppose we could play a few old favorites," he said. "Would you like that, Amber?"

Euterpe narrowed her eyes. "I want to hear the new one."

Rory sighed. "We'll see. It may not be ready."

She raised one eyebrow. "I have the feeling it will be ready enough to practice."

He glanced at the sheet music he had written and that was lying on the window seat. *Shite and double shite.* He didn't have time to compose a whole new song. "Fine," he ground out between clenched teeth. "We'll give it a try."

"Good. What time should I come back?"

"Eight."

"Wonderful. See you then." She waved on her way out the door.

Amber asked a question for the first time in an hour. "Do you prefer not to have an audience the first time you play a song?"

"Indeed. It would be like puttin' the first draft of a book into an unsuspectin' librarian's hands."

Suddenly an odor of gas permeated the room. They both sniffed the air.

"Do you smell that?"

Amber strolled to the kitchen. "Fuck!" She rushed to the stove and turned it off.

Rory ran in after her. Somehow the gas had come back on—by itself.

"I swear I turned it off. All the way. I heard it click."

Amber flicked the switch on the range hood and the fan roared to life. She ran to the living room and struggled to open the window. Rory was beside her in a second and easily opened the other two windows.

She whirled on him. "What the hell, Rory? Are you trying to kill me?"

"Of course not. I don't know what happened. I turned it off. I even went back after and served the stew. It was off. I swear it."

Amber crossed her arms and, mimicking his accent, said, "Did you now? It must be magic that turned it back on."

Magic… The leprechauns? He shook his head. *It couldn't be.* Why would they follow the dragons clear to Boston when they'd acted as if they'd like to wipe them from the map? Was that it? Were they so angry that they were trying to kill him and his sisters?

"Amber, me darlin', I don't know what happened, but I'll check the stove ever' hour until the others get here. You'll think I'm one of those OCD types I've heard about. If it happens again, we'll need to report it to the managers."

She stared at him and eventually let out a long sigh. "Fine."

"Come and eat your stew before it gets cold."

"Or blows up?"

She clearly didn't believe him, but he wasn't going to argue. He'd learned not to poke a hornet's nest, even when the bees appeared to be sleeping or away from home.

During dinner he tried to draw Amber out by making polite chitchat. That was like trying to pull railroad spikes from their ties. Even so, he sensed that she was beginning to relax a little.

Finally, she asked him another question. "So, your music… Have you ever recorded any of it?"

He tipped his head. "A few of our sessions wound up on YouTube, if that's what you're askin'."

"Well, no. I was asking if you have any CDs."

He stroked his chin. "Never even thought of makin' any. We play for our own joy and whoever showed up at O'Malley's during our sessions."

"What's O'Malley's?"

"The local pub. In Ireland, it's where everyone gathers. It's where news and gossip get swapped and often confused." He smiled. Playing kept the siblings out of the gossip circles.

Realizing that Amber had probably never spent much time in a small village pub, he thought he should explain the inside jokes that occur.

"About that new song…"

She pushed the stew around in her bowl. "What about it?"

"Well, it's not a serious ballad like the one you heard before. It's more of a jig with a humorous punch line."

"Okay." She sighed. "I'm going to change into something…else." She left him to his own thoughts and retreated to her bedroom.

When she finally emerged, he was stunned speechless. She wore a beautiful, silky white blouse that made her look virginal and sinful at the same time. Every man's fantasy. *Should I compliment her on it? Would she doubt my sincerity and insult me by sayin' so?*

Before he could decide one way or the other, someone knocked at the door. He knew it had to be one of his sisters, because they used the secret knock. One, then two, then three.

He opened the door and in strode Chloe. "Shannon will be right along. She set off upstairs to invite Sly, Morgaine, and Gwyneth."

Moments later, Nathan followed Gwyneth into the apartment. They each carried a bottle of wine. For some reason, Sly and Morgaine were late or staying away.

Euterpe was right on time though—which didn't surprise Rory a bit. She brought a six-pack of Guinness.

"Ah," Chloe said. "Now we'll have the craic."

Amber raised her brows.

Rory was quick to interpret. "'Craic' means fun. Nothin' more."

"Oh." Amber chuckled.

At last. He was glad to hear the welcome sound from her.

Before he closed the door, he heard Sly saying, "We're coming…with furniture." The vampire easily carried two chairs with him. When he entered and saw Amber, he slumped as if the weight were a burden. Morgaine was right behind him, also carrying two chairs. He saw her drop one, seemingly on purpose. A couple of candles rolled off.

"Oops," she said.

"I'll get it." Nathan handed his bottle of wine to Gwyneth and rushed into the hallway, then brought in the fourth chair.

Now, along with the futon and window seat, there were plenty of places to sit.

Amber settled on the futon with Euterpe.

Nathan and Gwyneth took two of the chairs. Sly and Morgaine sat on the other ones. That left the window seat, which already felt like the band's stage.

"What's this?" Chloe asked as she picked up the song from the padded bench. "A new song?"

He glanced at Euterpe. "I wish we'd had time to rehearse it."

Chloe sat beside her sister, and the two of them studied it to learn their parts. Soon they burst into laughter. He knew they'd have that reaction, but how would Amber take it?

"I'll have a hell of a time singin' me part without crackin' up," Shannon said.

"Do you want me to do it?" Chloe asked.

"Why don't all three of you give it a try?" Euterpe asked.

The siblings glanced at each other. "One of us needs to play a woodwind," Chloe said. "And that's usually me."

Euterpe shrugged. "Ah, well. It's your brother's song after all. I'm sure he wrote it with that in mind."

"I'm just to join in the chorus anyway," Shannon said. "And once you learn it, all of you are invited to join in."

"Oh, that sounds wonderful," Euterpe said.

"Feel free to clap along with the beat," Rory said. "The pub patrons often do." He hoped they'd clap so loud they'd drown out the words.

"Well, without further ado..." Rory picked up his guitar and Chloe her flute. This time Shannon played the squeeze box instead of her harp. The song needed a lively instrument, and he didn't need to tell her that.

Here goes nothin'.

After one round of the melody, the crowd joined in by clapping to the beat and he added his voice:

> *"They say you shouldn't covet your neighbor's pretty things,*
> *But mine has somethin' special. To me she nearly sings.*
> *Her skin is pink, her hair is soft, and her bottom is so round,*
> *I wish I had one like her. My joy would be unbound."*

Shannon joined in the chorus:

> *"I wish I had one like her, my joy would be unbound.*
> *Paddy's pig... Paddy's pig... I wish I had me neighbor's*
> *pig."*

To her credit, she didn't laugh or miss a note. The crowd burst out in giggles though.

> *"Me friend, he said she'd come to me as soon as pigs*
> *could fly.*
> *And so I made her special wings and tried to catch her eye."*

He winked at an astonished-looking Amber.

> *"I coveted that pig so much my heart it was a-achin',*

*I asked Paddy what her name was. He said he called
    her Bacon!"*

At this the crowd roared in laughter—just as he'd
hoped they would.

Shannon joined him in the chorus:

*"I asked Paddy what her name was. He said he called
    her Bacon.*
Paddy's pig… Paddy's pig. I wish I had me neighbor's pig."

Now even Amber was grinning.

—∿∿—

Chad the ghost chuckled. So far he hadn't pulled off
anything really dramatic, except turning the gas back on.
He had the two roommates confused and uncomfortable,
but he didn't want the other tenants pointing fingers at
him—yet. There was more fun to be had with these two.

The one thing he realized after watching them together
was that he didn't really want to accomplish his secret
goal. He didn't want to scare away one at the expense of
the other. These two belonged together. Being a man of
the sixties—the *peace and love generation*—Chad saw
another outcome he'd like to achieve. But could it be
done in the three days he'd been given?

A plan formed in his mind as the evening wore on.

—∿∿—

A few minutes after everyone had gone, the lights suddenly went out and Rory groaned. "Do American electric
companies need us to pay them a security deposit too?"

"I've never heard of anything like that," Amber said. She strode to the windows. "The neighbors have power."

He opened the door to the hallway. The impressive chandelier was bathing the stairs and hallway with light. "It's not the whole of the buildin'. Just us."

They faced each other and shrugged.

"I suppose Sly and Morgaine might know what happened," Amber offered.

"I've no phone to contact them all the way up on the third floor. I could shout for one of me sisters…"

Amber worried her lip. Finally she rose and said, "I'll call from my bedroom."

"Why wouldn't you just bring the phone out here?" He huffed. "You still don't trust me."

"It's not that. I want to plug it in to test the electricity." She whirled on her foot and marched to her bedroom. Arguing wouldn't help matters. She heard him mutter "Feckers," as she closed the door.

Amber plugged in her phone's charger and connected it to her phone. She didn't expect anything to happen, since no overhead lights probably meant no electricity in the apartment. But there it was…the phone's green light came on as if saying, "Hello. The electricity is alive and well."

To her relief, she watched the bars fill. "Ah…at last. Connection to the outside world," she whispered to herself.

She found the phone number for the managers in her call history and redialed it.

"Hello," Sly answered before Amber heard it ring on her side. It surprised her and she hesitated for a moment.

Click.

He'd hung up on her! Amber remembered that computers dialing random numbers often came with a delay before a human was connected. He must have thought... Oh, never mind. Amber simply dialed again.

This time it rang once, twice, three times, then went to voice mail.

She was about to leave a message, but instead of the usual recorded greeting and beep to leave a message, the recording said, "This voice mailbox is full."

"For the love of... Now what?"

Amber left her phone plugged in on the floor, but before she returned to the living room, she tried flicking on the overhead light. Nothing happened. *Weird.*

Rory had set pillar candles in the fireplace and was lighting them with matches. His sisters had included them in his groceries. Then he returned the futon to its usual spot facing the fireplace to enjoy the candlelight.

The lit candles added a romantic glow. Amber wished she was about to snuggle up with an attentive lover. Instead, she said, "I have good news and bad news."

"Always start with the good news," Rory said, staring at the candles. "It softens the bad news. You don't want the bad news waterin' down the good news."

Good to know. "Okay. Here's the good news—such as it is. We still have electricity. My cell phone is charging as we speak."

His auburn brows rose. "Electricity but no lights?"

"Apparently, yeah. I tried the switch in my bedroom and nothing happened. That's the bad news."

"That is odd. Try the kitchen light. I switched it off after dinner."

Amber took the few steps to the kitchen and tried the

overhead light there. When nothing happened, she just said, "Nope."

"Nothin' but candlelight then." He turned and gazed at her.

"Yup. For some damn reason, the only light in the whole apartment is from those candles." *Those lovely, romantic candles.*

As if he could read her mind, he slid over a tad on the futon and patted the space beside him. Rory's eyes seemed to flicker with a golden glow. *It must be from the reflected candlelight*, she told herself.

Chapter 8

Finn and Pat landed at Logan International Airport and disembarked.

"Okay, we're in Boston. Now what?" Patrick asked.

"Go get our luggage, I imagine." Finn began to look for the signs that would lead them to the baggage claim area, but Pat laid a hand on his arm.

"Before we stand around waitin' for our duffel bags, perhaps we should find a pub and talk about the next step in your grand plan."

"I like your idea of the pub, but don't worry about where we're goin'. I brought a map of Boston with me." The two of them began a stroll past the various shops and restaurants.

"Ah! I think I see a pub comin' up on the left," Pat said. As they neared it, he chuckled. "It's even called O'Malley's."

"Must be a sign," Finn said, grinning.

They strode in and found a small table. A waitress appeared a few moments later and took their order.

As soon as she left to get their Guinness, Pat said, "I'll feel better after a pint, but I'd feel really grand if I could hear this plan of yours."

Finn leaned back in his chair. "All we need to do is find Massachusetts Avenue and signs for Cambridge and MIT, and we'll be close."

"Oh, is that all? What about a place to stay? Are there any hotels there?"

"There's one only a block down from Mass Ave, on Boylston Street, and several a few blocks from there if that one's booked."

"I see you did your homework. Thanks for that."

"Of course. We couldn't just land in a city the size of Boston and walk around callin' for Shannon until our voices gave out."

Pat chuckled. "Knowin' how much you love her, I'd feared that was your plan."

Finn snorted. "No. All we need to do is find a street with brownstones in view of the sign that reads Massachusetts Ave. *Then* we start shoutin'."

Pat's eyes rounded.

Their conversation was cut short when they spotted three small men in business suits coming toward them.

Something was more than odd about these three. Finn had a notion that he'd seen them before...one or two of them, anyway.

The couple at the next table rose and left without having finished their food—or apparently paying their bill. Their waitress bolted after them, calling for them to stop. While everyone's attention was diverted, the three businessmen sat down at the table, and in the blink of an eye, it was perfectly clean.

Suddenly Finn recognized one of them. The leprechaun he'd caught in the cave. *Of course.* Leprechaun magic had moved the couple and cleared their table. Magic had probably turned the leprechauns' red hair black, too.

"Shamus?" he asked.

All three of them snapped their gazes on Finn.

"You must be mistaken," the leprechaun said. "Me name is Angelo."

A corner of Finn's mouth turned up. *So he's pretending to be Italian or Spanish—with a thick Irish accent.*

"I'm sorry. It's just that you look and sound like someone I met once. Someone named Shamus." Then he pointed to Lucky. "And you look familiar too. Lucky, is it?"

The only man he didn't recognize spoke up. "Lucky we may be, but you don't know us."

Little Lucky shook his head. "Those of us who are— uh, shall we say, 'vertically challenged' are often mistaken for each other. We must share some ancestors."

Finn narrowed his eyes. After a long, silent stare, the one he didn't recognize began squirming.

"It's no use," he said. "The lad isn't stupid, but these disguises and excuses are."

Shamus—or "Angelo"—whirled on him. "What are you talkin' about? We're businessmen from Barcelona." Then he leaned toward his friend and spoke behind his hand. "That's what we agreed upon."

"And we were just supposed to eavesdrop on their conversation," Lucky added in a loud whisper.

The one he didn't know extended his hand to Finn. "I'm Clancy. It's pleased I am to meet you. Unlike me friends here, I think we should work together and accomplish a common goal."

Finn shook his hand. "I'm Finn and this is Patrick."

Patrick leaned in and whispered, "Are these the little people you were tellin' me about?"

Finn nodded.

Pat cocked his head and spoke directly to Clancy. "A common goal? What might that be?"

"Why, to find the drag—Ow!" Clancy reached under the table and rubbed his leg.

Finn scratched his head.

"Who or what is the drag?" Pat asked.

"Drag races," Lucky supplied at the same time Shamus said, "Drag queens."

Both Finn and Pat raised their eyebrows. Finn finally chuckled. "I didn't know there are drag queens racing cars here. Unfortunately we can't help you with that. We're new here too."

Clancy laughed. "No. I-I got me names mixed up. It's Shannon Arish we be seekin'."

Finn snapped to attention. "You're lookin' for Shannon? Why?"

Lucky and Shamus hopped off their chairs and rushed around the back of Clancy's. One of them slapped a hand over Clancy's mouth, while they wrestled the little man off his chair and out of the restaurant.

Pat stared after them. "Well, it's clear they don't want to tell us what they're about."

Finn stood abruptly. "We need to follow 'em."

"But aren't they followin' us? If we go after them, the five of us will be goin' around in circles."

Finn gaped at his friend. "But what could they want with her? I have to know."

Pat sighed. "Relax and finish your beer. Didn't you say one of them told you she was in Boston? Maybe they're friends."

"And maybe I'm Batman."

"Then we'll slip out without them seein' us. Now that we know who they are and what they look like, they'll be easy to spot if they follow us again."

—⁓—

Amber yawned. It was clearly time for bed, and she wasn't looking forward to another long night on a hard floor.

"Well, g'night then," she said and strolled toward her room. "Thank you for the music—or the session, as you call it. It was a lot of fun."

Rory rose. "Ah, lass. Come here."

She halted abruptly. *What could he want? A good-night kiss? Not likely.*

He opened his futon and stood beside it. "I know there's not a stick of furniture in your room. I can't make a lady such as yerself sleep on a cold, hard floor."

He was offering up his bed? For her? "What's the catch?" She approached slowly.

"No catch."

"I-I don't know what to say." She stopped a few feet from him.

"No need to say a word. You can even have the side near the fire—such as it is."

"No funny business, right? I mean, I don't want to wake up in the middle of the night and find you wrapped around me like a python."

He stiffened. "You think I'm luring you to me bed for sex? I am not, lass. That would indeed make me a snake."

"I don't know many men who aren't interested in a fling once they get a woman into bed."

He narrowed his eyes. "Fine. I offered. Mayhaps I'll sleep guilt free after all." With that, he lay down on "his side" and faced away from the fire.

Damn it. Amber didn't think she could feel more foolish, but she did. A few moments ago, she was looking at a long sleepless night on the hardwood floor…and now she was again.

She'd been offered half of his comfortable mattress, and instead of expressing gratitude, she'd insulted him. Being suspicious of motives might have been appropriate if an American man was trying to talk her into staying overnight to "save her from" a short drive home. But she was stuck there with only one mattress between them, and he owed her nothing.

"I'm sorry," she whispered.

He opened his eyes, and he levered himself to a sitting position. "I understand. You don't know me. Not really. If you did, you'd know there was no ulterior motive involved."

She nodded sadly. "I think even though I don't know you, I sensed that you meant no more than generosity. Unfortunately my experience with men has been quite different."

"Ah, lass. It's unfortunate indeed. You're a beauty, and men will want you. But they've no right to trick you into somethin' you don't want."

She smiled.

"Come and sit. Perhaps we can get to know each other enough to get past this hump."

She raised her eyebrows. "Hump?"

"Ack! I didn't mean it that way. I-I…"

She chuckled and sat next to him. "I knew that. I just couldn't resist making you squirm—or in this country, we call it 'busting your balls.'"

"Oh. You've an unkind sense of humor, luv."

"I know. Sorry."

He smiled. "Not a'tall. I'm used to it. Most Irish

lasses are the feisty sort, and any one of them could have pulled that off…although not quite as well."

"Well, I must have reached into my Irish heritage for that one."

Amber sat on the futon, "leaving enough room for the Holy Spirit" between them, as her grandmother used to say.

He brightened. "Are you Irish then?"

"My last name is McNally. I'm as Irish as Paddy's pig."

They both laughed. It was a deep, cathartic thing that ended with giggles and grins over an inside joke.

Rory's eyes watered and he swiped at them. Then, by the funny way his face scrunched, Amber realized he was trying to stifle a yawn.

"We need to sleep," she said. "Is your kind offer still open?"

He removed his shoes, but left on his sweatpants and T-shirt. "Of course."

Even though he faced away from "her side," he was a big man and had to curl a bit to keep his feet from falling off the end. That pushed his firm-looking ass over the invisible line between them. She didn't dare complain.

Amber slipped off her shoes and padded over to her side of the futon. She didn't take off her blouse or jeans either. She thought about removing her bra, but the heck with it. She was exhausted and just wanted to drop down onto the comfy mattress and sleep.

Apparently they were both side sleepers. She lay on her side, facing away from him, and accidentally bumped his buttocks.

"That wasn't me," he was quick to say.

"I know. Sorry." She tried to scoot closer to the edge

but teetered, in danger of falling off. No matter how many times she adjusted, she just knew they couldn't fit that way.

Rory spoke up. "If you want to mimic spoons in a drawer, I promise I won't think anythin' of it."

She realized that curling the same way they'd fit much better. She sighed. "Okay, but I get to be the big spoon. I don't want to accidentally bump into your…"

"Knife?" he supplied.

Amber's face heated and she was glad he couldn't see her fair complexion, because it was probably turning red. Still she couldn't help giggling.

Ballyhoo was in an uproar. The village pub was exploding with locals, and tempers were beginning to flare. Finally, Mrs. O'Malley climbed up on the bar and raised her voice above the din. "Whisht! Be quiet, the lot of you. We've a man of the cloth here. Perhaps we should be askin' for guidance in this matter instead of arguing about whether or not magic is real."

"Father," Mrs. O'Malley said, looking down at the man wearing the white collar who was sipping his Guinness. "The whole village needs your opinion…not that there won't be some who'll ignore it, if their minds be made up."

The priest nodded. "Why should today be different from any other?"

"You'll address them, then?"

"I will."

At last. Mayhaps some sanity will return to our little pub.

While Mrs. O'Malley got down from the bar, Father Joseph Flaherty rose. He was loud enough to be heard by most, yet they crowded around him just the same.

"It seems as if there are two major questions," he began. "First, where did that castle up by Braydon Road come from? Did it just appear suddenly? If so, was magic involved?"

Despite that being three questions, polite affirmative noises came from the villagers.

"I haven't seen it yet, but I understand it looks ancient. Are you sure it wasn't there all along?"

"'Twas not, Father," one of the fishermen supplied. "'Tis built into the cliffs, so it could be missed from the road but not from the sea. One day it wasn't there and the next, 'twas."

"You couldn't really miss it from the road either," a sheepherder said. "I move me sheep over that way from time to time. The Arishes have no problem with it as long as I keep them a fair distance from the cottage."

"*Had*, you mean." Her husband Mr. O'Malley cleared his throat. "No one has seen the Arishes in weeks. Young Finn went lookin' for Shannon. One day he comes in and says she and her family are gone. They didn't say a word to anyone. We kept expectin' them to show up with their instruments, but Finn appears to have the right of it. They're missin', and next thing we hear is there's a magic castle behind their cottage!"

"Hmmm…" The priest glanced around the crowd. "Where is young Finn?"

Mrs. O'Malley placed her hands on her hips. "Now he's gone too, along with his shadow, Patrick. The two of 'em were plottin' some trip to Boston I heard."

"Ah, I have fond memories of Boston," Father Joe said. "I visited me aunt and uncle there when I was a lad." He smiled. "I developed quite a crush on me pretty cousin."

One of the village women gasped. "Father!"

He glanced at her. "What? I wasn't born with this collar."

One of the farmers spoke up. "There's somethin' else you should know, Father. The travelers are back." He spit on the floor. "Dirty heathens."

The next thing Mrs. O'Malley knew, all the villagers were spitting on her floor! "Ack! You'll be moppin' up that spit, Daniel O'Brien." If she were closer, she'd have boxed the farmer's ears.

Daniel ignored her and continued talking to Father Joseph. "We think young Finn consulted a fortune-teller, as he was *desperate* to learn where Shannon went."

"Ah, so you're thinkin' the gypsy sent him to Boston and the castle appeared by gypsy magic?" the priest asked.

"No, *we* don't," the fisherman said. "The two incidents could be completely unrelated."

"So, tell us, Father," Mr. O'Malley finally said. "Is magic real?"

The man of the cloth scratched his head and gazed at the floor. "If it is gypsy magic, there's a darkness to it. I'd counsel you all to stay clear of the travelers." Then he raised his voice. "Stay clear of those cliffs as well."

Everyone nodded and murmured their agreement, but Mrs. O'Malley knew there'd be a small army eyeing that castle come sunrise.

The minute the good father left the pub, the excited hubbub resumed. Mrs. O'Malley was right. The whole of Ballyhoo was heading straight to the castle.

—◈—

Rory woke when the sun began to shine through the windows. He had never closed the blinds. That was probably a mistake, considering he could have shifted into his dragon form in his sleep. He hadn't done that since he was a lad, but he'd had such an erotic dream last night that he was completely heated from within.

As his mind and vision cleared, he glanced over his shoulder and saw the reason for the dream. Amber was snuggled up against him with her arm draped over his waist. A slow smile stole across his face.

As much as he hated to move, he knew she'd be embarrassed if she woke in that position. He also had to use the bathroom, and if she saw him sporting morning wood… Well, her assumption wouldn't be far from the mark.

He gently lifted her limp hand and tried to slide out without waking her.

"Wh—what the?" She snatched her hand back as if she'd touched a hot stove. "Christ."

Instead of being embarrassed as he expected, she seemed angry. He swung his feet to the floor and sat up.

"I just woke up meself and found us in that position. I swear I had nuthin' to do with it."

"It's not that. Well, not entirely. You're burning up." She too sat up and reached for his forehead. "Are you sick?"

He quickly leaned away and said, "I tend to run hot. I'm fine." *Change the subject, you dolt, before she questions it further.* "Do you need the bathroom? I'll let you go first."

"I will, but I might take a while. Why don't you go first? I have to pick out some clothes to change into."

"Thanks." He bolted off the futon and jogged to the bathroom. *Clean clothes. What a luxury.*

He imagined his sisters had gone shopping for new wardrobes since they'd worn different things last night, but he couldn't leave the apartment to replenish his. Come to think of it, he'd have to call Chloe down and send her off to find him *something* cool to wear. Shannon would take too long. She tended to get distracted by shiny baubles. He wished he could try things on, but Chloe would probably have to guess at his size. The United States used inches, not centimeters, so he had no idea what to ask for.

Ah. Perhaps a bathing suit would be forgiving if she got it a bit wrong. Amber was right. He was scorching hot just from lying next to her.

———

Amber had just stepped out of the shower when she received a phone call from the moving company. They confirmed her request for an expedited pack and move of her whole apartment. It was going to be pricey, but she figured the fast service was worth it. The rent in this beautiful building was so ridiculously cheap that she *had to* have this apartment. She couldn't help feeling sorry for Rory, however, and that sympathy was getting in the way.

Maybe he could move in with his sisters. They seemed to get along, and his futon would fit in their living room as well as it fit in hers. She secretly hoped he wouldn't go far.

Mayday, Mayday, Mayday!

"Oh shit," she muttered.

She glanced at her pile of clothes on the toilet seat and imagined them already on her body. *Poof.* She was dressed. Smiling at her newfound power, she closed her eyes and zeroed in on the air emergency.

A small passenger aircraft, often referred to as a puddle jumper, was losing altitude fast. If she didn't act fast, a few dozen commuters wouldn't make it to work in the large Midwestern city they were headed to that day…and who knew how many innocent bystanders could be killed?

Fortunately the plane hadn't reached the city yet, and the pilot was frantically trying to line up with a highway. A busy highway.

The first thing Amber did was to slow the plane's descent and then stop the traffic behind her. Up ahead, she created an electronic sign that read: *Plane landing. Get off at next exit*, and that rerouted everyone off the nearest ramp. It was too late to push the puddle jumper back up in the air. The best she could do was to help with a soft-impact landing.

She leaned over the young pilot's shoulder and whispered, "Stay calm. You've been trained for this. Everyone will be all right." She knew he couldn't see her. She would seem like just a voice in his head. She hoped using a calm voice and solid reasoning was all she had to do to perform her job. There was little else she could help with. Correction—she didn't know what she could do yet. She hadn't fully tested her powers.

He took a deep breath and let it out slowly, seeming to gather his courage. The landing gear hadn't been operational, but Amber whispered, "Try the landing gear again."

He did, and his eyebrows shot up as it clicked into place just in time. Amber was fairly sure he'd do well from this point on, so she took a peek at the passengers.

Yup. All buckled in and braced for impact—including flight attendants. She returned to the cockpit and watched as the pilot hit the pavement and bounced. She slowed the plane some more, and the next two bounces were much less dramatic. Eventually the wheels gripped the pavement and the pilot steered the plane to a stop. The passengers cheered.

The pilot let out a deep breath in a whoosh, and then he closed his eyes and whispered, "Thanks."

Amber imagined he was offering thanks to whatever higher power he might have been praying to. She was humbled to realize it was her.

———∿∿———

Finn and Pat surfaced from the subway in Copley Square. Finn took the map out of his pocket and studied it.

"Okay. We should be right beside the Boston Public Library." He glanced up at the lettering on the side of the huge building, which proclaimed it was indeed the library.

"Right," Pat said. "Now what?"

Finn looked for the sun. It was still morning, so the sun would sit in the eastern sky, and according to the map, they needed to go west. He pointed down the long street. "Massachusetts Ave is that way."

"How far? I'm hungry."

"We just ate."

"You call a snack on the go eating? I need a sit-down meal."

Finn didn't need any more delays. He could almost feel Shannon in his arms. "I'm sure you can find food at our lodgings. It's only a few blocks down. Let's check in first."

Pat followed his friend's long strides. "Do you think the leprechauns are far behind?"

"I'd be surprised if they weren't ahead of us."

"How do they do that? Travel, I mean? I never saw them on the plane. Did you see them?"

"No. They're good at hidin' from people. We know that much."

After a few blocks, Pat's stomach growled. "I'm starvin'!"

"We're almost there, but if you can't wait, I found a place that sounds like a treat."

"What's that?"

"The Mass Ave Tavern."

Pat's eyes lit up. "That's it. That's where I want to be."

Finn chuckled. "So you'd rather lug our bags and keep 'em with us while we eat, rather than head straight to the hotel?"

"If it means eatin' sooner, then aye. That's what I want."

Finn shrugged. "Fine. Your stomach rules the day." Then, as if a lightbulb had snicked on over his head, Finn grabbed his friend's shoulders.

"What's wrong?" Pat asked.

"Nuthin'. In fact, somethin's very right. If I know Shannon's family, they'll find a pub to play music in." He shook his friend's shoulders. "Pat, you're brilliant!"

His friend chuckled. "And here I was, just thinkin' I was hungry."

———※———

When the movers showed up, they asked if Amber had any special instructions. Without explaining why, she told them to put everything that wasn't marked for the kitchen or bath in the bedroom. *Everything.* They looked at her strangely, but did as she asked.

As soon as all the boxes had been placed in either her closet or the neutral zones, Amber directed the movers to bring her sofa into her bedroom, along with the end tables, lamps, and two matching chairs.

"Do you really want it all in the bedroom?" one guy asked. "I don't think your bed will fit."

"I'll make it fit," she said.

While one guy pushed her living room furniture against the walls, the other one carried her queen headboard in. To her shock, Rory jumped up and said, "I'll help with that."

"Thanks, man. This sucker is heavy."

When they had set it against the only vacant wall, Rory came out of her bedroom and spotted the third guy bringing the bed rails up the stairs. He didn't set foot outside the apartment, but as soon as the item was over the threshold, he reached for it. "Here. I'll take that. You and your buddies can bring in the mattresses next."

Amber crossed her arms and frowned. *He's up to something.*

She followed him into the bedroom and watched as he fit the rails together.

"Do you think the movers would loan you a screwdriver if you asked nicely?"

"If I—" She wanted to sputter something about being very nice to people who were helping her, but he was helping her too. "Why are you being so cooperative? Are you giving up the apartment?"

He laughed. "Not on your life, luv. But it seems as if me standin' in the way wouldn't make a bit of difference."

She cocked her head. "No, it wouldn't. But you're actually helping. You don't need to do that."

"Well, of course I don't need to. You're not payin' me for it." When she hesitated, he added, "I'm just bein' a gentleman, helpin' a lady."

She tossed her hands in the air and returned to the living room.

The guys were struggling up the stairs with her box spring. She called out to the closest one. "Do you have a screwdriver we could possibly borrow?"

"Yeah. It's on the front seat in the truck," he said. "Help yourself."

She couldn't set foot out of the apartment and Rory knew it. *Aha! So that's his game.*

"Did you get the screwdriver?" he asked when he joined her in the living room.

She smirked. "Oh, you'd like that, wouldn't you?"

After a moment's hesitation he said, "You'd like it if your bed didn't fall apart."

She folded her arms. "I think I'll let the movers put it together."

He shrugged and strolled to his futon. "Suit yourself."

"I will." The movers came out of the bedroom wiping

sweat from their brows. She felt bad for them, but even that wouldn't tempt her to step outside.

Rory slid over to one side and said, "Have a seat, darlin'."

"Why?"

"Why not?"

"I know what you're doing."

He leaned back and crossed his ankle over his knee. "Right now I seem to be doin' a whole lot o' nuthin'."

She snorted. "Yeah, right. You're just waiting for me to put my big toe into that hallway. Well, that's not going to happen." She stomped off to the kitchen and began opening boxes. Everything was wrapped in newspaper. *Great. Soon we'll have a trash mountain.*

As soon as she had unpacked and put away the contents of her entire kitchen, she began stomping the packing paper into some kind of manageable pile.

Rory approached. "Why are you doin' an Irish stepdance in me kitchen, luv?"

As much as she hated herself for it, every time this infuriating man used an endearment like darlin' or luv—especially luv, her heart melted a little bit.

"In case you hadn't noticed, *my* place is becoming very crowded. I hate clutter, so I'm trying to act like a trash compactor. Eventually, I'll win this stupid standoff and be able to leave the apartment for a minute to throw the refuse in the Dumpster."

"Ah, bugger. I'll ask me sisters to get rid of it for you."

She gazed up at him in amazement. "You'd do that? Why?"

"If clutter makes you crazier than you already are, gettin' rid of it serves us both."

Her lips thinned at the insult and she stomped off to her bedroom. "Oomph!" She had tripped over something and landed, splat, on some boxes. Rory came running.

"Are you all right, lass?"

Other than feeling totally humiliated... "Yes, I'm fine." She struggled to push herself off the boxes, then felt strong arms lifting her as if she weighed nothing.

Suddenly, she flipped in midair. Before she had a chance to register what was happening, those same strong arms caught her. She grappled and clung to the first solid thing she could find. To her chagrin, it was Rory's neck and she gazed into his concerned face.

He carried her to the bed and laid her on the mattress. Then he sat next to her.

"Are you sure you're intact?"

"I might have a couple of bruises, but nothing really hurts—except my pride."

"Ah, pride is overrated."

"Says the proudest man I know."

He cupped her face. "You're beautiful."

She didn't know what to say to that. She just lay there with her lips parted, waiting to think of something.

Without warning, he leaned over and kissed her. And it was *not* a quick peck either. He laid his lips on hers with the perfect amount of pressure. Then he opened his mouth and caught her lower lip between his full, soft lips, tugging on it...but only slightly. A moment later he fondled her upper lip the same way.

It felt incredible. She couldn't help returning his sensuous kiss. To her own amazement, she slipped her tongue into his mouth. When their tongues met, they began a slow dance.

His hand slid to the back of her neck and he drew her closer. She slipped her arms around his broad back and savored his heat. It had been a long time since she'd been held like it meant something.

But it *didn't* mean anything. It couldn't.

She withdrew her tongue. When he didn't break the kiss, she moved her hands to his chest and gave a slight push.

He spoke first. "Ah, that was nice, wasn't it?"

She paused but couldn't think of a single way to disagree. "Yeah, it was. And—unexpected."

"'Tis the unexpected that makes life interesting." He brushed her hair away from her face with such a gentle touch that she wanted to sigh.

He bent over her and initiated his slow, drugging kiss all over again. She slipped her arms around his neck and let him sweep her away from all the tension of the past forty-eight hours.

Life was interesting, all right. And becoming more interesting by the minute.

———◦∾◦———

Conlan Arish entered the Belfast home he shared with his two brothers. "Aiden! Eagan! Where are you? I have big news about our bastard cousins."

Eagan appeared first. "What bastard cousins? Did our da have a mistress we don't know about?"

Conlan blew out a frustrated breath. "No, idjit. I just meant it as a feckin' insult. I'm talkin' about Rory, Shannon, and Chloe Arish. Our thievin' cousins."

"What about them?" Aiden asked as he strode in from the kitchen, wiping his hands on a dish towel.

"They've left the castle open and unguarded, and no one seems to know where they went."

The brothers glanced at one another. Eagan scratched his head. "How do you know this?"

"I just came from the pub. Everyone is talkin' about a castle on a cliff in Ballyhoo that just appeared out of nowhere."

"And you think it's *our* castle?"

"Who said this?" Eagan demanded. "Was it a reputable source?"

"Is a man of the cloth reputable enough for you? A certain Father Joseph is up here visitin' our Father Benedict."

"I suppose he has no reason to lie," Eagan said. "So…a castle built into the cliffs appeared in Ballyhoo. Is that right?"

"That must mean the leprechauns are no longer hidin' it." Aiden crossed his arms. "I wonder what happened."

Conlan shrugged. "Perhaps it was a mistake. Perhaps the Arish cousins insulted the wee shites."

Aiden smirked. "Aye. They could do that by breathin' wrong."

Conlan shook his head. "Feckin' leprechauns. So touchy. Last I heard, the lot of our cousins moved into a caretaker's cottage. Some nonsense about not wantin' to use their wings to get into the castle. Thought they'd cause a panic or somethin'."

"I was so young when we left the south of Ireland that I don't even remember what the castle looked like, never mind where it was," Aiden said.

"Aye." Conlan scratched his head. "I was the oldest and barely have any memory of it. Our ma was so afraid we'd be killed for the sins of our father that she whisked us out of there the very minute she became a widow."

Aiden grinned. "If our birthplace is exposed and unguarded, we can finally go to see it." His grin grew wicked. "And by 'see it,' I mean pillage it."

Conlan laughed. "I've never participated in a good ol'-fashioned pillagin'. Accordin' to our dear, departed nurse, the keep was full of treasure."

"How would she know?" Eagan asked.

Conlan just shrugged. "Servants always seem to know everythin' that goes on."

Aiden pounded his fist on his own palm. "Now that the castle is exposed and unguarded, we should go and take what's ours."

Eagan frowned. "I wonder if our cousins just moved to another house and are still livin' nearby."

"If so, we can take 'em. There's only Rory to worry about. The two females wouldn't stand a chance against the three of us," Aiden said.

"Ah, don't underestimate the lasses. Even as a child Chloe was a scrapper. They must be full-grown women by now—and dragons to boot. After all, it's been a few hundred years since we've laid eyes on 'em," Conlan cautioned his siblings.

"I've always wondered why our da didn't defeat his brother," Eagan scratched his head. "He was bigger and stronger."

"And younger," Conlan added.

"I suspect our uncle must have cheated to win. But with no evidence and no witnesses left alive, we may never know," Aiden said through gritted teeth.

Eagan smiled. "Perhaps there will be a clue in the castle."

"Perhaps the leprechauns know!" Aiden said.

"There's only one way to find out," Conlan said.

Aiden nodded. "It seems we need to take a trip to Ballyhoo."

Eagan's eyes widened. "And leave the safety of Ulster?"

Conlan snorted. "In case you didn't notice, Ulster hasn't always been safe."

"It's safe enough for us," Eagan insisted.

"Fine. You stay here then," Aiden said. "One of us should probably stay behind anyway—just in case the story is a ruse, and they plan to take this home and our whiskey-makin' business from us too."

"That's a fine idea," Conlan said. "Aiden and I should set off as soon as possible. Tourists and greedy locals might be carryin' off our family heirlooms as we speak."

"I'll go pack. What weapons should we take?" Aiden asked.

"We have our fire. Let's travel light and leave room in our baggage. If the story be true, we'll reclaim as many of our ancestral treasures as we can fit in our bags and then go back for the rest."

"That would be grand," Eagan agreed.

"Perhaps we can take back the castle that was lost in the wars so long ago," Aiden added.

Eagan nodded. "Our da would be proud."

Conlan stroked his chin. "We'll devise a surprise attack on the way. If our Ballyhoo cousins are still there, they won't know what hit 'em."

Chapter 9

"Mayday, Mayday, Mayday!"

Amber broke the hot kiss. "Damn it! Not now…"

Rory leaned away from her, looking concerned. "Did I go too far? I didn't think my hands were wanderin', but they coulda had a mind o' their own. If so, I apologize."

"No, no." She struggled to sit up. "It wasn't that. I-I need some privacy. Can you give me a few minutes?"

He levered himself off her mattress. "Of course. I'll be right—well, you know where I'll be." He chuckled and left the bedroom, closing the door on his way out.

Amber muttered, "Talk about bad timing… This had better be a genuine air emergency."

Without any further delay she disappeared into the ether.

A quick look at the scene had Amber's heart in her throat. Both the pilot and copilot appeared to be unconscious.

"Oh no! A flight attendant is trying to land the plane," Amber muttered. "That was always my worst fear."

She stayed out of sight in the ether, but leaned forward behind the frightened woman's shoulder. "You can do this," she said. "Tell the answering tower you're untrained and need detailed instructions to land safely."

The flight attendant searched the panel. "What the hell do I use to talk to them?" she muttered. "I don't think they heard me before."

"Try again."

The woman reached out a shaky finger and flipped

the toggle button on. "Mayday, Mayday, Mayday!" she shouted.

What could only be an air traffic controller answered immediately. "Flight 451, what is your emergency?"

"Oh, thank God," she cried. "I'm a flight attendant with no pilot training. I need help landing the plane."

"Why are you… What the hell happened to the pilot and copilot?"

"Both unconscious. Please, I need detailed instructions."

"Okay, 451, I see you coming in fast and low. Can you see the runway?"

She squinted. "Yes. Barely."

"Pull up on the steering column. You need to gain altitude and then we'll talk about landing."

"Okay," she said in a shaky voice.

She had a death grip on the steering column and just stared at it.

Amber said, "Tilt the top toward you."

The plane made a sharp ascent.

"You okay, 451?" the controller asked.

"Yes. I guess I pulled up a little abruptly."

"That's okay. You can level off now."

She did what he said, and this time moved the wheel more slowly.

"Good job," the controller said. "Now I need you to *gradually* turn the plane just a little while keeping her level. You don't want to turn the wheel like a car. *Gently* pull one side of the wheel toward you. I want you to get the feeling of turning. Think you can do that?"

Amber was relieved that the air traffic controller was calm and reassuring—plus he knew how to land a plane!

"Okay. Here goes," the flight attendant said.

The plane gradually headed toward the left.

"Good job, 451. Now turn back just as gradually and aim for the runway. I may have you circle if you're not lined up. Do you understand?"

Her voice broke as she answered, "Yes. But what if another plane comes in for a landing?" Tears were forming in her eyes, and Amber knew the flight attendant's composure was just about to give out.

"Already rerouted. We've cleared your path. You're doing fine, 451," the controller said.

"You need to stay calm," Amber whispered in her ear. "Take a deep breath."

The flight attendant sucked in a deep breath and let it out slowly.

"Now, I want you to locate the landing gear. It's the black switch on the left. Don't push it yet. I just want you to know where it is."

"I see it," she said.

"Good. Now, I need you to circle by turning gradually like you did before. Are you ready to circle?"

"I'm still a ways out."

"I know. But I want you to have plenty of room on approach. Okay?"

"Trust him," Amber said.

"Okay," the flight attendant said, and made a gradual left turn until she had made a complete circle.

"Good job, 451."

"Really?"

"Really. Now I'm going to have you do the same thing, while tilting the steering wheel down *slightly*."

"Oh, God," she muttered. Tears started to roll down

her cheeks, but with Amber's encouragement she did what was asked of her, every step of the way.

"I wish the pilots would wake up and take over," she muttered.

Amber wished they would too. They were alive, but unless she missed her guess, they had been drugged. This flight was never meant to land safely.

After another few minutes of detailed guidance, the plane was lined up with the runway and the landing gear was down.

"You're coming in hot," the controller said. "That means you need to pull back on the steering column."

"But I'm—Oh, never mind." She yanked back on the steering column as hard as she could and the engines stalled. The plane dropped and even though she had been over grass a few moments before, amazingly, she hit the runway. The flight attendant held on for dear life as the plane bounced hard enough for her feet to leave the floor. She saw fire engines at the ready. Lots of them.

She gulped and held on to the steering wheel with white knuckles. The plane bounced a few more times. The airport seemed to be rushing toward her as fast as the fire engines.

"Now turn in a circle again," the air traffic controller said.

"Yeah. Wouldn't want to come all this way and smash into your lovely tower," she quipped.

He chuckled. "Yeah, let's not do that."

The wing took a beating as they circled on the tarmac, but eventually, the damn thing stopped. The flight attendant dropped to her knees and burst into tears.

"You did it!" both the controller and Amber exclaimed.

"With a lot of help from you," the flight attendant managed to say between sobs.

"Hey, are you busy later?" the air traffic controller asked.

The flight attendant stopped sniffling and laughed. "I just plan to have a well-deserved nervous breakdown. Why?"

"I'd like to take you out for a drink—to celebrate."

She grinned. "I'd like that. Thank you."

Amber felt like she was eavesdropping at this point and remembered a certain sexy scene in her own bedroom. As soon as she got there, Euterpe was waiting.

"Now can you see why we need you so badly?" she asked. "As the muse of air travel you can help save hundreds of lives in situations like that. I might be able to play a sad melody on my lyre, but it would just be music to die by."

Chad the ghost had watched as Amber and Rory made out, and then he saw her push him away and ask for privacy. He was cursing Amber for being a "good girl" and ruining his entertainment when she disappeared!

He had been betting that she was *something* paranormal, just because this building attracted them like bears to beehives, but he had been thinking *witch* or *shapeshifter*. You know…something *normal*.

This chick was like nothing he'd seen before.

Who up and disappears? Vampires can run so fast they seem to disappear, but she wasn't nocturnal, and she hadn't fed on anyone—yet. Besides, the bedroom door and window were closed. So where the hell did she go?

He was about to give up and report the mystery to Morgaine when Amber's friend appeared, and seconds later, Amber reappeared. The friend may have been the one with supernatural powers, but Amber seemed pretty relaxed about it.

Then her friend called her the muse of air travel! What the…?

Apparently Amber possessed her own supernatural powers. That made more sense than having a human in the building. But a muse of *air travel*? He had to eavesdrop a little longer.

"She had plenty of help from the air traffic controller. I think she could have handled it without me," Amber said.

Her friend laughed. "I doubt it. You may not have landed the plane, but you kept her calm and focused."

"So did he."

"Yeah, yeah. He did a nice job too."

"I was wondering… Should I take some flight training classes?" Then Amber coughed. "When I can leave the apartment, that is."

"You can sit in on classes if you want. I wouldn't recommend enrolling, knowing you could be called out at any time."

"Could I audit the class from the ether and be free to answer a Mayday call?"

"Yup."

"What if Rory gets suspicious and starts searching for me? If he looks under the bed and in the closet, he'll know I'm not here."

"And that's a problem because…"

"Because if I'm not here and he is, he wins the

apartment. He'll do a jig and toss my stuff out on the sidewalk."

Euterpe chuckled. "I think he might have a different reaction to your absence."

Amber's brows knit. "What? Do you think he'd miss me?"

Her friend just winked and disappeared.

Hmmm… That gave Chad pause. He wondered how, when, and in what way to report this juicy tidbit to the tenants—most importantly how to provide himself with the best entertainment value. He used to run off potential renters when they looked at his old apartment, and it was fun. But that got boring after a few decades, and now Gwyneth lived there with his blessing. Hey, at least he got to see a beautiful redhead naked in the shower.

But the tenants weren't meeting again for a couple of nights. That meant he knew a secret for a little while. Maybe it was one he could use to have a little more fun.

———

Rory sat on the window seat, giving his sisters the futon. Chloe removed some things from a bag.

"I hope one of these is your size," Shannon said. "We got a variety. I think M is too small, but we got one anyway. It looks pretty close to a woman's size."

"Mayhaps you can wear it if I can't."

Shannon gasped. "You think *any* men's size would fit me?"

Chloe rose, strolled over to him, and slapped him upside the head. Then she returned to her seat on the futon. "That's for Shannon, since I know she wouldn't do it herself."

"Thank you, Chloe," Shannon said.

"Sorry," Rory mumbled. He took one look at the yellow polo shirt, then placed it against his chest so his sisters could see his torso showing on both sides. "I wouldn't dare stuff meself into this. I'd pop the stitches and then no one could use it."

"All right," Chloe said. "We also got you an L and an XL. They looked more like you." She pulled two more shirts out of the bag, both like the first one but in different colors.

Rory examined both. "This might do the trick." He left the blue L and took the red XL to the bathroom. After a quick, refreshing shower, he tried on the new red shirt. It emphasized the red stripe that grew from the widow's peak in his auburn mane.

The people of Ballyhoo had stopped questioning it long ago. So far, no one in the apartment building had mentioned it. Perhaps because they were friends with Drake, who displayed a yellow stripe, and knew it signified a dragon's clan. Besides, more and more humans were dying their hair with unusual colors. Rory liked to think dragons had started a fad.

The shirt fit just fine. Now, if his sisters had gotten something to fit his lower half, including a pair of boxers, he'd be forever grateful.

He emerged from the bathroom wearing a towel and the new shirt.

Shannon clapped. "It looks good on you, Rory."

"Did you happen to think of me lower half?"

"We did, but it was near impossible to guess what size you might be," Chloe said. "There were two sets of numbers on all the jeans and slacks."

"But we were in luck," Shannon added. "We found a store that carried everything Irish—from souvenirs to this!" She reached into another bag and pulled out a multicolored plaid kilt.

He chuckled. "It'll cover me while I wash out what I have on. That's good enough for now. At some point, when I can leave the apartment, I'll have to try on a few jeans and figure out what numbers to ask for." Then he gave them a quick bow. "I thank you."

Chloe folded her arms. "Amber hasn't given up yet, I take it."

"She has not. She's in the bedroom, along with everythin' she owns."

"What? You mean she had friends move all her things in there?"

"No, she hired a company. That's all they do apparently. Three strong men carried in every stick of furniture and box from her old apartment."

"Tell me you didn't help her," Chloe demanded.

Rory remained silent. What else could he do without tellin' her what she didn't want to hear?

"Bollocks," Chloe sputtered.

Shannon crossed her legs at the ankles. "Why is it you don't chide Chloe for her unladylike language?"

He gave his little sister a sly smile. "Because Chloe is a lost cause. You, there's still hope for."

Shannon giggled and Chloe elbowed her in the ribs. "Ouch!"

"You're just provin' me point, Chloe. Play nice."

"How about if we don't play a'tall?" She examined her fingernails. "And after I was nice enough to find clothes to cover your naked ugliness."

"Naked ugliness! And how would you know about me naked state? I always turn me back to you when shiftin'."

"All men are ugly naked. All hairy and gross with a shriveled—"

"Stop!"

~~~

Amber heard shouting and emerged from her bedroom. She gazed at the three siblings, who were frowning at each other.

"What's wrong?" she asked.

"Nothin'," Rory said quickly.

Chloe smirked. "We were just talkin' about me brother's hairy—"

Before she could finish her sentence, Rory was in front of her with one big hand covering her mouth. She mumbled something inarticulate and laughed.

Rory pulled his hand away but gave his sister the hairy eyeball.

"I'm sorry if I interrupted something. I can go back into my room so you can finish your argument."

"There's no need for that, lass," Rory said. "Me sister's had her fun."

He handed a bag to Shannon. "I thank you for your shoppin' skills."

"So there's no trouble in sibling paradise?" Amber asked hopefully.

"Not a t'all," Rory was quick to say.

"Good. I was figuring that after the managers let me keep the apartment, you'd just move your futon upstairs. After all, you can sleep in your sisters' living room as well as you can sleep in mine."

The sisters burst into laughter.

Chloe wiped her eyes. "As if we'd let him. Have you any siblin's, Amber?"

Amber nodded. "A sister. She's married and lives in Seattle—which is on the other side of the country."

"Imagine sharin' a room with her as an adult. That's what Shannon and I are doin'. We're gettin' in each other's way as it is. Add a big brother to the equation and you can imagine the chaos."

Amber shrugged. "It would be temporary though. I'm sure there's another place for rent around here."

"Not at a two-for-one rental deal," Shannon said.

Amber's brow furrowed. "Two for one? What does that mean?"

Rory slapped a hand over his eyes. "Now you've gone and done it, Shannon."

"Done what?"

"Told her she has the advantage. If they rent to me, they get no more than we've already paid. If they rent to her, they get what you're payin' plus what she's willin' to pay."

"Oh." Shannon bit her lip.

Chloe shoved her sister toward the door. "Me thinks it's time to leave." She faced Rory. "We're goin' out to explore the neighborhood."

"I don't suppose you could find me an apartment while you're out and about."

———

Finn, Pat, and the three little men had finally checked into the B and B. The leprechauns had followed them and approached them on the steps. They took the room across the hall from Finn and Pat after an uneasy truce had been reached. Since Finn wanted to waste no time, he'd work with them, if it meant he'd find his ladylove.

"So, there's been no sign of the Arishes?" Finn asked Shamus as they met up in the hallway.

"None. We don't have any real idea what we're lookin' for except Massachusetts Avenue. Perhaps there's a Massachusetts Avenue in another city or state."

Pat groaned. "Don't tell me we've got to search the whole country now."

"Probably not," Lucky said. "I've seen the area, and I'm fairly certain it's the same as what was in me vision."

Hoping against hope, Finn asked, "Can't you just close your eyes and pull up another vision? Maybe see where they are right now?"

"No, it doesn't work that way," all three leprechauns said at once and then they glanced at each other and chuckled.

"What way does it work?" Pat asked.

"Magic comes with some catches," Clancy said. "That's why sometimes it backfires and one must be careful with its use."

Finn focused on Shamus, remembering the way the word "caught" helped him catch the leprechaun when he *caught* him in a lie. Maybe he could catch one of them in another lie and force the matter.

"We need to coordinate our efforts," Lucky said. "Does anyone have a map?"

"In me pocket," Finn said.

Before he could retrieve it, Clancy waved his hand

and the map of Boston appeared. He opened it and laid it on the floor between them.

"Here's where we are now." He pointed and a red X appeared on the map to mark their B and B's exact location.

"Impressive," Finn mumbled. "I wish you could do that for Shannon's location."

"Alas, no."

"Why not?" he almost whined.

"Because we just can't," Shamus snapped.

"So, you want to split up and cover more ground?" Pat asked.

Shamus took charge. "You'll need one of us to go with you. Lucky, you take lover boy, and Clancy can take his sidekick."

"And what will you be doin'?" Lucky asked.

"The same thing you are, of course. Searchin' my third of the city."

"You mean to divide up the whole city?" Finn asked. "I thought we would concentrate on the Massachusetts Avenue area."

"For today that would be best," Clancy said. "If we have no luck, we can expand our search."

"This might take more than a day?" Finn cried.

Shamus humphed. "Who knows? Look at this Massachusetts Avenue. See how long it is?" He leaned over the map. "It goes clear across the river and doesn't appear to stop."

Pat kneeled to get a better look. "Is that the truth of it?" He traced the route with his finger. "Holy mother of God. We'll be walkin' with holes in our shoes if one of us doesn't find her soon."

He took a closer look. "Ah. It changes names here in

Harvard Square. And the other way it ends at Columbia Road. It's manageable."

"Whew," Finn said. "You had me worried, Shamus."

The little man shrugged.

Lucky said. "Finn and I will take this side of the river for the allotted number of blocks. I think she's close by."

That news was the best Finn had heard yet. "Come on, lads. Let's get started!"

The map magically tore into thirds and each party took a piece. Shamus grabbed the piece that started across the river. Finn wondered if there was any particular reason the bossy little leprechaun wanted to be alone and far from where they were now.

Amber approached Rory and said, "Can we talk?"

He scooted to one side and extended his arm across the back of the futon. "Of course, luv. Sit."

She smiled and sat next to him, leaving a respectful distance between. He scooted closer and wrapped his arm around her shoulders.

"Now that we've shared a kiss, there's no need to be shy."

And what a kiss it was. She had to fight to regain her objectivity. There were certain things that needed to be addressed—soon.

"Rory, I think we need to have the talk."

His brow wrinkled. "*The* talk? Is that somethin' Americans understand? Because I'm not sure what you mean."

"Um…" She felt her face heat. "I, uh…" She took a

deep breath and launched into it. "It's clear that we're attracted to each other."

He grinned. "That we are, without a doubt. And it's good to hear you admit that it goes both ways."

"Uh, yeah. And, well…" She had to get this out before she lost her nerve. "And just in case our, um… attraction—for lack of a better term—goes any further, we need to discuss certain things. Important things."

His brow wrinkled in confusion. "Hmmm… Say what's on your mind. I'm not so good at guessin' games."

She blew out a frustrated breath. "Like health concerns—birth control for one. I didn't come equipped with condoms, and I doubt you have a box of them in your pocket."

"Ah!"

Light dawns at last.

"You don't need to worry about that, luv. I can't get you pregnant."

"Oh?" She hoped he'd elaborate, so she wouldn't have to ask if he meant he was sterile.

"It's both a curse and a blessin', I suppose."

She suddenly felt too hot and scooted away from him a few inches.

"If all goes well between us and you want children, I'm not opposed to adoption."

Her jaw dropped. "No! I mean—let's not get ahead of ourselves. I was just concerned about an unwanted pregnancy or HIV."

He chuckled. "Ah. Fine. I don't know what this *talk* consists of so you'll have to forgive me if I answer wrongly."

"There are no right or wrong answers. Just tell the blunt and honest truth." *Forging on.* "I'm disease free and haven't been with a man since I was tested for sexually transmitted diseases."

"Oh? Why were you tested?"

"I found out my last boyfriend was a man-whore."

Rory's eyebrows shot up. "He lay with women for money?"

Amber laughed. "No. It's just an American expression, meaning he was promiscuous."

"Ah, I see. And did you know he was a 'man-whore' all along, or did you find out the hard way?"

"Definitely number two." *The shitty way.* "I overheard him making plans with another flight attendant, and when I confronted him, he admitted he had cheated on me—a lot." She knew she was frowning, but anger was better than tears.

"Ah, lass." Rory took her hand and gave it a gentle squeeze. "I'd never do that to you. Never."

Was this too much to hope for? Had she finally found an honest man who wouldn't hurt her?

"The only problem I foresee…" he began.

Of course. I knew it was too good to be true.

"I'm the head of me clan—small as it is. But I have certain responsibilities that I cannot shirk and cannot manage from here. At some point I must return to Ireland."

And there it is.

She sighed. "Of course. I would always come last. But, at least I'll eventually get this damn apartment."

She rose, but he didn't let go of her hand.

"Wait," Rory said. "We aren't finished with our talk."

She sighed. "I think we are."

—∿—

Shannon and Chloe had stopped at an outdoor vendor's cart to admire his handmade jewelry. Shannon was trying on a ring when sadness suddenly overwhelmed her.

Chloe happened to glance up as her sister's tears fell. "Ah, feckers. Don't start that again."

Shannon sniffed. "I can't help it. I miss Finn, and I can't help wonderin' what he thinks of me."

"He probably thinks you were kidnapped. He knows you'd never desert him on purpose."

Shannon rounded on her sister. "And that's supposed to help?" Off in the distance, over Chloe's shoulder, Shannon glimpsed a familiar-looking lanky lad striding along with his hands in his pockets just like Finn used to do. *Wait a minute…* She took off in his direction screaming, "Finn!"

"Hey!" the vendor yelled. "Are you gonna pay for that?"

Shannon didn't care what the man thought she was doing. If she had a chance of catching the love of her life before he disappeared, she would—or die trying.

Somehow, Finn must have heard her and recognized her voice. He stopped just before turning the corner. She saw him searching the street, and then his gaze landed on her. She saw the light of recognition in his eyes, and seconds later he was running toward her just as swiftly.

"Shannon!"

They came together in a tangle of arms and legs, lips and shoulders. Falling sideways, Shannon would have hit the pavement except that Finn turned at the last second to break her fall. So like the gentleman he was— even at the age of nineteen. He held her tight, as if he'd never let her go.

"Oh, Shannon. I thought I'd never see you again."

She was crying and couldn't speak.

"Oh, don't cry, luv. Whatever brought you here, I'll sort it out for you."

She glanced up and spotted one of the horrible leprechauns standing behind Finn, and then she found her voice. Pointing, she shouted, "Him. He's responsible for this!"

When Finn glanced over his shoulder, the little man shrugged.

Finn scrambled to his feet, pulled Shannon up, and demanded. "Is it true? Did you send her here?"

"I did not. Not exactly."

Finn held on to Shannon's hand but took a step toward the leprechaun, as if he could intimidate the little shite. "What *exactly* did you do?"

"Clancy's pot o' gold went missin'. Shamus said the Arish clan took it. A vote was taken and it was decided that they needed to be cast out of Ireland. For what it's worth, I voted against it."

"Oh. So that makes everythin' all right? Why didn't you stop them? What is wrong with you?"

The leprechaun raised his eyebrows at Shannon, and she gave him a subtle headshake. *Please don't tell him I'm a nine-hundred-year-old dragon...not a nineteen-year-old human.*

Chloe arrived, breathing hard. "I paid for your shopliftin', Shannon—and talked the man out of callin' the garda."

Shannon was barely paying attention to her sister. "Thanks," she mumbled.

Chloe acknowledged the others. "Finn? I don't know how you found her, but I'm glad you did. Mayhaps now

Shannon can stop blubberin'." Then she narrowed her gaze at Lucky. "And what might you be doin' here?"

"I helped the young lad here find his lady. You're welcome."

Chloe clenched her fists, "If not for you and your mates, they wouldn't have been separated a'tall."

Lucky folded his arms and ignored her comment. "We have business to discuss with your brother. Where might he be?"

Chloe tipped her head. "Why don't you discuss your business with me? Let these two lovebirds have their privacy."

"Because your brother is the eldest and the leader of your…" He glanced at Finn. "The head of the household."

"Shannon, Finn, why don't you go get reacquainted at a nearby pub. I'll handle this situation."

Shannon whispered in Chloe's ear. "I don't see any reason we can't take him to Rory. He needs to know they're here anyway."

Chloe folded her arms. She appeared to be in silent contemplation for a few moments. At last she answered, "Fine. I'll take you to me brother, but Shannon won't be there. She has more important things to do."

She smiled at Shannon and winked.

Heat flooded her face. Shannon knew she must be blushing furiously. Ah, the curse of the redhead.

Chapter 10

CHAD WAS WAITING BY THE FRONT DOOR WHEN IT flew open and a young couple raced up the stairs.

It was the younger Arish girl, but he hadn't seen the boy before. *Ah, young love. So impatient.*

Chloe tromped in behind them, followed by an extremely short fellow. He wasn't a child, since he sported a full beard. *"Hmmm... Who could that be?"* Chad wondered aloud—well, as "out loud" as a ghost gets.

The little man froze. "There's a spirit here," he said, rolling his *r*'s the same way the new Irish tenants did.

"You can see me?" Chad asked. He floated right in front of the man.

"I can see you and hear you—although I wish I was only hearin' you, spirit. You sound like a man, but you're wearin' a necklace and a long frock. Are you one of them cross-dressers then?"

At first Chad was offended, but then he laughed. This dude was obviously some old square from another country. *"They're called love beads and my pants are bell bottoms. I died in the sixties."*

Chloe's eyes rounded. "Lucky, are you talkin' to a ghost?"

"Apparently your buildin' is haunted," he said to Chloe. He turned back toward Chad and asked, "What is your purpose here, spirit? Be you friendly or...otherwise?"

"I don't see why my purpose is any of your business. Who are you, and what are you doing in my building?"

"Ah, I see. So it's like that, is it?"

"See what?" Chloe asked. "What is he sayin'?"

The little man put a hand on her arm as if to stay her questions. Then he bowed to Chad and introduced himself. "Me name is Lucky, and I come from Ireland on an important errand."

"What kind of errand?"

"'Tis really none of your business, though I don't suppose I can stop you from overhearin'."

"You got that right."

Chloe took a step toward her brother's door and knocked.

"Not yet," Lucky said. "I'd like to finish me conversation with the spirit first."

Chloe, who had previously seemed fearless, knocked frantically on her brother's door.

"I'm comin', I'm comin'…" Rory called out from inside the apartment.

At last his door swung open. "What the feck, Chloe?"

Chloe pushed her way in and slammed the door behind her.

Ignoring her, the little man continued talking to Chad. "All right. I suppose like others in this country, you don't believe in leprechauns, so let me save you from wastin' your breath. We're real. We have powerful magic. And 'tis true, we have pots of gold to protect. And *that's* why I'm here. Me brother Clancy's gold was stolen. Me other brother, Shamus, convinced us the dragons took it, so we ran them out of Ireland."

"Drove the dragons out, Saint Patrick style?"

"Somethin' like that. Have you heard them talk about where they might have hidden some gold coins?"

"No. And furthermore," Chad said, *"the dragons have been a groovy addition to the building. I don't want to see them hurt. It seems like you've done enough, driving them out of their homeland, so why don't you just be cool, go back to Ireland, and leave them alone?"*

"Well, here's the thing," Lucky said. "One of me brothers is hopin' to question them and find his gold. The other seems to have some kind of personal vendetta against the dragons in general. I'm the only one unconvinced that they took it in the first place."

"And where are the other two now?"

"We split up to look for the Arish girl. We told young Finn we wanted to help him find her. What we really wanted was to find her brother—their clan elder."

"So you lied to the kid."

"Hey. We found his ladylove, didn't we? Did you happen to see how happy they were?"

"And now you know where her brother is."

Lucky nodded. "Now I know where he is." He pointed to apartment 1B. "He's right behind that door. I'm supposed to call the others. They'll come and bring Finn's friend Patrick."

"Can you hold off on that? I have a little idea that might be worth exploring."

"An idea, you say? What kind of idea?"

"One that requires your magic. And if you really don't hold any ill will toward the dragons, I think it will help them be happy here. That way they'll stay in Boston and out of your hair."

Lucky removed his hat and finger-combed his messy

orange mop. "I suppose if they had a better reason to stay than to go home, it might just work out for all concerned."

Chad grinned. He was excited to see what would happen if he could pull off his plan, and now with a little help from magic, he had no doubt the pieces would fall into place—or backfire. Either way, the result would be highly entertaining.

───◦∿∿◦───

Chloe had grabbed her brother's arm and dragged him to the corner farthest from Amber's room.

"Where are you draggin' me, Chloe?"

"Shhh. I don't want Amber to overhear this conversation. Lord knows if the little shites outside the door can hear us or not."

"What little shites? Who's outside the door?" Rory asked in a whisper.

"Lucky's conversin' with a spirit hauntin' the place."

Rory gasped. "Lucky, the lep—"

Chloe clamped her hand over his mouth and whispered in his ear. "You don't want Amber to hear you talking about leprechauns. And you don't want the spirit hauntin' the place to overhear you either."

Rory reared back. He had to remind himself to whisper. "What do you know about this spirit?"

"Not much a'tall."

"So what does he want?"

"Who?"

"The ghost, of course… And where's Shannon, by the way?"

"Oh! I can't believe I forgot… She found Finn. Or rather, Finn found her."

Rory's jaw dropped. "Finn Kelley? From Ballyhoo?"

"That's the one. He came lookin' for her. Brought the feckin' leprechauns with him, but I suppose he'd never have found her without 'em."

Rory's suspicions were raised immediately. Leprechauns weren't overly fond of humans and tended to avoid them at all costs. "And why would they want to help him?"

"Lucky said they were lookin' for you. I guess Finn figured if they found you, he'd find Shannon. And if Finn found Shannon, the leprechauns would find you."

"Not a bad guess. So, if Lucky is lookin' for me, why is he talkin to a ghost outside me door?"

Chloe shrugged. "I don't pretend to know what goes through the little people's heads. They're as much a mystery to me as they are to you."

Rory smiled. "So Finn came after her. The lad just went up a few notches in my estimation."

"He's a good man."

"He's still a boy, but when they're ready, I'll be glad to give them my blessin' and call him me brother."

Chloe snorted. "You're daft. They don't need your permission to marry."

A sly smile crossed Rory's face. "Let's let them think they do. I want him to work for it a little longer."

"Work for what? Her hand in marriage?"

"That too. But I was thinkin' more along the lines of the weddin' night."

Chloe rolled her eyes. "Like I said…you're daft. They're together upstairs right now."

"What?" he roared. "Alone?"

"You see me here right in front of you, don't you?"

"I'll kill 'em both." He strode toward the door, then halted with his hand on the doorknob. "Shite! I can't leave the feckin' apartment. You'll have to go up there."

Chloe laughed. "And do what? Watch them sit next to each other with both feet on the floor, makin' sure there's room for the Holy Spirit between 'em?"

"Please…and be fairly lively about it."

"Why? They've been alone before."

"Outdoors. Not with a private bedroom just steps away. Jaysus!"

Chloe chuckled and strolled slowly to the door. "At least I'll be sure to knock before I barge in. Somethin' you wouldn't have done."

———⁓———

When Amber heard Rory yell, she opened the bedroom door and poked her head out. "Is everything all right?"

Chloe was just leaving and he slammed the door behind her.

Sheesh. Maybe they had a fight. She approached him slowly. "Rory?"

He ignored her completely. A moment later there was a knock at the door. He raked his fingers through his hair and sighed. Then he glanced in Amber's direction but didn't acknowledge her. He simply went to the door and answered it.

The tiniest man she'd ever seen walked in. "How's it goin', boy?"

Rory's lips thinned. "You have a nerve askin', but we're survivin'—despite your little stunt."

"And I'm glad of that."

An uncomfortable silence settled over them, so Amber strolled over to introduce herself. "Hi, I'm Amber. Rory's—uh—unintentional roommate. I guess."

Neither of them even glanced in her direction! It was as if she was invisible. *How rude.*

"Are you alone?" the little man asked.

Rory glanced at Amber's room and said. "Not entirely."

"What does that mean?"

Rory nodded toward her slightly open door. "There's a young lady in the bedroom who might be hearin' every word that isn't whispered."

"Ah. You work fast," the man said and winked. "Then we'll whisper."

"I'll just close her door. She'll probably yell at me, but we'll see."

"You found yerself a feisty one, did you?"

Rory snorted. "You have no idea."

"Hey, guys. I'm right here," she said. *Why the hell are they ignoring me?* It occurred to Amber that perhaps she'd teleported into the ether without meaning to. She looked down at her body, and to her shock, she wasn't there. At. All. *What the...*

Rory returned to the tiny man, who had climbed up onto the window seat. He dragged the futon closer. "What do you want, Lucky?" he whispered. "We don't have your feckin' gold."

Lucky? Was that the guy's name or a nickname he'd earned? Amber wondered what the hell was going on.

"This is for your ears only," the leprechaun said and glanced toward Amber's bedroom.

"Don't worry. She's probably too busy poutin' to come out. She's mad at me."

Lucky chuckled. "They're always mad at you. Women." He spat.

"Hey. None of that now. I'll have to clean it up."

"She won't clean for you?"

Rory laughed.

"I'll do it," the little man said. Then, to her shock, he waved a hand and the spittle disappeared. The whole floor shone as if it had just been washed.

"Nice. I wish I had your magic sometimes."

"And I wish I had your size and power to fly. We all get what we can handle."

Power to fly?

"By the way, it's a bit chilly in here. Can you build a fire?"

"It's not allowed. All I can do is light the candles."

"Please do, then."

Rory didn't get up. Instead he stayed where he was and breathed a column of fire! The candles caught and Lucky smiled.

"So what is it you want?"

"We want Clancy's gold, of course."

"We don't have it. Never did. You blamed the wrong dragons."

"Are there other dragons?"

Rory fell silent.

Dragons? Flying? Fire? Holy shit! I've been falling for a genuine fire-breathing dragon! She wouldn't have believed it if she hadn't seen with her own eyes.

"So, you still haven't said why you're here."

"I'm gettin' to that."

"Then get to it."

———

Rory heard a *thunk*. "What was that?"

"Oh, probably just the ghost."

"Chloe mentioned a ghost. What do you know of it? Is he hauntin' this buildin' after livin' here?"

"I don't know any other kind of ghost, do you?" Lucky asked.

"No." *Now it makes sense.* He *had* turned off the gas, but a ghost had turned it back on. That was unsettling. Maybe the spirit was also responsible for the lights that wouldn't work.

"I take it you didn't know the place was haunted," Lucky said.

"I didn't, though I might have suspected. Tell me about our spirit. Is he dangerous?"

Lucky shrugged. "He's an odd man. Says he died in the sixties."

"Is that all?"

"Other than a very strange way of dressin' he seems harmless enough."

Rory stroked his chin. *I don't know about that.* "Can he communicate with anyone but you leprechauns?"

"Don't know. I didn't ask."

Rory dropped his head in his hands. "Holy mother."

"Look at it this way. What can you do about it? Nothin'."

Rory raised his head and scowled. "That's supposed to make me feel better?"

"No. It's just a fact. If you want to talk in private, we can go outside. I saw a nice strip of green with some benches not far from here. Cars are speedin' by so I doubt we'd be overheard."

Rory leaned back. "Here's the rub… I can't leave the apartment. The young lady I mentioned wants it and so do I. We're goin' by the old adage that 'possession is nine-tenths of the law' until the management says otherwise."

"Oh."

Lucky didn't seem as surprised as Rory had expected he'd be. Did he know more than he was letting on?

"We're gettin' off the subject again," Rory said. "I still want to know why you're here—and it makes no difference whether we're bein' overheard by a spirit or no. We have no gold."

"All right. Here 'tis. We cannot find Clancy's gold in Ireland. He wants to talk to you. Mayhaps you found a way to bring it with you, or you found another type of magic to hide it from us."

"Neither. We don't have your feckin' gold."

"So, if that's true, you won't mind if I pay a visit to your sisters now."

"I didn't say that. Leave me sisters out of it."

"We can't do that. If one of them knows somethin'…"

"They know what I know. We *didn't* take your feckin' gold!"

Lucky raised his palms to calm the dragon. "All right. All right. Relax. To tell you true, I don't think you took it either."

"Then why did you come?"

Lucky screwed up his face as if it pained him to admit something.

"Tell me," Rory encouraged.

The little man sighed. "I may be the only one with me head screwed on straight, and I came to make sure me brothers behaved. Shamus and Clancy are convinced you either have it with you, or you've hidden it somewhere deep."

"Jaysus. How could we have it with us? You cast us out on a boat with nothin'. We were lucky to get our other treasures to sell. Do you know how hard it was to part with priceless family heirlooms like that? I had to take a tenth of what we could have sold them for, just to feed me sisters and get them to a comfortable new home."

Lucky wouldn't admit they'd made a mistake. Leprechauns never did. But the look on his face could only be called contrite.

"I'll have to tell me brothers that I found you."

"That would be grand," Rory said as sarcastically as he could.

"They will be here in a few minutes. Would you like to prepare your roommate for their arrival?"

Defeated, Rory nodded and slowly approached Amber's room as if going to the gallows.

He knocked on the partially open door. "Amber?"

When he heard no answer, he nudged the door open a few inches. "Amber? Where are you, luv?"

He glanced over his shoulder at the bathroom in case she'd gone in there when he wasn't looking. That door stood wide open. She should be able to hear him from there, but he went to investigate just the same.

No Amber in there. He sighed. She must be in the bedroom and simply ignoring him. But if their place was about to be overrun with little people, he had to be sure she was warned and would agree to stay in their bedroom with the door closed.

Since when have I been thinking of this as our *place?*

Well, if it was *theirs*, he had a right to go into the bedroom and find the stubborn lass. He pushed his way into the bedroom and glanced around the boxes, looking for those shiny strands of amber hair.

She must be in the closet. He stepped over boxes and around the bed, and eventually wove his way to the walk-in closet. "C'mon, lass. There's no need to hide from me. I have somethin' important to tell you."

No Amber.

"Where the feck did she go?"

Suddenly, he realized she must have left the building, and that meant he won the apartment!

So why did that make him sad?

"It must be a trick. She's got to be in here somewhere…"

"Chad, is it?" Lucky had closeted himself just inside the door leading to the building's basement.

"I'm here, Lucky."

The leprechaun folded his arms and looked pleased with himself. "Did you see what we did?"

Chad chuckled. *"Yeah. I'd say it's working. You did a groovy thing, little guy."*

"I'll thank you not to call me 'little guy.' It sounds like somethin' you'd call a child. As for groovy—I'm not even goin' to guess what that means."

"It means you did something great."

Lucky smiled. "So, I didn't see what happened after I left. Has he looked for her? Does he know she's invisible?"

"Yes. He looked for her, and I'd say he has no idea she's invisible. Right now he's sitting on the floor of her bedroom looking a little stunned."

"Hee, hee, hee," Lucky giggled. "How long should we let him stew?"

"Until it's no fun anymore." And that could take a while, Chad thought, as he poked his head into the apartment and saw Rory muttering something about composing a song.

"Ah, I wish I could watch," Lucky said when Chad returned.

"I'll watch for you and let you know if anything special happens. Meanwhile, weren't you going to talk to the sisters?"

"Yeah, yeah. I'll get to that. When it comes to a leprechaun's priorities, mischief always takes first place."

Amber came to on the hardwood floor. *Did I faint?*

Rory walked out of her bedroom. *What was he doing in there?* All the thoughts that had overwhelmed her shortly before she fainted came rushing back. *Shit!* She held up what should have been her hand, right in front of her face. She even waved it back and forth, but saw nothing.

I really am invisible.

Rory walked right past her and picked up his guitar, then sat in the middle of his futon and strummed a few sad notes.

Why isn't he celebrating? He must realize I'm not in the apartment. It's not that big a place, and he just came out of the only spot where I could have hidden myself if I'd wanted to.

She had tried to speak to him and his friend before, but neither acted like they'd heard her. *Oh well. It's worth another shot.*

"Hey, Mr. Stubborn! Yeah, you, with the big...handsome...face." *Damn it. He can't hear me.*

He began to sing, haltingly at first.

"Me Amber is the woman I always dreamed about."

Huh? It's as if he's composing a whole new—

*"Her lips they are incredible, especially when she
    pouts..."*

"No, that's not it." He strode to the paper and pencil he'd left on the window seat and flipped the paper over. Then he sat down and resumed his song, writing the lines as he composed them.

*"Me Amber is the woman I always dreamed about.
Her lips are soft and beautiful, even in a pout..."*

"Ah, that's better."

*"Makin' love to her lips is all I got to do,
'cuz me Amber is a missin', and I'm missin' Amber
    too."*

Amber slapped her invisible hand over her mouth. *What? I thought I was the only one feeling something, and I-I... Oh God. I was so horrible to him. How could he possibly miss me?*

"Feckers," he muttered. "How can I sit here and wait for the leprechaun committee when Amber might be in trouble?"

He rose, set his guitar aside, and raked his hands through his auburn hair. "There must be somethin' I can do."

"Ah!" He snapped his fingers, tipped his face toward the ceiling, and yelled, "Euterpe! Euterpe, I need you!"

The muse strode from the bedroom. "Did I hear my name?"

He folded his arms. "You did. Now, mayhaps you can tell me what's goin' on here. And don't pretend I don't know exactly who you are. I know that you were *not* in that bedroom chattin' with Amber one minute ago."

She cocked her head. "What are you talking about?"

"I'm on to you. Not to Amber. I don't know what she's about—or where she's gone off to, but I mean to find out."

"Where she's what?"

"I searched her room. Hell, I searched the whole apartment. I looked in and under every box and behind every door."

Euterpe frowned and muttered "uh-oh" under her breath.

"You see? It's no use lyin' to me anymore. I want to know what's goin' on."

"Did you two have a fight?"

"You mean besides the one we started the minute we walked into this feckin' apartment?"

"Hmmm… You seem on edge."

He raked his hands through his hair again. "You could say I'm on the edge of sanity. Now, if you've any pity in your heart at all…"

Euterpe shrugged. "What does it matter? She's gone. That's what you wanted, isn't it?"

"No," he mumbled.

"No?"

"Not anymore."

She beamed. "Well, isn't this an interesting turn of events. If I help you, what will you do for Amber?"

"I'll give her the apartment. I don't care about anythin' except findin' the lass and makin' sure she's all right."

"Well, I don't know where she is, but I'll do my best to find her." Euterpe walked toward the bedroom, totally ignoring Amber, who was right beside her. Then she halted and faced Rory. "I don't suppose keeping up the ruse matters anymore." She snapped her fingers and disappeared.

Amber froze in shock. Rory knew Euterpe was supernatural? And he didn't freak out—or even bat an eyelash when she disappeared.

Did Euterpe really not see her? Would Brandee or Bliss pop in if she called to them?

Knowing they'd want to stay out of sight, Amber returned to her bedroom and shouted, "Bliss! Brandee! I need you!"

She waited, but no one appeared. She leaned out the door to see if Rory had possibly heard her this time, but no. He had just picked up his guitar and resumed his composition.

Do I dare call on the Grand-Momma of all?

She was just about to when she heard a voice.

"Yelling won't do any good. I should know."

"Huh? Who's there?"

"My name is Chad. I'm one of the residents of

apartment 3A. You'd probably think of me as a spirit haunting the building, but I prefer to think of myself as a corporeally challenged resident."

"Do you pay rent?"

"Fuck no."

"Then I don't see how you're a resident."

"Funny. I don't see you at all."

"This is just a temporary glitch. I'm not dead…" A sudden terrifying thought entered her head. "Am I?"

He laughed. *"You're just now wondering?"*

"Well, I don't see my body anywhere…but I did lose consciousness for a bit. Who could have snatched my body right out from under Rory's nose? And how can you hear me?"

"Shouldn't the better question be why can't anyone else?"

"I don't understand what's happening. Do you know?"

"I know more than you do."

"Great. So tell me, wise spirit."

Chad chuckled. *"Look, I don't have to explain a thing to you. One of the best things about being a ghost is that there's absolutely nothing you can do about me. If I want you to know something, I'll tell you. I come and go as I please. I can be nice to those I like, and I can devise all kinds of unpleasantness for those I don't like."*

"Okaaay… Maybe we got off on the wrong foot. Hi. My name is Amber McNally. I was… I mean, I *am* a flight attendant and a resident of apartment 1B."

Chad laughed out loud.

"I'm sorry. Is something about that funny?"

"Yeah. You don't exist. At the moment, you're a soul with no body. I'm picturing you trying to fly the

friendly skies and interact with passengers in your current state."

Amber's lip trembled. At least she thought it must be trembling. It felt like it was. She took a deep breath and commanded herself to stay calm. "Can you make yourself known to everyone? Or just a select few?"

"There are people who call themselves 'sensitives.' They don't like the old-fashioned word 'psychics,' but that's what they are. I can let them know I'm around if I want to. Or I can be quiet and let them wonder."

"It must get very lonely. I don't imagine that many psychics visit."

"I see what you're doing."

"What?"

"You're trying to sympathize and get on my good side."

"Well, why wouldn't I? It looks like you're my only friend at the moment. Maybe I'm all you've got too."

"Nope. I have friends all over the building. I even have a roommate."

"That's right. You said you lived—er, that you reside in 3A. Isn't that Gwyneth's apartment?"

"Yes. She's my roommate and a friend."

"She can hear you?"

"I'm not taking any more questions right now. I just wanted to check on you."

"Can I ask just *one* more question? Please?"

He sighed. *"As long as it isn't stupid."*

"Okay. I was wondering if the little man who visited Rory before—I think his name is Lucky—if he has anything to do with this."

"Ding, ding, ding! Give the girl a kewpie doll!"

—∼∼—

Rory marched to the door, threw it open, and called upstairs, "Shannon! Chloe!"

He waited and when there was no answer, he tried again. "Shannon! Chloe! Hell, I'll even take Finn at this point!"

Eventually a door opened upstairs, but it wasn't the one to his sister's apartment. It was the door to the paranormal club. A big, blond man holding a pool cue strolled over to the banister.

"Is everything all right down there?"

"Fine. I'm sorry if I disturbed you. I was hopin' one of me useless sisters would open their door across the hall."

The door in question flew open, and Chloe leaned over the banister. "Useless are we?" she shouted.

Rory smiled. "Ah, I knew that would get your attention."

"I'm chaperonin' Shannon, just like you told me to. Now apologize, you big oaf."

"Sorry." He was grinning and wasn't sorry at all.

"Now that you've got me attention, Rory, what did you want?"

"I want to find Amber."

"What?" Chloe exclaimed. "Isn't she there with you?"

"No. I was wonderin' if she was up there."

The guy from the paranormal club leaned over the banister. "Is that the woman my wife is friends with? She's a flight attendant, right?"

"She is."

"So you were visiting her and she stepped out? How long ago?"

"I-I don't really know. I thought she was in her bedroom, but when I checked, it must have been an hour or more since I'd seen her last."

"Oh boy," the guy muttered under his breath.

"You must have missed her, Rory. Go back and look again," Chloe said.

"I'm tellin' you, I looked. I opened every box and drawer she might have managed to cram herself into."

The guy at the top of the stairs laughed. "Do you want my professional opinion as a private investigator?" He continued without waiting for a response. "It sounds like she left the building."

Rory shook his head. "I know you must be right, but I cannot fathom it. How did she get past me when I was sittin' in view of the door the whole time?"

"Were you nappin?" Chloe asked.

"Not a'tall." Rory tried to tamp down his frustration.

Finn called out. "Is that Rory?"

"Where are you, lad? I want to see the man who followed me sister all the way from Ireland."

Finn rounded the banister and descended the stairs. He grinned as if Rory might pin a medal on his chest. Shannon followed him. At least they were dressed. Rory didn't know what to do with these two yet, but he needed to have a serious talk with Finn soon—alone.

"Where are you stayin', lad?"

"At a bed-and-breakfast over on Elliott Street. The hotels on Boylston are too expensive."

"Good man. With your trackin' skills, I'd ask you to participate in a search party—but unfortunately I'm lookin' for a woman you've never seen."

He focused his gaze on Finn. "So, how did you manage to track down me sister?"

"I had a *little* help." He leaned in on the word "little" and gave Rory an intense stare, as if he'd know what he meant.

If Finn knew about the little people, did he know they were leprechauns?

"What help specifically?"

Lucky materialized between them.

"Specifically, me."

"No! You showed your magic?"

"Relax, Brother," Shannon said. "Lucky met Finn a while ago. Back in Ireland."

"And you told him what you were?"

"Not me. Shamus did that."

"Why?" Rory asked, still in shock.

"I never did get the full story," Lucky said and gazed up at Finn.

"I'm sorry. I promised I'd never divulge a word of that conversation."

The guy who was still leaning over the railing said, "I've never met a leprechaun." A few others who were curious had joined him. He glanced behind him at his friends. "Have any of you?"

The other guys all murmured "no" in various ways.

"Why don't you join us? I'll invite you into the club and introduce you."

"That sounds grand," Lucky said. A moment later he materialized next to the big guy who'd identified himself as a PI.

"Wait!" Rory said. "What about findin' Amber? I want to hire you, but we should get lookin' right away."

"Sheesh," Lucky said. "She's still in the apartment."

"Where?" Rory demanded.

"Chad?" Lucky called out. A moment later he began whispering to thin air.

Ah. The ghost has somethin' to do with it.

At last, Lucky grinned. "Why look. There she is!"

Rory snapped his head around and found himself staring into the most beautiful hazel-green eyes he'd ever seen.

"Ah, lass." He took her in his arms and she embraced him willingly.

There were chuckles from the upstairs gallery, but Rory didn't care. He lifted her so he could enter and kicked the door shut with his foot, then his lips descended to hers.

Chapter 11

AMBER HAD TO MENTALLY SHAKE HERSELF OUT OF Rory's drugging kiss. She had a few questions for the fire-breathing dragon.

She leaned back, reluctantly.

Rory opened his eyes. "What's wrong, luv?"

"Uh… We need to talk."

Rory groaned but followed her to the futon and sank down next to her.

She cocked her head. "What is it you don't want to talk about? And why?"

"Everythin'. At least not now." He shifted uncomfortably in his seat, and she noticed the erection tenting his pants. Her eyes must have bugged out, because he followed up with, "And *that's* why."

She chuckled. "We'll get to that—maybe. I heard a few things when I was invisible."

"Is that where you went? You became invisible? Am I to assume you can eavesdrop on me anytime you like?"

"No. I didn't do it. The little guy—Lucky—did it. Well, he and the ghost were the ones who thought it up."

Rory hit himself upside the head. "I should have known. Feckin' mischief-makers."

"It sounds like you know what they're capable of. So, how was he able to do that?"

He sighed. "Magic. How much did you overhear?"

"Enough to know you can fly and breathe fire. I

wouldn't have believed it if I hadn't seen the fire coming out of your mouth with my own eyes."

Rory gazed at the floor. "I suppose you want nuthin' to do with me now that you know I'm a shapeshiftin' dragon."

Her eyebrows shot up. "You're a shapeshifter too?"

"Well, o' course. Me wings aren't hid beneath me shirt."

"Shift for me."

"What?" He leaned back and stared at her as if she'd grown two heads.

"I should see what you look like in all your forms, especially if I'm sharing an apartment with you."

A slow smile spread across his face. "You're not afraid?"

She shrugged. "Depends. You won't light me on fire if you get mad, will you?"

He laughed. "Darlin', you've already made me as mad as I get, and you're still standin'. Or rather sittin' right beside me."

"For some reason, I feel like I can trust you."

"Grand. Then you should trust me with your secret too."

"*My* secret?"

"Don't treat me like I'm an idjit. Your friend, Euterpe…snapped her fingers and disappeared. Don't tell me you didn't know she's a muse."

Amber tried to look contrite. "I knew. I'm not an 'idjit' either."

"And because this buildin' seems to house and host a number of paranormals, tell me. What are you?"

She sighed. "I'm a muse too. The modern muse of air travel."

She could see she'd surprised him. He looked like she could poke him and he'd fall on the floor.

"Modern muse, you say? Are there others?"

"Yeah, but I'm not supposed to talk about them."

"Can you give me a general idea of what's covered?"

"I don't know yet. I'm new. I was just recruited, so I guess you could call me a rookie."

Suddenly, Mother Nature herself appeared in their living room. She didn't bother to hide her identity with modern clothing. She wore her white robe, belted with a vine.

"Mother! I mean, Gaia!" Amber exclaimed. "What are you doing here?"

Rory rose swiftly. Reverently, he whispered, "Gaia? Mother of *All*?"

She smirked. "At last. Someone who treats me with the respect I deserve."

He bowed. "I'm honored by your presence."

"I like you, dragon."

"…and I'm humbled by your opinion."

She smiled sincerely this time. "He's a charmer. I hope you know how lucky you are, muse. By the way, I'm hearing good things about you, and I enjoyed your description of yourself as a rookie. It's always good to know your place."

Amber found her feet and rose too. "I—uh… Thanks? What can I do for you, Goddess?"

"Nothing at the moment. I was just making sure you two were aware of how important it is not to share this sensitive information with humans. There are a couple of them in the building."

"Ah," Rory said. "Finn for one. Perhaps you can help me, Goddess of All."

Her unplucked eyebrows rose. "Help? In what way?"

"I need your wisdom, and advice if you're willin' to give it."

She nodded. "Go ahead with your question."

"Me sister. She's in love with a human. He loves her back thoroughly, but there will come a time when he grows old, and though she's much older, she doesn't look it and never will."

"Ah, yes. Your sister is almost a thousand years old, I believe."

Amber's jaw dropped, but Gaia must not have noticed because she continued talking.

"You're saying he doesn't know she's a dragon…"

"I forbid her from tellin' him, but you can't forbid a lass from fallin' in love."

Mother Nature chuckled. "Yeah. That was my doing, I'm afraid. I invented love to populate the planet and as an amusement for myself, but I didn't install a lick of logic with it. Sorry about that." She folded her arms. "Well, dragon. I'd say you did well, but you do have a dilemma on your hands."

"Indeed I do."

"Wait a minute. If Shannon is about a thousand—and Rory is her older *brother…"*

"Oh, for goodness' sake, muse. He's a thousand and ten," Mother Nature said.

Yup, she must be able to read my mind. Then Amber realized she was staring at Rory with her mouth open.

He looked at her and grinned. "But I don't look a day over twenty-eight, right?"

"R-right."

"I imagine the solution your parents chose will be Shannon's eventually."

How can she continue on as if I just heard that the weather is fair?

"Oh." He looked thoughtful.

He had Amber's attention again, and she placed her hand gently on his arm. "What happened to your parents?"

"They had to move away and only come back after all the humans they knew were long gone. Unfortunately, they never came back and it's been hundreds of years now. Once the villagers catch on that we're not gettin' any older while they're not getting' any younger, well…" He sighed. "We stayed hidden for several generations and only blended in with the current population recently. We wanted to stay close in case our parents came back, but…"

"I see. It's all part of not letting humans know about the paranormal then."

Mother Nature patted her on the head. "I'm glad you took that lesson to heart, muse of air travel."

"Do you even remember my name?" Amber didn't mean to be irreverent, but she couldn't help wondering.

"Of course I do. It's Amber. Or is it Jade? I get new names confused at times. That's why I just go with something safe until it sticks. Look, I'm not going to stay long. I have air currents to stir, waves to undulate, volcanos to keep under control…"

Rory let out a reverent breath. "All that, and humans too."

Gaia smiled and nodded. "I'm delighted someone finally understands all I do." She faced Amber and said with a wink, "He's a keeper."

Then she was gone.

Rory nearly collapsed on the futon.

"You look like a fanboy who just met his idol."

He gazed up at Amber. "Aren't you a little awestruck as well? You just met the Goddess. *The* Goddess!"

"I didn't *just* meet her. I met her the other day when she recruited me."

Rory slapped a hand over his eyes. "She handpicked you? Don't you realize what that means, lass?"

Amber was genuinely puzzled by what she considered his overreaction. She sat down next to him. "I guess not. What does it mean?"

"It means you have a destiny. Like Joan of Arc. I-I don't know how to feel about lovin' a woman with a destiny. It's confusin'."

He loves me? She'd expected him to try to backpedal. To say he was just writing a song, nothing more.

She set one hand on his knee. "Do you believe that *this*...could possibly be destiny?" She wagged her index finger back and forth at the two of them.

He hesitated, then slowly smiled. "I suppose it could be. I mean, you know I'm a dragon and I know you're a muse. It seems as if we're suited to each other and unsuitable for humans."

"I know."

They stared at each other for a few moments, then fell on each other as if ravenous. She opened her mouth and welcomed his tongue. As he cupped her head, he yanked her body closer, and they collapsed half on and half off the futon's long cushion.

A flurry of fingers yanked at zippers and buttons until they practically fused together, hot skin to skin that was heating rapidly from the inside.

Amber managed to pull away to murmur, "My bed..."

Rory smiled and scooped her up in his arms.

He carried her to the bedroom, then had to pick his way between the boxes so he wouldn't drop her. "We need to spread this furniture around the rest of the apartment."

"So, I'm not confined to my—I mean, *our* bedroom anymore?"

He grinned. "Not if this next part works out."

He had a point. They should probably find out if they were sexually compatible before they decided to share a bed. Would he roar fire at the moment of climax? That might be good to know.

They finally made it to the bed without incident, although both of them were still wearing socks and underpants. Rory sat up to rip his off and then Amber's. It was the first glimpse she had of his erect cock.

Holy... Wow! No wonder he was unsuitable for humans. He was probably too big for most girls. Amber smiled, remembering she was a minor goddess and could probably stretch herself to fit.

We'll find out.

Resuming where they'd left off, he stroked and caressed her as they locked lips. He cupped her bottom and pulled her tight against his staff.

She lost her breath for a moment.

When he leaned back, they were both panting hard. Amber hadn't realized how much she'd needed this until now. Perhaps most of their fighting hadn't been about the apartment at all. Maybe it was due to their overpowering sexual tension and attempts to resist its pull.

She grasped his cock and stroked, to which he reacted with a pleasurable-sounding groan. She couldn't come close to touching her finger to her thumb because of his girth, but that didn't seem to lessen the effect.

He quickly rolled her onto her back and bent over her nearest breast. He suckled deep, and she experienced a visceral tug that made her think she might come apart right there and then. She arched and moaned, only stopping when he switched to her other breast. He gave that one the same attention and increased her pleasure tenfold as he cupped her mons and added a massage to the apex of her thighs.

When he zeroed in on her sensitive bud, Amber let out a strangled cry. She grabbed the red streak in his hair and held him still.

"Wait," she whispered breathlessly. "I want us to come together."

"What's wrong with you comin' twice, luv?"

She chuckled. "Nothing at all. I just thought you might like to get in on this."

"Oh, I'd like to get *in*, all right, but first let me love you good and proper."

She wondered what that entailed, but she had a feeling she'd never forget once she knew. She let go of his hair and grasped the sheets instead.

He brought her to the brink and backed off. She swatted him and cried, "That's not fair. If you want to wait, that's fine, but I shouldn't have to."

Rory chuckled but respected her wishes. The next time he took her to the breaking point, he didn't stop. Amber let go, shattering. She felt like she was flying without a plane. She soared so long that she thought she might never land. When she couldn't take anymore, she latched on to his hair and gently pulled him away. Her orgasm slowed and gently touched down.

He smiled. As soon as she'd had a short rest, he continued to make love to her for what seemed like hours before taking his own pleasure. She must have climaxed half a dozen times by then. At last he looked her in the eyes and said, "I can't wait any longer, luv."

"Go ahead," she panted.

He grinned and positioned himself between her knees. She was as relaxed as if she'd had a few glasses of wine. Slowly she guided him in, and when fully seated, he let out a sound of pure relief.

Rory began a slow rhythm of thrusts. Amber lifted her hips to meet him in welcome each time. As he increased the tempo, she did too. No matter how relaxed she had been a few minutes earlier, she could feel the tension building again like a spring being coiled tighter and tighter. He built their mating to a feverish pitch, and then she was flying apart.

He grunted and jerked several times, and she knew they were climaxing together. She hoped his orgasm was as satisfying as all of hers had been.

At last, they stilled. He collapsed onto his side, and breathing heavily, he lay with his arm across her abdomen.

"That was…" She didn't have sufficient words to describe what she was feeling, but Rory seemed to understand.

"'Twas incredible," he said and chuckled.

"I-I guess we're compatible in bed."

He laughed out loud. "Bejeezus. Sure'n no truer words were ever spoken."

———

They were roused from a short nap by frantic knocking on the apartment door. Rory shot to his feet. He strode to the living room and found his kilt.

"Hold on…" he called out. "I'm comin'."

By the time he had his kilt fastened, Amber had tossed on a robe and joined him.

"I'll get it," she said.

"You'll do no such thing. Put some clothes on. The last thing I want to do is damage a lass's reputation. I'll find out what's what and call you if you need to be here."

She whirled on her bare feet and marched back to the bedroom.

Whew. The last thing I want to do is damage a young lass's reputation.

When he opened the door, four leprechauns stood before him.

"There's four of you?"

"Sorry to disturb you, but our king, Fagan here, has some news."

Fagan was the only one dressed in brown. He looked uncomfortable and kicked at the floor. "I'm sorry to tell you after the castle reappeared, I couldn't hide it all by meself. I thought I could, but I may have overestimated me magic. Sure'n it's still strong, but not as strong as it used to be. And hidin' a castle…well, that takes a lot of power."

Rory gritted his teeth. He had a feeling he wasn't going to like what was coming next. "Have you told Chloe and Shannon this yet?"

"No. We needed to approach you first as clan leader—of *this* branch of Arishes."

Confusion warred with a sense of dread. Something had happened. Did their cousins still nurse the age-old grudge between their fathers? *Ha.* Why wouldn't they? The Irish had long memories.

"Get on with it, Fagan. What's happened?"

"Can we at least come in and sit down?" Lucky asked.

"No. I have—company."

"Ah. Your roommate," Lucky said.

Amber strode into the living room, fully dressed in jeans and a sexy white blouse.

Three of the leprechauns leaned in to get a better look. Small smiles played on their faces. One of them whispered behind his hand. "She's a beauty. No wonder he doesn't want to leave."

"True, but what's keepin' *her* here?" Shamus asked, and they all tittered.

All except Rory. He had had about enough of being trapped in this place. He and Amber had finally come to some kind of agreement but hadn't had a chance to formalize it and talk to the apartment managers.

"Amber. May I speak with you a moment?"

"What's wrong?" she asked.

"Nothin', luv. I have to go upstairs, and I want to know if I'll be welcome when I come back down."

She laughed.

Why is she laughin'? "I wasn't meanin' it to be funny. I really need to know."

Her face fell. "Are you serious? After… You still don't trust me?"

"I trust you just fine, but we've not discussed—"

She turned and strode to the bedroom and slammed the door. He rolled his eyes, realizing he had to make a fast decision. He could either go after her and wrestle a promise out of her, or trust that she'd let him back in... even though now she was angry.

"Ah, feck." He stepped into the hall and slammed the door behind him.

———

Amber had to ask herself why she was so angry. She had just spent the best afternoon of her life in the arms of a very skillful lover. So, she unpacked her boxes as she thought over everything that had happened in the last three days.

He had said he loved her, both in song and with his body. What the heck did she want?

Maybe that was the problem. She didn't really know what she wanted. She had envisioned her life a lot differently.

One thing was for damn sure—she had never imagined sharing an apartment in this neighborhood with a dragon! Of course, she had never imagined she'd become a muse either.

She still had a lot of questions about that. She needed to have a long talk with Euterpe, but she didn't even like the woman, and she was already in a pissy mood.

Maybe Bliss or Brandee would have time for me.

She set down the box marked "linens" and took a quick glance around the apartment. No dragons or little people were lurking in any of the rooms.

She looked at the ceiling and called, "Bliss?" When

there was no answer, she tried Brandee. Still no answer. Maybe she had to shout.

"Bliss!"

At last Brandee appeared. "Sorry for the delay, Amber. Bliss is having her baby."

She gasped. "Now?"

"Yeah. It took forever. She refused to do anything to hurry the labor, so she's exhausted. Drake is with her, and the muse of childbirth is taking care of the baby."

Amber straightened. "There's a muse of childbirth?"

"She's not one of the modern muses. Actually, she's not a muse at all and knows nothing about modern medical technology. Eileithyia is known as the divine midwife."

"Shoot. There's a god or goddess of everything, isn't there?"

Brandee chuckled. "Just about. Don't worry. You won't meet most of them."

Amber wiped her brow. "Whew. I still have to bone up on my Greek mythology."

"There's plenty of time for that. Now, before we get sidetracked…why did you call Bliss and me?"

"I feel like there are still a lot of things I should know, and Euterpe isn't teaching me much."

Brandee nodded. "Yeah, it's hard for the ancient ones. Our world has changed so much that they've kind of given up."

"But they won't admit it."

"Bingo."

"So, how did you learn whatever you had to know?"

"I asked a lot of questions. My muse trainer was Erato. Really sweet, but always daydreaming. I had to yank her back to the here and now, and force her to answer my questions."

"Where was she?"

Brandee chuckled. "Oh, she didn't go anywhere, but her mind did. I didn't know it at the time, but she was helping couples fall in love while she was sitting right next to me."

"Wow. That's a talent."

"Yes, and she's quite busy. It helps if you can find a tactful way to ask your assigned muse those many questions you have. If she can't answer to your satisfaction, Bliss or I can share what we know. We've had to figure out a lot on our own."

"But at least you have each other," Amber said wistfully.

Brandee set a hand on her shoulder. "You have us too. Today is pretty unique. It's not every day a baby is born—especially a miracle child like this one."

"What do you mean?"

"Well, dragons and humans can't create life. Female dragons have to mate with another dragon to get pregnant. When Bliss initially refused Mother Nature's offer, Drake gave up his immortality and became human. He loved Bliss so much that he chose to sacrifice his long life-span so he didn't have to continue on for centuries without her."

Amber slapped a hand over her heart. "Oh my God. That's so…incredibly romantic."

"Yeah, well. The choice was short lived. As you know, Bliss had a change of heart. But while Drake was human, they did the deed and she's about to have a perfectly human baby—we think."

"You think?"

Brandee shrugged. "This has never happened before, but if it was going to happen, it would happen to *her*. Bliss has a tendency to react first and think about the consequences later. Oh, and she's a blurter, so if she says something a little tactless just give her a couple of minutes. She'll usually backtrack and find a nicer way to say the same thing."

"Good to know."

Just then an angry voice yelled, "Brandee! Where the hell are you? I just had your godchild here!"

Brandee giggled. "See what I mean? I gotta go, but I'll come back when all the drama is over."

"Wait!"

Brandee was already gone.

I wanted to know why humans and dragons can't create life. Not that Amber wanted to. She just wanted to know why. Not that it mattered. She wanted to be a dink, right?

She snorted. Maybe she already was.

———

Rory took a seat in his sisters' apartment. They also had bought a futon, as well as a chair that looked like it might convert into a bed. Lord knew what they were thinking at the time. Maybe that all three of them would wind up together. The leprechauns sat along the window seat. Chloe brought a plate of scones from the kitchen and placed it on the storage trunk, which doubled as a coffee table. Shannon followed with a tray holding a steaming teapot and a sleeve of foam cups. While she poured, Rory glanced around.

He'd never seen their apartment before he got stuck in his.

He noticed a similar layout to his place downstairs, but there was a nice hall closet right where he didn't have one. The kitchen and bath looked a little more spacious too. Sly had mentioned that his place was the smallest in the building—correction. His *and* Amber's place. He still had a hard time believing he hadn't just stepped out the door and into homelessness. Time would tell if she'd let him back in.

Right now he had to stop thinking of Amber and start thinking about the feckin' leprechauns—if he could.

"So, where is Finn?" he asked.

"He and Pat went out to get a few things for us," Chloe said.

"It was probably smart to send them away."

He focused on Fagan, the king. "You mentioned somethin' about not bein' able to hide the castle anymore. So, has anyone discovered it?"

Fagan covered his face with his hands. "The whole feckin' country knows about it now. I hate to be the one to tell you this, but the place is overrun with newspeople, tourists, and curious locals. Everyone wants a piece of it to carry home as a souvenir."

Shannon cried out and almost dropped the teapot as she slapped her hand over her mouth. Chloe swore.

Rory held up his hand. "Before anyone barbecues the lot of you, tell me we're to be allowed home to take back what's rightfully ours."

King Fagan shot a sidelong glance at Shamus. "We have nothin' against you returnin' to the castle. It seems as if Clancy's gold isn't there."

"It has to be somewhere," Shamus said. "We didn't find it at home, but what if they hid it well? We came here to question them."

Rory rose and leaned over the little man. Speaking through clenched teeth, he growled, "We didn't take your feckin' gold."

"Well, someone did," Clancy said.

Chloe rose and stood beside her brother. She folded her arms as if to form a united front. "It weren't us."

Shamus advanced a step, but before he could go any further, Fagan snapped his fingers and the little trouble-maker was back on the window seat. "Hold your tongue, Shamus, or I'll stuff a rag in your mouth."

"Look, we mean you no harm," Fagan said. "Never did. It was just a misunderstandin' of sorts."

"A misunderstandin'?" Chloe laughed. "A misunderstandin' is when the barkeep brings you light beer instead of ale. Because of you little feckers, we lost everythin' we had. And now you're tellin' us the land our ancestors fought so hard to win is gone too."

"No, not gone," Fagan said and smiled. "The good news is your cousins came and claimed it. They kicked out all the fortune hunters. It's still standin' in the same condition as when you left it... Well, minus a few pieces."

All three of the Arish siblings cried out. "Our cousins?"

Fagan leaned away and his brow wrinkled. "Did you not want someone in the family to protect it for you?"

Rory shook his head. "For a thousand years, we've protected it from *them*."

"Ah, dear. A little family feud is it?"

"If you call an all-out war that killed half the kingdom a family feud, then we had a little family feud."

"Our father was the eldest of three brothers," Shannon explained. "The castle, lands, and everythin' belonged to him. His next younger brother thought he'd steal the crown simply by assassinatin' our father. He failed in each attempt. Finally he gathered men who swore their loyalty, and all were ready to fight for a cheat who promised them a noble title and some land when he became king."

"So, what happened to the third brother?" Clancy asked.

"Ah, he left the country before that got out of hand," Rory explained. "He had no hope of becoming king, so he went off to seek his own fortune."

"So he stayed out of it?" Fagan asked.

Rory nodded.

"No one ever heard from him again," Shannon said.

"So the only two families with claims to it are you and the other Arish brothers," Shamus said.

Rory stiffened. "They have no claim to *our* home." His fists clenched and the sting of emerging talons signaled he needed to calm down before he shifted.

Chloe was right there with him. Her eyes blazed and a curl of smoke wafted from her nose.

"Relax," Fagan said. "Nothin' good can come of you shiftin' and burnin' down your new home."

Shannon sighed. "Our da would suffer a heart attack if he heard our home went to his brother's sons after all the blood spilled to keep it for us."

Rory dropped back onto the futon and bent over, his head in his hands. He didn't want to say it aloud, but he had no idea how to reclaim the place if his cousins refused to leave. It's not like they could declare another war on Irish soil. They'd all land in prison.

"Mayhaps you could share?" Clancy said.

All three siblings stared at him as if he had ten heads.

Chloe recovered first. "Are you daft, little man? Share with the idjit sons of the man who tried to murder our father?"

Clancy folded his arms and pouted.

"'Tis your feckin' love for gold that put you in this position," Shamus said.

"*Our* love for gold?" Rory ground out. His nostrils flared and smoke escaped.

King Fagan pointed at his fellow leprechaun. "Stop yammerin' right now. I don't know what you have against the dragons, Shamus, but whatever it is, put it on the long finger. Now, the reason I came here meself was to lift the magic we four used to keep *these* Arishes out of Ireland. After they return, they can deal with sendin' the others back to Ulster."

"Shite," Rory muttered.

Chloe placed a hand on her brother's knee. "What are you thinkin', Prince?"

She *never* used his title. It must have been her way of swearing her loyalty while at the same time reminding him of his obligation.

He was thinking he had lost interest in the crumbling ruin that had once been their beloved home. The idea of leaving a certain sexy flight attendant to oust a rival clan filled him with dread. What if she found someone else to move in with her while he was gone? His green eyes were probably turning greener.

As far as he was concerned, his Ulster cousins could have the damn castle. It was an empty ruin, but his sisters would never forgive him if he gave up without a fight. *At least a verbal one.* He wouldn't pit his sisters against male dragons.

"I need to talk to them." Rory narrowed his eyes at Fagan. "I don't suppose you have their phone number?"

"Sadly no. But now that we're together, we can lift the spell that kept you from returnin' home."

Rory nodded. "Do it then. I'll go pack."

"And I'll go with you," Chloe said, getting to her feet.

"No, you won't. You'll stay here and keep an eye on the youngest."

Shannon rose and jammed her hands on her hips. "What do you mean by that? I'm not helpless. Besides, I have Finn to stay with me now."

Rory snorted. "Sure'n *that's* what I mean, me darlin' sister."

"You can't be serious," the women said at once.

Rory got to his feet, raising himself to his full height. "You'll both stay here. As head of this clan, I order you."

Their eyes rounded, but neither said a word. They couldn't. Their leader had given an order, and to disobey would mean treason. He'd never used his powerful position with his sisters, but this was for their own safety.

--~~--

Chad the ghost couldn't wait to give his report to the tenants. Wouldn't they be delighted to learn that the rivals had become lovers? No hard decisions. No ugly scenes. The hippie in him just loved this outcome.

He searched for witch Morgaine, but she wasn't in her apartment. He floated across the hall, looking for his southern belle roommate Gwyneth. She was missing too.

Where the heck did everyone go?

A cheer went up from the paranormal club down-stairs. *Ah. They must be having a tournament or something.* That worked just fine. He could probably call an impromptu tenants' meeting on the spot.

He sunk through the floor into the club and saw a bunch of smiling faces huddled around a phone. Gwyneth and Morgaine could hear him and Nathan could see him, but Sly wouldn't know Chad was there unless he flashed the lights or something.

"Congratulations, Drake," Sly said.

"I knew y'all were havin' a boy." Gwyneth hugged Nathan. "They say the goddess only gives ya what y'all can handle. I can't think of anyone better to raise a rowdy boy than Bliss."

The phone was on speaker and Drake laughed loudly. "You got that right. The little tyke won't get away with anything."

"I'm so happy for you two," Morgaine said. When Chad cleared his throat, she looked up. "Oh! Chad is here. Did you want to add your congratulations to the new parents, Chad?"

"Sure. But then I have something even more important to discuss with the whole room. Don't let anyone leave."

"More important?" she echoed.

Gwyneth glared at the ceiling. "What the heck could be more important than the birth of our good friend's baby, Chad?"

Drake's voice interjected. "It's okay. I should get back to Bliss. I just wanted you all to know that everything went well. Both mother and baby are fine."

"Y'all don't have to hang up just because of Chad. It's not like he has anywhere to be."

"It's okay, Gwyneth. Another visitor just popped in and I should be social. I'll come by the club later with cigars."

Gwyneth scrunched up her nose as if she'd smelled something foul.

"See you later," Drake said, and as soon as everyone had congratulated him again, they finally hung up.

Chad couldn't have waited much longer without shorting out the ceiling fan or something.

"Okay," Morgaine said. "What's so important that you had to interrupt?"

"It's the new tenants in apartment 1B."

Morgaine rolled her eyes. "Are they at it again?"

"Amber and Rory have become lovers. There's no need to decide who gets the apartment!"

For some reason Morgaine wasn't jumping up and down. Considering she'd be the one to eject one or the other tenant, Chad thought she'd be happier than this.

"Why aren't you excited? I thought you'd at least say something like 'groovy.'"

Morgaine placed her hands on her hips. "I didn't say 'groovy' because I'm not from the sixties like you are, Chad. Also, just because they're making love doesn't mean they want to share the apartment long-term."

"True," he admitted. *"But free love went out in the seventies. I didn't know it was back in. If so, well... Groovy!"*

"No. Free love isn't back in. I think people realized

it sometimes hurt others and haven't been doing that for a while."

Sly cocked his head at her. "What are you talking about? Who's hurting who with free love?"

"Nobody is hurting anyone." Morgaine's posture relaxed and she smiled. They shared a few moments of silent communication and punctuated it with a kiss.

"Well, I don't really know what we can do with this information. It's not like I'm going to march down there and ask if their recent bedroom activities were a declaration of undying love."

"That's a cop-out. I'd do it, but neither of them can hear me." Then Chad got an idea. The leprechauns! They could hear him—and see him. *"Never mind. I'll continue to watch them and see what happens. You may return to your regularly scheduled…whatever."*

Chad floated through the wall and followed the sound of raised voices across the hall.

He stopped and listened outside the apartment for a few minutes. It sounded like an Irish Sunday dinner. Lots of heavily accented English with a few voices trying to speak over the others.

Suddenly all became quiet, then four distinct munchkin voices began chanting.

No matter how hard he listened, he couldn't make out the words. *They must be chanting in Gaelic or something.*

After they finished, one of the leprechauns said, "There. Now you can go home."

Chapter 12

ON THE OFF CHANCE THAT FAGAN WAS WRONG, Rory strode across the hall and used the phone in the paranormal club. He had to place an international call to his cousins' home in Ulster. He was relieved when one of them answered the phone.

"It's Rory Arish. Which one of you am I talkin' to?"

"Rory? The operator said it was a call from the United States."

"So? I asked which one of me cousins I'm talkin' to."

There was a brief pause on the other end. "What does it matter?"

"I'd like to know what to call you."

"It's Eagan."

"Ah. The youngest. Is Conlan about?"

"Anythin' you want to discuss with Conlan you can say to me," Eagan blustered.

Rory found a comfortable chair and sat down. "It's an important matter, and I think Conlan and I should speak as heads of our clans."

"Are you referrin' to our ancestral castle that's been discovered? The reason I can't put you in touch with Conlan straightaway is because he and Aiden are in Ballyhoo now."

This time Rory was speechless. *Bollocks. It's true.* Perhaps Amber, being a flight attendant, could help him get to his destination quickly.

"Fine. I'll meet them there."

"Why did the operator say you were callin' from the United States?"

"It's a long story."

"I have time, and I enjoy long stories."

"Most Irishmen do—except this one. If you speak to Conlan before I arrive, tell him I'll be there presently. There's a B and B in town where he and Aiden can stay until I can welcome them properly."

"But—"

Rory hung up the phone and ran downstairs.

"Amber?" When there was no answer, he went to the bedroom.

He poked his head in and didn't see her. *Shite.*

"Amber?"

No answer.

"Jaysus." A few hours ago, neither could leave; now apparently they both could.

Rory strode across the hall and knocked.

After another set of knocks, Nathan eventually answered the door. "So, she threw you out already?"

"Who?"

"Amber. Your…um—?"

Rory didn't have time for explanations. "I'm lookin' for her. I was thinkin' she may have come over here."

"Nope. She's not here. Did you check the hospital?"

Alarm slammed through him. "Why? What happened?"

Nathan leaned against the doorjamb. "Don't get your panties in a twist. She'd be on the maternity ward, visiting a friend who just gave birth."

"Oh. Is it Bliss?"

"Yeah. Bliss and Drake had a completely human boy."

Rory scratched his head.

"I… Well, I'd better go. I'm in a hurry. I'll see you in a bit." He retreated to his apartment to pack the few things his sisters had bought for him.

When he walked through the door, a smiling Amber greeted him.

"Hey, Rory. I guess you realized I'd let you back in."

He plunked his fists on his hips. "And where were you?"

Her smile slipped, as if she'd been caught doing something underhanded. "I—uh…I guess you were here before I got back."

"Correct. I looked everywhere for you. Well, not everywhere. I just covered the first and second floors."

"So you didn't speak to Morgaine and Sly?"

"No. And I wouldn't have." He noticed she let out a deep breath and relaxed. He took his own deep breath and blurted out the highlights. "I have to go back to Ireland. There's an emergency I need to take care of. I was hopin' you could help me get on the next plane. There must be a trick to travelin' at the last minute."

"Oh! What kind of emergency?"

"Well, nobody died."

"That's too bad."

His eyes widened. "What?"

Her hand flew to her chest. "Oh! I didn't mean it that way. I just meant you could get an emergency bereavement seat."

"Ah. I thought for a moment we made about as much sense as the neighbor next door."

She smirked. "I don't know exactly what that means,

but you can tell me later. Right now it sounds as if you're in a pickle and need to get home fast."

"That's the right of it. The little man you met earlier, Lucky... He was one of a few that were helpin' us at home, but now they've deserted their posts and all hell has broken loose."

"I see. Well, if it's really that important, you don't need a plane." She strode over to him and grasped his hand. "Where do you need to go?"

"Ireland. Specifically me home on the western cliffs of County Kerry in the town of Ballyhoo."

She tipped her head. "Never heard of it."

"No. I don't suppose you have. It was a sleepy little village until recently. Mayhaps you can get me to Galway, and I can find a taxi to take me to Ballyhoo."

"Or you can picture the place you want to be in your mind. Pick a spot that's usually deserted. We can't be seen materializing out of the blue."

"The pub is out then," he said.

"Are you in a hurry or aren't you?"

"I should think me old bedroom would be empty."

"Close your eyes and picture it as if you're there."

He did so. When she gasped, he opened his eyes. They were in some kind of haze. Peering out of it, he saw two people sleeping in his bed and a few others in sleeping bags on the floor. *Feck. What's this?*

The next thing he knew, they were standing in their Boston living room again.

"What's with the slumber party?" she asked sharply.

"Hell. That's probably why I need to get back there. It looks like me place has been overtaken by others who think possession is nine-tenths of the law."

She shook her head. "Well, now that I know where you want to be, I can poke around a bit and find a deserted spot to take you to."

"There's a shed out back. And a sheep's paddock with a deep lean-to. I doubt anyone would be sleepin' out there."

She nodded, dropped his hand, and disappeared.

He was at a loss. Should he try to bring Chloe with him? Her take-no-prisoners attitude would roust the interlopers quickly. Did she really need to chaperone their sister? Shannon was, after all, only a young lass in looks. But acting the part of her elder and protector had become such an ingrained habit...

While he was debating, Amber reappeared.

"The good news is I found a spot. The bad news is there are people almost everywhere. Tents are pitched all over the place."

"Feckin'..." He couldn't come up with a curse word strong enough, which left him frustrated.

She grasped his hand and suddenly he was surrounded by sheep. Surprised, the animals began bleating.

"Shhh..." Rory crooned. "'Tis only me."

They crowded around, nudging Amber away.

"They must think it's time for grazin'," he said. "I don't suppose you could watch them for me while I go toss out a number of trespassers, could you?"

"I've never tended sheep before, but how hard can it be?"

He stifled a snort.

A throat cleared and Rory's gaze met a familiar face. "O'Neil. What are you doin' here?"

The man's expression turned from surprised to

annoyed. "Tendin' your bleedin' sheep. Where've you been all this time?"

Rory ignored the question, and Amber elbowed him in the ribs. "Ah, forgive me manners. Amber McNally, this is Far O'Neil."

"Father?" Amber asked.

O'Neil laughed. "Not hardly. Me first name is Farquar. Everybody just calls me Far. I think they've forgotten me real name."

"Far is a teacher and plays sessions with us in the pub when he's not tendin' sheep. Thanks for lookin' after 'em."

O'Neil shrugged. "They'd probably take a bite out o' the tourists if they got too hungry. I may have done you a disservice."

Rory would have laughed, but the idea of tourists within his sheep's reach infuriated him.

Just then, Amber muttered, "*Damn* it. Not now."

He tried to read her face. "Do you have to leave?"

"Yeah. I—uh… Nature is calling."

He gave a quick nod.

"Far, why don't we take a walk? You can fill me in on the shenanigans happenin' on me property."

Rory quickly ushered his acquaintance away, letting Amber answer her Mayday call.

As he strolled behind the lean-to, frowning at the tents, Farquar O'Neil told Rory that a mysterious castle had been discovered built into the cliffs just *off* his property.

Rory halted. "Bollocks. That castle *is* me property. It belonged to our Arish ancestors. Now it belongs to Shannon, Chloe, and me."

"Not accordin' to county records," O'Neil said. "You've been payin' taxes, they said, but not enough to cover two dwellin's. Only the one is listed and it's the cottage."

"So who is sleepin' in me bed, and how is it they think they've a right to it?"

Far shrugged.

"It's time I go see." Rory whirled on his heel and marched toward the caretaker's cottage. *If it's me no-good cousins and they think they've a right to stay there, they have some bad news comin'...*

Amber struggled to keep her mind on her muse job. A helicopter instructor had apparently suffered a stroke, and a brand-new student was at the controls. Amber didn't know a thing about helicopters, so all she could do was keep the student calm.

"You can do this…" she said.

The helicopter rocked a bit.

"Steady," she whispered in his ear.

The student managed to stop the rocking and return the helicopter to a perfect hover. Amber looked down. They seemed to be over a farmer's field, but the corn was only a foot or so high. She supposed he could land. Even if he took out a few stalks, he might live to pay the farmer for the loss.

"Sh—should I cut the engine and try autorotation, even though I've never done it before?" he asked aloud. The instructor wasn't answering and probably couldn't.

What should I tell him? Damn it. I have no idea. They were at about one hundred feet, but this kid needed help. They could flip end over end if a propeller hit first.

"What does your gut tell you?" She whispered in his ear.

He glanced down. "It looks too high."

"Then go lower."

He swallowed hard. They descended, but even Amber knew they were going too fast.

"Shit!" she cried and then slapped a hand over her mouth.

Fortunately the student stayed relatively calm and muttered, "Autorotation it is." He steadied the craft and cut the engine as he murmured a prayer. It was "Now I Lay Me Down to Sleep," but she imagined that was all he could think of under the circumstances.

Instead of a dead drop as Amber would have expected, the chopper slowed dramatically and then the blades began rotating in the opposite direction. They were almost on the ground.

"You're going to be all right," she said excitedly.

He finished his prayer moments after they came to a full stop with a mild thump. The chopper was in one piece, as was the student.

Amber saw the farmer rushing over and knew she could leave. There was nothing she could do for the instructor. He was still alive, and something told her he'd be all right. The kid dragged a cell phone out of his pocket and dialed 911.

Amber's relief only lasted a moment. Where should she go now? Back to Rory, but where was he? Surrounded by squatters?

She had a feeling Rory might need help ejecting his

unwelcome visitors, but he'd never ask for it. Maybe she could round up some muscle at the paranormal club and bring him reinforcements.

He might be angry if his pride was hurt, but that's all she could think of to do to help. *So, tough noogies, Rory. Your paranormal family is coming to the party!*

She reappeared in their apartment, which seemed deserted without him in it. Throwing open the door and charging up the stairs, she decided to stop at his sisters' place first. Then she could take them across the hall and talk to everyone she could find at once.

Rory flicked on the lights in his cottage and stomped up the stairs to the two bedrooms. Chloe and Shannon shared the one at the back of the house, and his was in the front. He threw open the door to his room, and with only the light from the moon, he could see two figures in the bed and two more on the floor.

He threw back the covers on the bed, and two men about his size sat up quickly.

"What's this?" one of them cried.

"That's what I'd like to know," Rory said.

The man closest to the bedside lamp reached for it, but Rory clapped his hands and turned it on. The two men squinted while their eyes adjusted to the light.

Rory didn't recognize them.

"Who the hell is this, Conlan?" one of them asked.

Rory leaned back and crossed his arms. "Ah. You must be me Ulster cousins. Conlan and Aiden. It's been so long, I hardly recognize you. I spoke to Eagan on the phone."

"Rory?" asked the one referred to as Conlan.

"I am. Now tell me, what's wrong with the B and B in Ballyhoo? That's where I asked you to wait for me."

The one who must have been Aiden snorted. "There's been no room at the inn since news of the family castle got out. You're lucky we're here protectin' it."

Rory's eyebrows shot up. "Protectin' it, are you? It seems you're doin' a rather poor job of that, considerin' there's an army camped across the street from me property."

Conlan shot out of bed. Rory couldn't help noticing he was wearing boxers made of the Arish plaid.

"And you did so much better…leavin' it completely exposed and unguarded. And where have you been all this time?"

Rory just remembered they weren't alone. He glanced at the sleeping bags. Two terrified faces looked back at him, and it was only then that he noticed duct tape over their mouths.

"Who the feck are these two?"

"Reporters," Conlan said as if the word tasted foul. "These bastards didn't listen to the fact that they were on private property."

"They keep sendin' 'em two at a time, and we keep tyin' 'em up," Aiden supplied.

"Didn't you see all the news trucks on the road?" Conlan asked.

Rory stepped over one of the reporters on his way to the window. There were half a dozen news trucks from various parts of the United Kingdom and Ireland.

Conlan crossed his arms and stared at the two on the

floor. "There's a few women in the other bedroom and more men in tents across the street outside."

"Are you askin' to get arrested?" Rory yelled. "This is the same as kidnappin'."

The two men on the floor started nodding madly.

Conlan puffed up his chest. "You've no right to criticize how we handled things. Seein' as you were no help a'tall."

"'Twas no fault of ours." Rory wished he could elaborate, but arguing would waste precious time.

"Then whose fault was it?" Aiden demanded.

Rory sighed. "It doesn't matter right now." He nodded toward the reporters on the floor. "How long have they been here?"

"A day at most. Thank goodness word spread slowly."

Rory gasped. "These people probably need food, water, and a bathroom to relieve themselves."

The two on the floor nodded vigorously.

"Now that you finally decided to join us, you can help with that," Conlan said.

"I wish me sisters were here to cook and help with the lasses."

No sooner had he said that than Amber, Chloe, and Shannon marched through the door.

"What the feck is going on?" Chloe shouted.

Rory blew out a breath of relief. "Ah, me darlin's. Your timin' couldn't be better." He hugged his sisters. "I'll introduce you to our cousins later, but right now we have a problem to fix."

Shannon gazed at the men on the floor. "So it seems. What can we do to help?"

Rory wanted to kiss her. There really wasn't time for

lengthy explanations. "Shannon, would you be so kind as to start cookin' a big breakfast for our—um…guests? And Chloe, there are lasses in your bedroom. Can you untie them and let them use the toilet? No hogging the bathtub though. They can do that later when everyone is accounted for."

"I don't believe this…" Chloe muttered under her breath as she stomped off down the hall.

"What can I do?" Amber asked.

Rory grabbed her arm. "Come with me." As he was leaving the bedroom, he glanced over his shoulder. "Untie them, and let them use the outhouse."

"They'll run," Conlan said.

"And I'll let 'em go if you don't do as I say. Now me lady and I have somethin' to discuss in private. Take them one at a time."

His cousins didn't look happy, but at least they moved toward the men on the floor, albeit slowly.

Amber was sure Rory was angry. But she had only brought his sisters, not the entire paranormal community like she'd wanted to. Still, she didn't appreciate being manhandled. "You don't have to drag me. I need to talk to you too."

"Oh bejeezuz." He dropped her arm and took her hand instead. "I'm sorry."

At the bottom of the stairs he glanced left and right… probably looking for more tied-up bodies. There didn't seem to be any, thank goodness.

"Let's speak outside," he said. As soon as he opened the door, reporters rushed up to their little cobblestone walk with microphones and cameras pointed at them, already calling out questions. Rory noticed they were careful not to step onto his private property. Perhaps he had something else to thank his cousins for.

"Are you the owners of the castle?"

"Why won't you let people explore it? Is it unsafe?"

"Don't you agree it belongs to the Irish government?"

Rory slammed the door. "Feck. Maybe me cousins had the right of it. Stay here. I'll tell them to keep the captured reporters upstairs." He dashed toward the stairs.

"Wait. I have an idea."

He halted. "And I'll listen to you. Just give me a moment."

He all but flew up the stairs, taking two at a time. Amber smelled something wonderful and drifted toward the kitchen. Shannon was humming and whipping up something in a large bowl.

Amber peered over her shoulder. "What smells so good?"

"Ah, that would be bacon. I was lucky to find some in the fridge," Shannon said, smiling. "And wait until you taste me biscuits… Best in Ballyhoo, they are."

Amber's mouth watered. When was the last time she'd eaten? With all the excitement, it must have been several hours since her breakfast with Rory.

Speaking of whom, the man himself appeared in the doorway. He filled the opening and even though he looked stressed, he was still the handsomest guy… dragon…whatever she'd ever seen.

"Ah, Shannon, luv. I can't thank you enough for what you're doin'."

She grinned. "The way to forgiveness is to break bread."

"I'm not sure we're the ones who need forgiveness," he groused. "Amber, you had an idea to tell me about?"

She glanced at Shannon. "Didn't you want to speak privately?"

"Mayhaps Shannon ought to hear this too. She keeps me from making decisions based on me anger sometimes."

"Aw… Thank you, Brother. And you keep me from making decisions based on me sentimentality sometimes."

"You mean, your two hearts," Rory said.

Before Shannon had a chance to get everyone side-tracked, Amber interjected. "Does anyone want to hear my idea?"

"We're listenin'."

"Everyone at the paranormal club is ready to help," she said. "I just found out that vampires can do something called mesmerism. Then they can tell people to do, forget, or believe anything they want them to."

Rory nodded. "I've heard of this, but I thought it was a myth."

"It isn't," Amber said. "Sly and Morgaine are willing to help any way they can."

Rory's eyes rounded. "You involved the managers?"

Shannon spoke over her shoulder. "Damn right she did, and you ought to be grateful. 'Tis a fine mess we have here. I can't think of a better way to get out of it. Can you?"

"No." He hung his head.

Amber wondered what he was thinking. Was his pride hurt that he had to ask for help—and from the two people he most wanted to impress? She hoped he'd realize they were already impressed and willing to stick their necks out for him.

At last he nodded. "'Tis a fine idea, Amber. Can you bring them straightaway?"

"I can bring them all. Just say the word."

"All?"

"Everyone. The leprechauns, the shapeshifters, the witches, the wizard…"

"Whoa. Let's not turn this into a circus—or more of one than it is already. Bring the ones who can mesmerize the reporters and stop the secret from leakin' any further. And get those feckin' leprechauns back too. I need them to hide the castle again. That way anyone who comes after will think it was all a hoax."

"Um…about the leprechauns. Lucky, Fagan, and Clancy are willing to help, but Shamus said he won't." She didn't add his final comment—that he wasn't interested in helping thieves.

"Bollocks," Rory said.

"Yeah. He's really angry. He has to face some type of questioning—or whatever it is they do when a leprechaun is suspected of using their magic wrongly… The good news is that the others are willing to try the spell without him."

"Good. Hopefully it will work. Now, you said everyone is just waitin' on me word?"

Amber smiled. "Yup."

He simply said, "Word," and she popped back into the ether.

"Is he ready to accept our help?" Morgaine asked.

"Absolutely. He'd like all those who can mesmerize the reporters to come right away. Some major damage control is needed, since his cousins have the reporters bound and gagged."

Morgaine gasped.

Sly grabbed Amber's hand. "Take Kurt and me first. He can freeze time."

"Well, not time exactly, but people. If you untie them and they run…"

"Got it," Amber said, and she grabbed his hand too. A moment later they were in Rory's living room. Shannon was looking in their direction, but Amber didn't care at the moment. The dragons had their own secrets to keep.

"Where are they?" Kurt asked.

Rory spun around in the doorway. "Upstairs, out front, and in the tents."

"Kurt can freeze people if anyone tries to run," Amber said.

"Perfect. Why don't you start with the reporters on our front walk? The others are tied up—for now."

Kurt gave a quick nod and strode out the front door. The minute he stepped outside, reporters rushed toward him with their microphones raised. He extended his arms and they froze.

Amber followed him. "Cool! I didn't know anyone could do that."

Rory was right behind her. "Ah, you're a very good wizard, Kurt. I haven't seen the like since Merlin."

Amber turned slowly and stared at him. "You knew Merlin?"

"A story for another time, luv. Now, are there any other friends in Boston who can mesmerize these idiots? I imagine it could take Sly all day."

"Besides Morgaine, there's my wife, Ruxandra," Kurt said. "She was on her way to the club when I called her. She's a vampire."

"I'm on it," Amber said and disappeared, only to appear a moment later in the club.

Materializing in front of other paranormals was disappointingly anticlimactic. She always expected that popping out of thin air would at least raise an eyebrow or two, but…nope. The female vampire strode right over to her.

Amber had never met Ruxandra, and she'd say the blond bombshell in a red dress with full, red lips was model beautiful…until she opened her mouth.

"It's about fuckin' time."

"Uh. I'm sorry?"

"I thought you had a paranormal emergency." Ruxandra crossed her arms under a full bosom. "I hope you're not the one to respond if *I'm* in trouble."

Morgaine touched her shoulder. "Amber knows what she's doing, Ruxandra. Let's just get there and see if we can help." She took Amber's hand.

Amber reluctantly reached out to Ruxandra, who gripped her hand almost painfully. She couldn't drop them off fast enough.

When she got to the caretaker's cottage, she explained to the Arish cousins that the two women had come from the neighborhood and were talented hypnotists. That way she wouldn't expose strangers to more paranormals. She didn't know these men—or dragons—or whatever…

The next transport involved the leprechauns. She could probably take all three of them because they were so small, but did she want to insult them by suggesting it? She had heard that they could be easily offended.

She landed in the paranormal club and saw three of them huddled in the corner, whispering furiously.

Should I interrupt?

"Ah! There she be," said Lucky. He climbed onto Clancy's shoulders. "We're ready, lass. Can you take all three of us together?"

She smiled. "I can try," she said humbly, realizing they had complete faith in her.

She strode over to them and took Lucky's and Fagan's hands, while Clancy held on to Lucky's legs.

Reporters were beginning to come down the stairs, so she materialized in the kitchen where Chloe was guarding the door.

"Ah, Shannon," Fagan said. "Your kitchen smells wonderful. What are you makin'?"

She whirled on them and frowned. "None of your business. We wouldn't be in this mess if not for the lot of you."

Lucky gasped. "That's no way to speak to our king!"

"Whatever. Where's the other one?"

They all hesitated until Clancy spoke up. "Uh, he stayed back in Boston. Said he liked it there."

"I'll bet."

Amber cleared her throat. "I think the important thing is to get that castle hidden again."

All of them agreed.

"Where's Rory?" Amber asked, peeking out the kitchen window. When she looked back to where the leprechauns had been standing, she was shocked to see empty space. "Where did they go?"

Shannon snorted. "Don't know and don't care. As soon as they hide the castle, I hope to never see the little bastards again."

Chloe poked her head in. "Rory's outside with Kurt. Shannon, is the food almost ready? We have some hungry mouths to feed."

"Almost. Get them seated in the dining room and set the table."

"Can I help?" Amber asked.

"No, thank you. See if you can help Rory." Shannon turned back to the stove to remove her lightly browned biscuits.

Amber left the kitchen with her mouth watering.

—⁓—

Rory didn't know whether to thank his cousins or kill them. They'd stopped gawkers from pillaging their ancestral home, but if it hadn't been for his paranormal friends from Boston, he hated to think about what would have happened.

All the tents had been emptied of unwanted guests. The people had been magically cleaned up by the wizard while he had them frozen in place, then they'd been mesmerized by the vampires. They'd been told there was nothing to see, that the whole thing was a hoax. Then they were told to go inside the cottage for a hearty breakfast—and be grateful the owners were so nice. After that, they were to go home.

Now the leprechauns stood at the edge of the cliff, holding hands. Rory watched while they chanted. They'd said four would have been better, but three should do.

Rory hoped they were right.

He felt a tap on his shoulder and turned to see Amber grinning up at him. Every time he looked at that gorgeous smile, he wanted her.

He wrapped his arm around her and pulled her close. Nuzzling her hair, he whispered, "I've missed you."

"I missed you too." She tipped her face up, and he swooped in for a deep kiss.

Someone cleared his throat.

It was all Rory could do to tear himself away. At some point they needed to talk, but right now all he wanted to do was… Well, it didn't involve talking. Before he looked to see who was intruding, he whispered in her ear. "Ah, darlin'. If only we were invisible. I'd take you in me arms and make sweet love to you right now."

Kurt stood beside him, smirking. "Sorry to interrupt. I was wondering if you needed anything else from us, or if I can take my impatient bride home now."

Rory considered asking him if an invisibility spell existed—and offering to pay him a million dollars if he could perform one that very second—but how would he tell the wizard when they were ready to become visible again? Then he remembered Amber's gift. She'd transported him here in some kind of fog. No one saw them while they were in it.

Suddenly he couldn't get rid of his helpers fast enough.

"Ah, we're fine now. Please accept me humble thanks."

Kurt clamped a hand on his shoulder. "We all look out for each other. You never know, I may need your help someday."

"And I'll be there for you. Count on it."

Ruxandra joined Kurt, then looked to Amber. "Ready for takeoff?"

"Sure thing," she said. No sooner had the wizard and his vampire bride grabbed her hands than they all disappeared.

Amber would be right back. Rory was sure of it. Meanwhile, he gazed across the large expanse of bright-green sod to watch the leprechauns at work. They were chanting in ancient Gaelic.

The castle had faded, but only slightly. It was still visible, but looked even stranger than before. A pile of stone ruins stayed, but the only remaining turret was transparent. *This better work.*

It faded a little more and a little more, and finally winked out completely. Rory let out a deep sigh of relief. He strode toward the leprechauns, but before he could reach them, they vanished.

"Little feckers," he muttered. "I was goin' to thank them, not that they deserved it."

At last Amber reappeared. "Sorry it took me so long. I checked in on the others and transported Sly and Morgaine home too."

"So now it's just Chloe and Shannon, plus dozens of guests?"

Amber chuckled. "The guests are wolfing down breakfast and chatting about how they wished the story were true. Apparently Shannon's cooking is the only reason they're not upset about wasting their time."

"Ah, she's a grand cook. Finn will be a lucky man."

"A lot luckier than you, unless she teaches me a few things back in Boston."

Bollocks. An opening to discuss livin' arrangements. Well, he wasn't ready to do it yet. He'd just do what he was aching to do.

He pulled her into his arms and held her tight against his erection. Then he whispered in her ear, "Can you transport us someplace private for an hour or two?"

"Don't you want to make sure Chloe and Shannon are all right?"

"Me cousins are there if they need anyone ejected."

"Do you think they'll stay? Your cousins, I mean."

"I know they will. They still think the castle is holdin' priceless family heirlooms that they'd like to get their hands on."

"And are they apt to steal them?"

"Not if there's nothin' there. I haven't looked, mind you, but I'm pretty sure we sold most of it in Iceland."

"Won't they be upset when they find out?"

"Oh, I'm sure they will. But for now we can rest assured they won't shift and use their wings to find out. When everyone has gone and night falls, they may try it."

"What are they apt to do then?"

Rory snorted and a curl of smoke exited his nostril. "I'm expectin' the second Battle of Ballyhoo, but I can't think about that now." He couldn't think of anything now except getting horizontal with Amber.

He nuzzled her neck. "That's my problem for tonight—which gives us plenty of time to disappear for a while."

She giggled. "True. Where would you like to disappear to?"

"Anywhere—or nowhere. Can we stay in that lovely foggy middle part?"

"The ether?" Her voice made the idea sound incredulous.

"I guess not…"

"The truth is, I don't know. I can stay there to talk a troubled pilot through an emergency, but I've never tried to keep anyone with me in there. I'll probably have to hold your hand the entire time."

"I don't mind." He grinned.

She shrugged. "Let's try it. What's the worst that could happen?"

He wished she hadn't said that.

Chapter 13

AMBER WAS SECOND-GUESSING HERSELF AS THEY floated naked in the ether. Maybe she should have asked Brandee or Bliss if they'd tried it. Chances are they had. The lure of zero-gravity sex was pretty tempting.

Not letting go of Rory's hand also made the experience interesting. Using only one hand to caress each other made that touch easier to concentrate on and appreciate.

He trailed his finger down her cheek and neck, following the path with his lips. Occasionally he tasted her with his tongue. She shivered, but not because of a chill in the air. Ether wasn't real fog and she was far from cold. In fact, she was warming quickly.

She caressed Rory's strong arms, back, and—um—other muscles. A gratifying groan let her know he enjoyed her touch as much as she enjoyed his.

Their lips fused while stroking each other's highly sensitized erogenous zones. Amber couldn't help moaning into his mouth. He almost let go of her hand, but then gripped it harder. She twined their legs together. Still, they couldn't get quite close enough.

When she couldn't stand waiting anymore, she transported them to their bed in Boston. *Their* bed. She still had to convince herself her luck had finally turned and their love was real. But how long would it last?

She pushed that thought to the back of her mind to enjoy the moment. They let go of each other's hands and

Rory positioned himself between her knees, bracing his hands on either side of her shoulders.

"Is this how you want me, luv?"

"I want you in every way, but this will work."

He grinned.

Lowering himself onto his elbows, he lined up his hard cock with her damp opening. Then he gently guided himself in.

She sighed with pleasure and raised her hips to meet him.

When he was fully seated, he began his rhythm. She arched and moaned blissfully. He murmured beautiful words she didn't understand. He must have been speaking in Gaelic, but it didn't matter. The soft cadence of his voice and warmth on her cheek told her all she needed to know. He was speaking words of love.

She loved him too. How she had fallen so fast was a mystery—especially with her rotten luck in relationships. It didn't matter now. All that mattered was this moment. This beautiful moment. She felt tears burn behind her eyes, but she knew he'd understand it if they appeared. She "just knew" a lot of things now. Maybe because she was a muse, but she suspected she'd know they belonged together even if she were a mere human again.

That knowledge sent her over the edge in ecstasy, flying as she never had before. Rory jerked with his own release at the same time.

When they both were spent, he placed his lips on hers for a tender kiss. Then they gazed at each other. Rory's eyes were glistening too, so she wrapped her arms around his neck and let her happy tears flow.

After they'd showered—together—and dressed, Rory said, "We'd better get back to Ireland and make sure Chloe and Shannon are doin' all right. I know Shannon will want to return because Finn is here in Boston."

Amber reached out and took his hand. "Ready for takeoff?"

"Go ahead, luv. Do your thing."

Landing was a bit bumpy—not because Amber did anything wrong, but because when they stepped out of the ether, they seemed to have landed in the middle of a loud family feud.

"You're feckin' out of your minds," Chloe yelled.

Conlan yelled back, "'Tis as much ours as yours. If you don't give us half of our ancestral treasures, we'll take them—by force."

"Bollocks," Rory muttered under his breath.

Amber looked up at him with a quizzical expression. He knew what she was probably thinking. *What treasure? Why not share it? Is it worth another war?*

Rory leaned down and whispered in her ear. "We don't have it anymore. We had to sell all we could to get to Boston, pay for the apartments, and have enough to live on for a while."

"Shit," she muttered.

"Stay here," he ordered and strode into the kitchen, where the argument was taking place. Unfortunately, Amber didn't like being told what to do and followed right behind him. He should have known that would happen.

"I'm the clan leader. If you have a difference of opinion, Conlan should take it up with me."

Shannon looked relieved, but Chloe glared at him.

"I was handlin' it just fine, *Prince*," Chloe said.

He wasn't sure if she used his title to emphasize his status or if she meant it sarcastically. Knowing his sister, it could have been both.

He saw Amber's shock out of the corner of his eye. *Oh well. No time to explain now.*

"We're all feckin' princes," Aiden said. "You just happen to be the eldest."

"And our father was the eldest of his generation," Shannon reminded them.

"And the victor in the Battle of Ballyhoo." Chloe jammed her hands on her hips.

Shite. Why did she have to mention the war? It had ended so badly for both sides, and it was so long ago.

Conlan's eyes narrowed and his fists clenched. "Is that how it's to be then? You want another war, it seems."

"We do not!" Rory held up his palms, then lowered them quickly. He didn't want his gesture to be mistaken as surrender…as much as he wanted to avoid another battle.

Conlan folded his arms. "It seems as if your brother can be reasoned with better than you can, Chloe."

"Aye," Aiden added. "We should sit down and discuss this." He glanced at Amber. "Man to man."

He doesn't think she's aware we're all dragons. That could be an advantage. Rory also doubted they knew about her muse status. She'd kept a low profile, so he had a couple elements of surprise, if he needed them.

"Shannon, Chloe, Amber. I need you to excuse me while I speak to me cousins privately." Hopefully Amber would follow his sisters' lead. They were required to obey him…albeit under protest sometimes.

Chloe snorted. Shannon simply turned around and went back to washing the breakfast dishes. Amber seemed to understand and asked Shannon if she could help. Chloe grabbed a dish towel and said, "If you'll dry, I'll put away."

Rory led his cousins to the living room. It was cozy. Nothing had changed much over the years, unless a chair's springs poked up uncomfortably or a rug became threadbare. He was glad they'd kept the eclectic, humble-abode look, so it wouldn't hint to strangers of the wealth beyond their wildest dreams. The silver and bronze antiquities may have been sold off in Iceland, but unless the leprechauns had melted all of it down, there were still items made of gold in their keep. A lot of them.

Conlan and Aiden sat on the sofa, and Rory took the adjacent armchair.

"I'm afraid I have bad news for you," he began.

The two uninvited guests remained silent, but their stiff body language betrayed their apprehension.

Rory cleared his throat and continued. "The treasure is gone."

Conlan and Aiden gasped in unison.

Conlan recovered first. "How do we know we can believe you, and if it's true, where the feck did it go?"

Rory shrugged. "It must have been stolen." He was able to pull off that lie because it was partly true. The collector in Iceland had practically robbed them with his less-than-generous offer.

"We need to see the keep," Aiden said.

Rory nodded reluctantly. "I understand your request, but the leprechauns hid the castle again." He almost suggested they wait until nightfall, shift into dragon form, and use their wings and talons to find the cave openings by feel. But he'd rather keep his cousins out until he'd had a look himself.

"We know where it is, Cousin," Conlan said.

Aiden folded his arms. "Aye. And you can't keep us out."

Rory forced himself to relax and call their bluff. "If you can get in without callin' attention to what you're doin', go ahead."

Conlan and Aiden stared at each other.

"We'll find it tonight," Conlan said.

"Grand," Rory said sarcastically. "Since I need me bed back, you can pack up and go to the B and B now."

"I hope you know we wouldn't have helped ourselves to your bed if the B and B wasn't filled to the rafters," Aiden said.

Rory nodded solemnly. "No need for apologies."

"Who's apologizin'?" Conlan asked. "Someone had to protect the castle, so it's a damn good thing we came. You never told us where you were and why."

"Because it's not your business." Rory leaned back in his chair.

His cousins just stared at him, probably waiting for him to grow uncomfortable and say something he shouldn't.

"I suggest you let any remainin' B and B guests know the whole thing was a hoax and send them on their way. The sooner that's done, the better."

"And what if some of them saw the castle before it was hidden again?"

It's doubtful, yet possible. Could Rory sneak the vampires back over the ocean a second time and pass them off as neighbors? That was unlikely. "You can make them think they saw an illusion—or say it was built of mud as an amusement, and when the earth dried, a strong wind blew it into the sea."

The brothers looked at each other. "There's been no rain for a few days."

"A blessin' to be sure," Rory said. "Surely the locals will have noticed that."

Conlan smirked. "Not that I think it'll work, but a sand castle it is."

"A dirt castle is more likely, with our elevation and no sand to speak of," Rory said.

Aiden threw his hands in the air. "You expect people to believe a lie like that? It'll never work."

"Not if you don't try to convince them."

The middle brother shook his head. "We can try, but they'll want to see for themselves as much as we do."

Conlan became Rory's unexpected advocate. "We'll say what we said before. 'Tis private property."

Aiden snorted. "And look how well that worked. Tents appeared on the turf across the road."

Suddenly Rory panicked. "Did any of 'em take pictures?"

"Only from a distance," Conlan said. "I suppose the rock could be mistaken for dry dirt. Of course, some may have had telephoto lenses."

"Shite," Rory muttered. "Can you think of a better idea?"

The others puzzled it over silently.

Chloe called out from the kitchen. "If they doubt you, tell them they're daft and laugh like you've never laughed before. They'll drop it if they think they're reportin' a lie."

"That's a grand idea, Chloe," Rory said. Then he thought about some of the tabloids he'd heard about—especially those in England. Apparently they had no respect for the truth. All they cared about were headlines that sold their newspapers. They had even been accused of using photo tricks to make things look however they wanted them to look.

He decided not to worry. Now that the castle was hidden again, anyone who believed the reporters' blarney and came to check would be disappointed.

"Cousins, as much as it was nice to see you after such a long absence, I think you need to be on your way to the B and B. It's a fine thing you did for us, and we're grateful."

Aiden narrowed his eyes. "So you're tryin' to get rid of us. Don't forget we'll be back tonight."

Rory sighed. "How could I forget a thing like that?" He quickly added, "I'll be anxious to hear what happened with the guests at the B and B." The memory of his mother's advice floated through his head right at that moment: *"It's often a person's mouth that breaks their noses,"* meaning, be careful what you say.

———

Rory breathed a sigh of relief when he closed the door behind his cousins. As a bonus, no new reporters had appeared. Perhaps Chloe was right, and reporting a hoax would be an embarrassment to a genuine journalist.

He leaned against the door and let his mind travel ahead. One of them should remain on the property to keep trespassers from getting close to the hidden castle. Otherwise, someone would fall off the cliff and onto the rocks below.

Chloe would keep people off the property to be sure, but she could make enemies in the process. Not only that, but her reaction would cause suspicion.

Shannon was the obvious choice. He ticked off the reasons in his mind. First, she wasn't happy about sharing a room with Chloe in Boston. A falling-out would mean Shannon would surely end up sleeping in the closet. Then there was Finn. He would want to take her home. He was a good lad. Even though he worked at the local grocery store, it was a job, and Shannon loved him. Since a nest was enough for a wren, Finn would be happy to join her in the caretaker's cottage.

His sister was a thousand years old. How much longer could he go on sheltering her? Finn would discover her secret in time, when he aged and she didn't. Would he keep their secret if he discovered it sooner?

Ah, well. It has to be discussed—and soon.

He strolled into the kitchen. "Amber, I need to talk to me sisters. After that, I need to discuss somethin' with you too."

Her eyes widened, but she quickly schooled her features. "Sure. I'll go check in with Euterpe. It's been a while since I've seen her."

"You know where to find me when your visit is finished."

She kissed him and disappeared.

Chloe chuckled. "Are you sure you can handle bein' in love with a muse? I'm wonderin' if a minor goddess outranks a dragon prince."

Rory wasn't going to rise to the bait. Instead he cleared his throat and launched right into the matter at hand.

"Chloe, Shannon, one of us needs to stay behind and watch the property. If gawkers don't try to trespass, our cousins certainly will."

Chloe crossed her arms. "And who did you select for this responsibility? I cannot possibly guess," she said sarcastically.

Hopefully, that meant she'd be relieved to hand it over to Shannon.

"I've decided that Shannon and Finn should live here and take care of the place—and each other."

Open-mouthed, Shannon dropped the spoons she was holding and they clattered to the floor. When she recovered, she whispered, "Do you mean it? You wouldn't play me for a fool, would you?"

He frowned. "Of course not. When have I ever done such a thing?"

A grin slowly spread across her face, and she launched herself into his arms. She kissed him on the cheek and hugged him hard. "Thank you, Brother! Thank you, thank you!"

He chuckled as he peeled her off and set her on the floor.

Chloe's eyebrows were raised. "Can I talk to you, Rory? Alone." She glanced at Shannon, who was dancing a jig.

"It won't do any good," he said. "Me mind is made up."

"So you're goin' to let them live in sin?"

He took a step back. "Certainly not. The promise ring she's been wearin' hasn't escaped me notice. I assume Finn will marry her straight away."

"Without a birth certificate for Shannon?"

Rory sighed. "We'll figure something out. One problem at a time."

"And where does Finn think she is at the moment?"

"Uh…" He glanced over at his youngest sister. "Shannon, where does Finn think you are? Did you tell him you were goin' to Ireland?"

"I didn't have time to tell him anythin'. I left a note sayin' I'd be back soon."

"Shite. Then we'd better get you back. That boy will turn over heaven and earth lookin' for you. Chloe, will you stay here until I get Shannon and Finn sorted?"

"Of course."

"And you won't infuriate anyone while I'm gone?"

As she was sputtering, he called out, "Mayday, Mayday, Mayday," and Amber appeared.

"What the hell, Rory? Did your wings catch on fire?"

He laughed. "No, me darlin'. I have an emergency of a different kind. Sure'n I knew you'd come if I called that way."

She folded her arms. "How about from now on you just yell, 'Yo, Amber. I need you.'"

He sidled up next to her and whispered, "I'll always need you."

She looked like she was trying to suppress a smile, but she eventually gave in and grinned at him.

Ah, she takes me breath away every time she smiles.

———⁓———

Shamus snickered as he planted the items he'd gathered from the other residents' apartments in the female dragons' Boston lair. He had to hide them, but not very well. The managers would have to discover them when searching for their lost possessions, but not the dragons.

He took the cash from the swear jar and placed it under the couch cushions. Now he had to identify it as the redheaded witch's money, so he took the sticky note off the swear jar and tossed it next to the money, as if it had fallen off.

The crystal ball would be harder to hide, but after looking around, he found some empty shoe boxes in the closet. The shoes were on display in a built-in shelving unit, so he doubted the dragon sisters would need the boxes until they moved—or were tossed out, whichever came first.

Hopefully they'd be evicted for stealing, which would back up his story…that the *dragons* had stolen Clancy's pot of gold.

Now to find a place to stash the few gold coins he'd brought with him. The lion's share was back at home in Ireland. He'd had a heck of a time finding a new place for the pot of gold because the meddling lad who'd trapped him knew where it was. He'd had to bury it deep in the bowels of the castle—in what was once the dungeon. Nobody would go down there. It flooded from time to time, and the air was so musty it was disgusting.

"Hmmm…" Shamus stroked his beard. The gold needed to go in Rory's place. As the clan leader, he'd naturally keep the gold in his possession. Shamus snuck down the stairs and put his ear to the dragon prince's apartment door. He heard nothing. *Good. They must be out.*

He materialized on the other side of the door and tiptoed around, checking each room to make sure the place was deserted. When he was satisfied that no one would catch him, he began his search for a place to stash the gold coins.

———∿∿∿———

Chad floated close to the ceiling to prevent the little criminal from spotting him. He didn't think he would, but why take a chance? The leprechaun was obviously setting up the dragons to look like thieves, but why?

Shamus lifted the lid on the built-in window seat. Apparently, he rejected that hiding place and moved to the fireplace. He leaned over and peeked up at the flue, but moved on without placing any coins there. He glanced around and scowled.

Chad could have told him there were a ton of places to hide the coins in the bedroom, but the little guy must not have wanted Amber to be involved. Instead, he focused on the kitchen and bathroom.

He quickly dismissed the kitchen muttering, "All these things probably belong to the lass. I can't see Rory cookin' for himself."

Moving on to the bathroom, he checked the medicine cabinet and found only two toothbrushes and toothpaste. "Looks like neither of them gets sick."

Just then, the door to the apartment opened and shut. Shamus glanced around in a panic. Then a smile spread across his face. He lifted the lid off the back of the toilet, tossed the coins into the water, replaced the porcelain top quietly, and disappeared.

What now? Chad thought to himself. Should he immediately tell the others what he knew? Or would it be more fun to see how it played out?

Being the bored ghost that he was, he decided to watch the fireworks. And with dragons involved, *fire* was the operative word.

Chapter 14

"WHAT WAS THAT NOISE?" AMBER ASKED.

Rory frowned. "It sounded like it was comin' from the bathroom."

They both leaned into the bath and glanced around. The shower curtain was drawn back, and the pedestal sink left no place to hide.

Rory opened the medicine cabinet. "I don't see anythin' amiss."

"Neither do I." Amber shrugged. "It's an old building, and it probably comes with a variety of creaks and groans."

"To be sure. I don't have time to worry over it. I need to have a man-to-dragon talk with Finn about marryin' me sister."

"Are you going to tell him you're all dragons?"

"Christ, no! And if you're apt to slip up, I'd suggest you stay away from the lad altogether."

Amber sighed. "It's not my place to divulge that, so you don't have to worry. But I'm curious… How are you going to explain Shannon's extreme longevity?"

Rory hesitated, then headed to the kitchen and grabbed a Guinness out of the fridge. Amber waited, hoping he was just taking a few minutes to think and not ignoring her.

Finally he sighed. "It's difficult when dragons try to become part of the human community. At some point, we have to pick a fight and leave, or fake our deaths and hide. Either way, someone gets hurt."

Amber's heart hurt for poor Finn. And knowing what she did about Rory's sister, Shannon would be devastated too.

"Does Shannon know this?"

"Only too well. I tried to discourage their relationship from the start. She insisted she'd rather love for a short time than not at all. I think it was too late the moment their eyes met for the first time." He strolled to the living room and she followed. They sat on the futon in *their* living room.

Amber smiled. "We call that love at first sight."

Rory smirked, then pulled her onto his lap and kissed her. When he released her, he said, "So do we." Then he murmured something in Gaelic and nuzzled her neck.

The Irish had so many colorful expressions, and Amber had no idea what they all were. Knowing Rory, she imagined she'd learn quite a few of them eventually.

She slid off his lap and sat next to him. They needed to talk and were finally alone. But she needed to ease into the conversation. "So how old was Finn when they met?"

"He was about sixteen. She told him she was sixteen too."

"And now she says she's nineteen. So does that mean Finn is nineteen?"

Rory nodded. "Just turned nineteen."

"Isn't that young to be getting married?"

"Not in Ireland. Ballyhoo is a small, isolated village. Few if any children go to college. Most stay home and work the farm they grew up on or join their father's fishing business. About the only time they leave home is when they get married."

Is now the time to bring up our 'living in sin'? Do I want to? If it's okay for him, but not for his sister, isn't that a double standard? Amber still wasn't sure what to say, so she'd put it off a little longer.

"Does Finn work on a farm or fish?"

"Neither one. His father is the only grocer in town. Finn and his friend Patrick have worked there since they were tall enough to stack cans. At first, it was just after school. Now they've finished their schooling and work full-time. It's how it is."

"I thought Pat came here with Finn. Does that mean Finn's father is running the store alone?"

"I imagine he had his wife pitch in for a bit. But Patrick was good enough to keep their son out of trouble, so I don't think they'll fire him."

"Is he still here in Boston? I haven't seen him."

"No. He went back to Ireland as soon as Finn found Shannon. Pat'll be back at the store by now."

"So did they all meet in school?"

"No. We had to stay out of sight for decades, so I home-schooled my sisters meself. It wasn't until the last caretakers died that we left the castle and moved into the cottage. The caves were crumblin', since gravity always wins over time."

"Speaking of time…maybe I can make you all appear to age naturally."

"You could do that?"

"I don't know. I'll ask Euterpe. If the ancient muses can still look young, maybe young dragons can be made to look old."

"That would be grand."

"So what happened after you moved to the caretaker's cottage?"

"Shannon took to the kitchen like a duck to water. She wanted to try a new recipe, and it called for an ingredient we didn't have."

"So she went to the grocery store," Amber guessed.

"Quite right. I blame their whole relationship on molasses."

Amber chuckled. "That was the ingredient she didn't have?"

"Indeed it was."

Amber said. "Do you think she wants to get married?"

"Without a doubt. Me sister has a soft heart—or hearts. She has two."

Amber raised her brows. "Two hearts?"

He nodded. "So it seems. She's had two heartbeats since birth."

Amber wondered if Shannon didn't just have a heart murmur. That might sound like a second heart beating. "Did you ever have her checked out by a doctor?"

"No. Me mother and father didn't believe in doctors. They patched us up when we fell on the rocks as we learned to fly." He smiled, appearing nostalgic. "Besides, we're very hard to kill." He winked.

He leaned down and was just about to kiss her again when a knock on the door ended their discussion.

Rory groaned, then strode to the door and opened it to reveal a very happy Shannon and a very nervous Finn.

"Can we come in?" Shannon asked. "Is this a good time to talk?"

"I'd like to see Finn alone."

Shannon's face fell. "What could you say to him that you can't say in front of me?"

"It's not up for negotiation, luv. Go upstairs and pack whatever you want to bring home to Ireland with you."

Shannon stuck out her lower lip, making her look even younger than she was supposed to be.

"I'll help you," Amber offered. She gazed at Rory. "Maybe I should take her shopping for a *special* dress? One she might need *soon*?"

At first he just stared at her, blankly.

What? Doesn't he understand the concept of a wedding dress? Or did he change his mind about wanting her to get married?

Shannon rolled her eyes. "Me brother's thick when it comes to matters like weddin' clothes."

Finn stared at her open-mouthed. "Weddin'?"

Apparently, Shannon hadn't told him what his talk with Rory was about.

Finn's eyes rounded, then he grinned. "Is that what this is, Rory? Are you givin' us your blessin'?"

"I might. Now get goin', Shannon. Take Amber up on her generous offer to help." He sidled up next to Amber and whispered, "We'll need plane tickets this time." Then he tipped his head toward Finn.

Shannon grabbed Amber's hand and stopped just as they reached the hall.

"Wait. I need some money."

"Chloe has plenty. Isn't she upstairs?"

"Ah, no. You told her to stay—um…where she was."

"Ah. I forgot. Well, mayhaps Amber can take you to Chloe, and all three of you can go shoppin' or whatever it is you lasses want to do. Your sister has the bulk of our savings hidden away."

Amber nodded.

"All right then." Shannon strode to Finn and kissed his cheek. "I'll see you shortly."

He took her hand and laid it against his cheek. "Don't take so long this time. I miss you like crazy when you're gone."

Rory rolled his eyes and Amber hurried her out before Finn realized he couldn't live without her for a minute.

Ah, young freakin' love.

Shannon and Amber landed in the cottage's kitchen, within earshot of a family squabble.

"You've no right to set foot on our family's land!" Chloe shouted.

Conlan folded his arms. "It's our family's land too—or did you forget? We're of the same family."

"You are not. You moved to Ulster centuries ago. I barely know you. You could be anyone."

"Our parents *had to* move to Ulster. You know that. Our mam was driven out of Ballyhoo after our da was slain."

"Exactly," Chloe said.

Aiden advanced on her.

"Stop." Conlan grabbed his brother's arm and held him back. "The whole thing happened so long ago that no one can be sure of anythin'."

"One thing we're all sure of is that meddling Saint Patrick decided it was his mission to rid Erin of all snakes and dragons in the fourth century," Aiden bit out.

Conlan snorted. "Drove them into the sea, he did."

"Thank the Goddess our grandparents and a few others spotted the caves on their way over the cliff and managed to save themselves. Else none of us would be here," Shannon said.

"Which is where our fathers were born." Conlan crossed his arms. "You see? It's our ancestral home too."

"And we came here to protect it," Aiden reminded her.

"Are you forgettin' the Battle of Ballyhoo?" Chloe asked. "You lost the ancestral home when your da got greedy and wanted to be king—*if* you're even his sons. As I said before, you could be anyone."

Aiden began peeling off his shirt and pants.

"What the hell do you think you're doin'?" Chloe yelled.

"Provin' we're related," Aiden said. Then his eyes began to shimmer and his skin turned scaly and greenish. Wings emerged from his back as his neck and face lengthened.

Amber had never seen anything like it in her life. She took a few cautious steps back. Chloe didn't seem terribly impressed. She just folded her arms and waited. When the transformation was complete, Shannon started to giggle.

"What's so funny?" Conlan asked.

Shannon pointed to Aiden's tightie whities straining at the seams. "He's too embarrassed to shed his knickers. Soon, they'll burst."

Chloe joined her sister in laughter. "Why don't you just shimmer off your clothes magically and shift at the same time, like we do?"

Conlan growled and Aiden quickly transformed into human form again.

Amber couldn't help but wonder if Rory shifted into

the same *thing*…or creature. She also wondered if the Arish siblings shed *all* of their clothes when transforming. It appeared as if they did.

Amber had to intervene. Mother Nature would *not* be happy if things escalated too far. A neighbor could visit and look in the window at the wrong moment.

"I'm sorry to interrupt," she said. "And I don't want to get in the middle of this, but I need to remind you all of a very basic rule."

They glanced at her with raised brows.

"What might that be?" Conlan asked.

Do they really not know? "Gaia's rule, of course. Never reveal your paranormal nature to humans."

All of them gawked at her.

Finally, Conlan asked, "Who did you say said this?"

"Gaia… You know…Mother Nature. You've heard of her, right?"

Shannon looked like she was about to faint. For once, Chloe was speechless, and the two cousins just stood there with their mouths hanging open.

"How do you know this?" Conlan demanded.

Amber straightened to her full five-foot-six-inch height and said, "She told me."

Shannon found her way to the sofa and sat down.

Chloe shook her head and muttered, "All this time we've worshipped her, and yet she shows herself to—to…*her?*"

"Excuse me?" Amber said.

"Nothin'. I was just…" Again, Chloe had no words.

"You're makin' the whole thing up," Conlan stated.

"I am not. Who do you think gave me the powers I have?"

Aiden tipped up his chin defiantly. "And what powers do you have? Whatever they are, a dragon can put you in your place."

Conlan stopped his brother with a hand on his arm. "Even if what you say is true, what will Gaia do if a human sees us shift into the form she gave us?"

Amber winced. "You don't want to know."

"It can't be that horrible. We're her children, after all," Shannon said.

Amber remembered being turned into a baby and told she might have to start all over again. Yet Brandee and Bliss seemed to think it was an empty threat.

Mayday, Mayday, Mayday…

"Oh crap," Amber muttered. *Could these emergencies be timed any worse?* "I've got to go." With that briefest of explanations, she followed the voice into the ether, disappearing in front of everyone there.

Uh-oh…

Mother Nature met her with arms crossed and a stern scowl on her face. To Amber's surprise, she was back in her apartment.

"Ah, was that you who called, Gaia?" Amber asked.

"I had to do something before you spilled every bean in Boston. Now go to your room and stay there, young lady. You're grounded!"

Amber wanted to commiserate with someone—and that someone was Rory. But she didn't know where he was.

"I am in soooo much trouble," she mumbled on her way to the bedroom.

"I am in soooo much trouble," Rory muttered from his sitting position on the floor of their kitchen.

She halted. "What are you doing down there?"

"Ah, lass. I'm all right." He struggled to get up. "My knees went out from under me."

Concerned, Amber rushed to his side to help him up. Of course, lifting a two-hundred-pound man wasn't really something she expected to accomplish. He got to his feet and wrapped an arm around her.

She guided him to the futon. "What happened?"

"Your boss happened."

"Mother… I mean, Gaia?"

"Yes. The big boss of everything."

Amber gasped. "What did she do to you?"

He leaned forward and clasped his head in his hands. "Just threatened to rip me a new arsehole."

"What for?"

"For givin' me sister permission to marry a human."

Amber glanced around the apartment. "Where's Finn?"

"He's upstairs in the girls' apartment. She said she'd made him sleep, and when he wakes he'll think the whole thing was a dream. Now she wants me to undo it with Shannon."

"Undo the engagement?"

He nodded sadly. After a long sigh, he said, "You might as well take me to her. Puttin' it off won't help."

Amber grimaced. "I can't."

"What do you mean, you can't?"

"She grounded me."

"Ah, feckers. We're feckin' fecked now." He sprang to his feet. "I don't suppose I can borrow your phone…"

"Of course you can." She went to the bedroom and grabbed it from its charger.

He looked so beaten as she handed it to him. She couldn't stand seeing him this way.

After several rings, a hysterical-sounding Shannon answered. Even if Amber didn't have goddess-like hearing, she'd be able to understand her.

"Relax, luv. What's happenin'?" Rory asked.

"You've got to get here right away!" Shannon blubbered. "Chloe tried to stop Aiden from flying down to the caves. He shifted to get away and she shifted to catch up to him. Then she sunk her fangs into his leg and he screamed, and they went over the edge of the cliff together! Oh, Rory. I can't see them! I think they hit the rocks and fell into the sea!"

"Where's Conlan?" he shouted.

"I don't know. Probably at the B and B. They said they'd go and come back when you were here to reason with. Aiden must have snuck back on his own."

"Well, go get Conlan. See that you calm down, and don't scream the story to the whole town."

"Why can't you come and get him? Just get Amber to bring you."

"Amber's sittin' right here. But she's lost her powers."

Shannon shrieked. "Lost them? How? Oh, never mind. If you can't get here, we're well and truly fecked."

"Go get Conlan. I'll be on the next plane."

"What about Finn? Where is he?"

He slapped a hand over his eyes as if he'd forgotten all about the young man he'd promised could marry his sister.

Amber placed a hand on his shoulder. "Go to Ireland. I'll see what I can do to help Finn."

Rory gave her a quick nod. "Finn's fine. All right, Shannon. Listen to me well. Get Conlan to help you with the others, and feck it if he wants to see the castle. Let him look. There's nothin' to see."

She sniffled. "And you'll get here tonight or tomorrow?"

"At the latest," he promised.

Rory said a quick good-bye and disconnected the call.

"Can you get me on the next flight to Ireland? Sayin' it's a family emergency should help, right?"

"It might. But I have another idea. Let me make a quick call."

He handed her the phone. She stopped and thought a moment before punching in the number.

Hell, it's an emergency and he owes me.

⁓

Rory took the steps two at a time and entered the private jet. He met the pilot at the top of the stairs and shook the man's hand. "I thank you fer helpin' me to get home in a hurry. I'm glad Amber knew a pilot with his own plane."

The guy chuckled. "It's not mine. Well, not completely. A group of us own it and fly private gigs. It's mostly to impress the ladies." He winked.

Rory took an instant dislike to the guy, but he'd have to take what he could get.

"Why don't you sit up front?" the man said. "We don't have a copilot. Hell, we don't even have a flight attendant. Just don't touch anything. The view will give you a thrill."

"Sure," Rory said. He didn't tell the guy he could sprout wings and get a dragon's-eye view any time he wanted—as long as no one witnessed it.

The pilot did a cursory flight check, then communicated with the tower. Before long, they'd taxied down the runway and taken off.

As soon as the plane leveled off, the pilot turned to Rory and seemed to be appraising him. "So, you're Amber's new fella…"

Rory didn't know what Amber had said to the guy. She'd closed her bedroom door when she spoke to him. Now Rory just nodded and kept quiet.

"Yeah. I regret cheating on her," the pilot said. "I hope you'll be smarter than I was. She was a great girl."

Rory's eyes rounded. "What?"

"Oh, she didn't tell you? Yeah, we dated for about a year. I tried to keep it in my pants, but hey—sometimes there's just too much temptation."

Rory was infuriated. He knew he wasn't her first, but how could anyone treat his Amber that way? This bastard was probably the reason why she'd wanted nothing to do with men when he'd first met her.

It was all Rory could do to keep himself from bashing the pilot's head against the controls and causing the plane to crash.

The pilot droned on about this new flight attendant he was seeing, and how he was trying to learn from his mistakes with Amber. But after a short time, Rory knew the pilot hadn't learned much at all.

"Well, it appears I've arrived in Amber's life at the right time," Rory finally said.

"Huh? Oh yeah. Timing is everything," the guy said and grinned.

What he meant by that, Rory could only guess, but he didn't really want to know either.

He gazed out the window and didn't say another word until they landed at the airstrip near Ballyhoo. Rory was relieved when his feet hit the tarmac.

The pilot's parting words were, "For what it's worth, Amber thinks the world of you. No one has ever threatened my balls if I didn't help a new boyfriend before." He'd laughed and slammed the door.

———

For some reason the damn toilet wouldn't stop running. Amber jiggled the handle, but that didn't help a bit. She sighed. She didn't know a thing about plumbing. That's one reason she had always rented. Maintenance was definitely not her thing.

Fortunately, nice buildings came with people to maintain them. She didn't know who that would be here, but the managers certainly would. She found her phone and called Sly.

He answered on the second ring. "Sly Flores," he said.

"Hey, Sly. It's Amber. I seem to have a plumbing problem. Can you tell me who I need to call for maintenance?"

He chuckled. "Yeah. Me. What kind of problem is it?"

"The toilet won't stop running. I've jiggled the handle…"

"I'll need to take a look at it."

"I'll be here," she said and mentally rolled her eyes. *Thanks to Mother Nature grounding me like an errant teenager.*

"I'll come right down."

A few seconds later Amber heard a knock on her front door.

Sly was there, toolbox in hand.

"Wow, that was fast!"

He smiled.

"Let's see about that toilet…" He went to the bathroom and removed the porcelain cover on the back of the tank. His eyebrows shot up. "Well, here's your problem." He carefully set the cover down on the bath mat and fished out a gold coin. "This was blocking the drain from closing."

"What the…"

"There's more in there." Sly collected all the coins and showed her six in the palm of his hand.

She bent over them and tried to identify the writing. "I can't make out the denomination or what country they're from."

"They look quite old." Sly rinsed them under the tap and laid them on a towel.

Amber picked up one of the coins and turned it over in her hand. "I think there's a picture of a crown on one side. And maybe that's a horse on the other side?"

Sly plucked the coin out of her fingers and put it in his mouth, then bit down on it.

"Ewww… That was in my toilet."

He laughed. "But not in the potty. It was probably cleaned every time you flushed. How long has this been happening?"

"It just started. Do you think they've been in there all along?"

"It's hard to say."

"Who used to live here?"

He laughed again. "I did. Before that, my daughter's best friend, and before that, my daughter. I doubt any of us had solid gold coins."

"How do you know they're gold?"

He held the one he had bitten out to her. A sharp puncture mark marred the surface. She was going to ask why it didn't look more like the line of a tooth, but then she realized…her maintenance man must have fangs. He could probably use and retract them at will. *Oh lovely.*

"Well, I guess that mystery is solved. Thanks for coming down on such short notice."

He pointed to the towel holding the rest of the coins. "What are you going to do with these?"

She shrugged. "I'll show them to Rory in case he's knows something about them." Then she smirked at him. "You can keep the one you put in your mouth. If he misses it, I'll tell him to talk to you."

----~~~----

By the time Rory got to the cottage, all hell had broken loose. Apparently the ruckus had been heard by a neighbor who came to investigate, then probably ran to the pub to announce the Arish girl was having a complete knock-down, drag-out fight with a stranger whose shouted accent gave away his Ulster citizenship.

More like a knock-down, dragon-out *fight.*

Who knows what the man saw, but by the time half the village arrived, Chloe and Aiden *had to be* back in fully human form. Rory jumped into the fray, trying to pull Aiden and his sister apart. Chloe wasn't doing half badly, he was proud to observe.

One of them accidentally swiped him with their talons. "Shite," he yelled. "Stop this right feckin' now!"

Chloe had to obey. Who knows if Aiden would recognize him as the prince. Conlan was the one he was more apt to follow. The Ulster elder had been hanging back and observing the whole thing.

Rory whirled on him. "A little help here?"

Conlan snapped his fingers. "Aiden!"

Aiden fell away and landed on his back in the bright emerald grass. Chloe went the other way and landed on her side. Her nostrils flared and her fangs were still bared.

"Human. Now!" Rory said.

They both retracted their talons and fangs, then launched themselves at each other again.

"For feck's sake!" Rory cried.

People from the pub were pouring over the slight rise. His sister and cousin were still locked in mortal combat—but thank the Goddess, at least they were human.

Without a second thought, the local sheep-farming brothers tackled Aiden and gave Chloe the advantage. She got in a good right hook before Aiden shook off the farmers. Rory was mortified that the entire village was seeing his sister's temper, and—ahem *everything*. Shannon rushed over to her with a robe.

Before he knew it, the fishermen charged, yelling, "Protestants!" and jumped Conlan.

"Stop!" Rory shouted. Unfortunately, the villagers didn't know he was a prince and didn't have to obey. They were just itching for a fight, and a stranger from Ulster was fair game as far as they were concerned. More villagers followed the fighters' lead. Even Mr. O'Malley got in a couple of punches.

Thank goodness Rory had superior strength and managed to yank the villagers off Conlan two at a time. Aiden wasn't faring as well until Chloe jumped in to help.

An Irish cousin was family and had to be protected from nonfamily.

"Christ Jaysus, Chloe," O'Malley yelled. "Do you want this bastard taught a lesson or not?"

"Sure'n I do, but by *me*. None of you touch 'im further."

Aiden got up slowly. Shannon helped him into Rory's robe, and he nodded his thanks to her.

"Everyone into the house now!" Rory ordered.

The villagers began to walk toward the cottage until he said, "This is a family matter. The rest of you can go home."

There was a collective whine, but the villagers fell away and plodded back toward the pub. They'd be discussing the matter all night—probably all week. Maybe all month. It was the most excitement anyone in Ballyhoo had seen for a while.

Rory held the door open as each Arish made their way into the living room and found a place to sit. Then he slammed the door shut and locked it.

Hands on his hips, he glared at the entire group. "What the hell were you thinkin'?"

Aiden was starting to speak when Conlan held up his hand.

In a calmer voice, the Ulster elder said, "He was standin' up for what he felt was our right. I didn't stop him because he's not wrong."

"What *right* are you talkin' about?" Rory asked.

"The right to examine the caves. You said yerself if we came back this evenin' we could have a look."

"But it's not dark yet, is it?" Rory stated. Then he pointed to Chloe and Aiden on opposite sides of the sofa. "And the two of you know better than to shift in daylight. Have you lost your minds?"

Neither one answered. They stared off in opposite directions.

Rory shook his head. Conlan rose and faced Rory. "I think we need to have an elder-to-elder talk."

As much as it hurt to hear that his cousin didn't consider him *the* elder, Rory had to swallow his pride and make peace with the other Arish family.

He nodded. "Let's go outside. We can keep an eye out for curious villagers who might sneak back and try to spy in the windows."

Before he opened the front door he said, "If we hear a peep from any of you, we're comin' back in and it won't be pretty."

He looked to Conlan for confirmation and he nodded. *Finally.* Rory sensed some kind of truce, however tenuous. Outside he said, "We should look around the place to be sure we're alone first."

Conlan accompanied him without speaking.

When they returned to the front of the house without seeing anyone lurking about, Rory sighed. "I think the first thing we need to discuss is what we are to each other."

"What do you mean?"

"Are we family or enemies?" Rory stared at his cousin and waited.

At last, Conlan said, "We're family. But until we face a common enemy, it can appear to be the other." He smirked.

Rory had to chuckle. "So it seems. But peace has to be struck, and it has to happen before one of us is maimed."

Conlan returned to his serious demeanor. "Sure'n that would make things far worse."

"Exactly." As much as he dreaded it, Rory had to tell his cousins that he had sold off the majority of their ancestral treasures. "Now, I have some bad news, and it may come as a shock."

Conlan groaned. "Speak your mind, Cousin."

"I'm afraid the caves truly are empty."

Conlan's eyes widened. He seemed to be wrestling himself under control. At last he let out a deep breath. "I see. That's why Chloe didn't want Aiden flyin' into them."

"To be sure."

"So, you must have moved the treasure…"

Now the moment of truth had arrived. Rory prayed that his cousin would understand. He had to present the news as only an Irishman could.

"I have to tell you a little story."

Conlan's eyes narrowed. "It better be a true story."

"I assure you, it may seem unlikely, but it's the God's honest truth."

Rory leaned against the door and slid down until he was seated on the stoop. He hoped his cousin would follow suit, in case the story grew long. He waited.

At last, Conlan slid down the clapboards until he was seated beside him.

"Ah, now here's where the story begins." He took a deep breath and covered all the important details. How the leprechauns dragged them out of bed and magically marched them to the edge of the cliff. How the leprechauns accused them of stealing Clancy's pot of gold. Most important, how the accusation was untrue.

How the four of them were transported to a raft.

How Chloe had accused the little bastards of attempted murder and secured a seaworthy vessel for them. And at last, how any treasure that wasn't gold coin had been tossed aboard—else the leprechauns could be accused of stealing too.

Conlan listened patiently to the whole thing, until Rory got to the part where they had to sell some of the items in Iceland to survive.

His posture stiffened. "So you sold off our priceless inheritance for lodging, food, and some spendin' money?"

Rory sighed. "It was necessary. If it helps matters, we held on to what we could."

"So, where is the rest? In Iceland?"

"Buried deep in a cave."

Conlan shot to his feet. "How can you be sure it's still there? What if it's been discovered? Or washed away by the tide? You said the cave was within sight of the ocean, didn't you?"

"I did, but it was high tide and dry when we arrived."

Conlan spat on the ground next to him. "Damn leprechauns." After a long pause, he finally said, "I'm not sure what I'd have done in the same situation. But I do understand one difference… I have brothers. You had to protect two sisters. Although one of 'em can take care of herself and then some."

The cousins smiled at each other, since Chloe had just demonstrated the truth of that statement.

"Still, she is me sister and deserves me care and protection."

Conlan nodded. "I'm fairly sure we can work this out," he said.

Rory almost sighed in relief, but it was too soon for that. "What did you have in mind?"

"Me brothers and I will go to Iceland and fetch what's left of the treasure. That way, we'll be sure nothin' else is taken, if discovered."

Rory opened his mouth to protest, but Conlan raised his hand. "Let me finish, Cousin."

Conlan had given him a chance to tell his whole story, so Rory had to afford him the same respect.

He nodded. "Continue."

Conlan took his time phrasing what he wanted to say. "You know what's there. We don't, and as you witnessed, me brother Aiden isn't the most trusting soul. Now I propose we bring back the remainder, without retribution for what was lost, and then we divide the remainder equally."

Rory had to admit *to himself* that what Conlan proposed might be the only way to end the family feud. Even though he expected that the loss of some items might cause hard feelings.

"Can you guarantee your hotheaded brother will accept the compromise—*if* I agree to it?"

"You know as well as I do that you can only do so much to control another—but I'll try to ease his temper."

"Mayhaps if you remind him you could've wound up with nuthin'…"

Conlan scowled. "Sharin' what belongs to all of us has been too long comin', and you know it well."

Rory wanted to say he knew no such thing, but he was afraid a statement like that would escalate the tension and what little peace they were forging would fall apart. Instead, he rose and brushed off his pants. "Let's go. It's time to break the news to your brother."

Chapter 15

AMBER SAT ON HER BED, POUTING. SHE REALLY DID feel as if she were a child being punished. She'd called out to Bliss and Brandee at least half a dozen times with no answer.

She hoped she hadn't lost her powers forever. She was just getting used to them and had to admit that air travel without a plane was pretty darn cool. She also enjoyed her new job. Never had her efforts been so satisfying. It was tough to fail, sure, but to succeed as she had… There was nothing like it.

"Oh hell," she muttered. As much as she wanted to avoid her assigned mentor, she had to talk to *someone*.

"Euterpe?" she called out.

The muse appeared in front of her. "It's about time. I wondered how long you were going to suffer before you reached out to me."

Amber hung her head. "I'm sorry. Have I blown it completely?"

"Oh, you messed up good, but I think you can repair the damage and get back into Gaia's good graces."

"How?"

Euterpe sat next to her and took her hand. "You've already made a start by asking for my guidance."

That's encouraging. She hoped the rest of what she had to do was that simple, but she doubted it.

"First, you must look inside yourself and see where

you erred. Then admit what you did wrong and apologize. Wholeheartedly."

Amber gulped. She wasn't sure who she had to apologize to, but she had a sinking feeling Euterpe meant to the Goddess of All herself.

"Okaaay…"

"Next, you must promise never to repeat your mistake. You're new and still learning. I can ask for leniency on that basis *this* time, but…"

She didn't have to finish the thought. Amber knew she couldn't claim ignorance much longer. "I really do feel bad about boasting and showing off. It's up to Mother Nature to reveal herself to those she chooses. I guess my ego got the better of me."

Euterpe smiled. "That's the insight you need. Now you can take responsibility for your actions. How about I leave you alone to think…"

Amber grabbed her hand. "No. Please don't leave yet."

Euterpe tipped her head. "What else do you need from me?"

"I don't know. Reassurance? Will Gaia turn me into a baby and make me start over?"

Euterpe's brows shot up, then she laughed. "Of course not. What gave you that idea?"

"*She* did. She even did it for a few seconds to show me that she could."

Euterpe giggled. "That's a new one. She usually threatens punishments that would hurt. Look, she needs you, and you're part of the family. You know too much." Euterpe winked.

"Not if I go back to being a zygote in some poor woman's uterus."

"I see what you mean. Hmmm… I've never known her to carry out her threats. Of course, that doesn't mean she won't if you keep pissing her off."

Amber started to bite her nails.

"Oh, relax." Euterpe wrapped her arm around Amber's shoulder. "Just do as I advised and you'll be fine. The only reason she'd carry out a threat like that is if you defy her and become a total liability. I don't think you'd do that."

"Absolutely not." Then Amber thought about how easily she'd broken a cardinal rule. "At least, not on purpose."

"I think you've learned your lesson. Let me talk to her." Euterpe stood and this time Amber let her go.

Rory was fortunate that the peace between himself, his siblings, and his cousins seemed like it would hold. At least long enough to get the remaining family treasures out of Iceland and divide them.

Now he had to meet with the leprechauns and be sure this whole thing wouldn't happen again. Early in the morning, while everyone else slept, he wandered over the bright-green expanse toward the cliffs.

"Fagan? Lucky?" he called. After waiting an overly long time, he tried again. "Clancy?"

"Ahem."

A throat cleared behind him and Rory whirled around.

Clancy stood there with his arms crossed. "You called me, dragon?"

"I did." Rory didn't know what to do with his hands. If they were on his hips, he'd appear hostile, and that was the last impression he wanted to give. He ended up tucking them into his pockets. "I'd like to speak with all of you."

"I don't know if the others will come, but here I be. What do you want?"

"I want you to know I wish to make peace with you. All of you. If we'd taken your gold, I'd have given it back. I wish I knew what happened to it, but I don't. I hope you know that by now."

Clancy stared at him. His lips pressed together in a thin, stubborn line. At last, he relaxed a bit. "I suppose the accusation was a bit hasty. We never did find any evidence against you."

"To be sure, because there was none."

Clancy scratched his head. "I wish I knew what happened to me gold. I've been collectin' it me whole life."

"I hate to mention this, but Shamus seemed to be pointin' fingers and accusin' us more loudly than the rest of you. Could he have taken it and used us to divert attention from hisself?"

Clancy's brows rose. "Me own brother?"

Rory waited while Clancy mulled that over.

When he didn't speak for too long, Rory asked, "I always wondered… Are you really brothers? Not that you don't look similar enough."

Clancy shook his head. "It's a term of familiarity rather than family. There be precious few of us in existence and no women I know of, so I doubt there'll be more."

"I see. So you've come together as a band of brothers would. But without the blood ties, can you be sure the loyalty is there?"

The little man gazed off toward the ocean and remained silent.

Rory shrugged. "'Tis just a thought."

Clancy nodded but didn't offer a hint as to which way his mind was leaning.

Rory glanced back toward the cottage, and when he faced the cliff again, Fagan and Lucky stood there too.

"We didn't want to accuse our brother without evidence," Fagan said. Fagan again was the only one wearing brown, to show his status as king of the leprechauns. "But we've noticed the behavior you mentioned, Rory."

"Yet you had no problem accusin' us dragons without evidence."

They simply shrugged. At last, Fagan said, "It's our opinion that no matter how painful it be, we need to investigate our own."

"Has he returned from Boston yet?" Rory asked.

"Not yet." Fagan kicked the sod. "We'll have to go fetch him before he hides. He knows somethin' is amiss."

"Do you think your mate, Amber, can give us a lift?" Lucky asked.

Rory frowned. "I doubt it. She said she's in some kind of trouble and can't leave our apartment right now."

"Your apartment? So you may be goin' back?"

Rory let a slow smile spread across his face. "I'd like to bring her here, but if Boston is where she's meant to be, I will try to keep a foot in each place."

Lucky smiled. "I'd do the same. She's a jewel, all right."

Rory reminded himself of the amber stone his grandmother had given him upon his birth. She'd said he'd know his true love if the color of her eyes matched the stone. Unfortunately, his stone had been lost when he was too young to remember it.

His sisters had smartly hidden theirs away. He'd played with his as if it were a toy.

Amber's eyes were green with flecks of gold and would have been a match—if the stone was green. He wished he could remember. He'd never risk losing *her* by playing with her affections like her pilot ex-boyfriend had. "She is indeed."

"You must be anxious to get back to her," Fagan said.

"As anxious as we are to get to Shamus," Clancy added.

"I am," Rory said.

Fagan smiled slyly. "You know, even with magic it's hard to cross an ocean."

Rory tipped his head, wondering why the leprechaun leader looked coy.

"But it isn't impossible," Lucky said. "If we all know the exact spot where we're goin', we might be able manage it."

"With all our magic combined," Clancy said.

"Might?" Rory asked.

Fagan shrugged. "We've never tried it with a passenger, but if we drop you in the ocean, we'll fish you out and try again."

"Drop me?" He pointed to himself. "You think you can transport me to Boston?"

"Mayhaps," Fagan said.

"I'm quite heavy."

"It shouldn't matter to magic what size you are," Lucky said.

'Tisn't very reassuring. Still, he was tempted to let

them try. "What about Finn? Since he knows what you
are, could you bring him back with you?"

"Mayhaps," Fagan said.

Knowing how much Finn and Shannon loved and
needed each other, he had to consider the offer.

"What do you think, Rory? You're the elder dragon
and prince of the area. Are you ready to take a chance?"
Lucky asked.

"I need to talk to me sisters and cousins. If all will be
well here…I'll fly by plane."

<center>~~~</center>

*"You'll find your crystal ball in the Arish sisters' apart-
ment,"* Chad told Morgaine as the residents from the
third floor met in the hall. *"And your bread is under
their couch cushions,"* he said to Gwyneth.

"Bread?" Gwyneth asked. "Why would they want
that? Besides, it would be squished flat by now."

Morgaine chuckled. "I think he means cash, Gwyneth.
They called it 'bread' in the sixties… The money from
your *swear* jar." She couldn't stand the irony anymore
and laughed out loud.

"Oh hush. I know it's funny to y'all, but there's
somethin' more important not to lose sight of. There's
a thief among us!"

Morgaine wasn't reacting because Chad had already
told her he knew where her precious crystal ball was. He
couldn't stand watching her mope and suffer anymore.
Besides, the Arish chicks weren't even around. It was
like hoping for a good catfight with only one cat.

"You have the key to their place, right?" Gwyneth
asked the managers.

"Yeah. But they're not home, and it feels wrong to invade their privacy," Sly said.

Morgaine opened the door to her own place. "I don't have a problem with it if Chad's right and my crystal ball is in there. I want it before it can be hidden again." She grabbed the skeleton key off a peg in their coat closet.

"Who took it?" Gwyneth asked.

"It was one of the leprechauns, but I never caught his name."

"We'll deal with him later," Morgaine said. "First I want my crystal ball, and then we'll ward our apartment against intruders—supernatural ones included."

"Sounds good to me," Gwyneth said.

They all marched down the stairs, and Morgaine slid the key in the lock. Chad hadn't prepared them for the fact that a young man was sleeping on the couch. They all startled when he sat up.

"Who are you?"

"Shannon's…"—he blinked and hesitated—"friend. Is she with you?"

"No," Sly said.

"Chloe?" he asked and tried to peer around the trio in the doorway.

"We're the managers. We need you to stand up so we can look under the couch cushions." Sly advanced into the apartment.

Finn rubbed the sleep from his eyes. "Whatever for?" He appeared annoyed now.

"We think there's money under 'em," Gwyneth said.

"Is that what managers do now?" Finn asked. "Look for money under the residents' cushions while they're away? Are you lookin' for some kind of tip? Here's a tip for you. Don't touch a thing until one o' the lasses is with you. Otherwise, you'll have to deal with me."

Gwyneth sighed. "Just lift the cushions. My money was stolen, and we have reason to believe it's under your butt."

Finn rose. "I doubt that highly, and just to prove it…" He flipped over the cushion revealing several dollar bills and a sticky note that read "Gwyneth's swear jar."

"Holy mother," Finn mumbled. "Why would they do such a thing?"

"We don't think it was them," Morgaine said.

"It was the lep—" Gwyneth began, then slapped a hand over her own mouth. "I mean…it was the lepers."

Finn's eyes rounded.

"Yeah. There's lepers round these parts, so y'all better scoot home."

Morgaine and Sly shook their heads as if giving up on Gwyneth's ability to filter.

Gwyneth shrugged. "What?"

"Damn," Finn said. "I thought you were goin' to say it was the leprechauns. Now *that* I would believe."

All three of the residents stared at each other with open mouths.

Sly cocked his head. "Leprechauns?"

"Sure'n you believe in leprechauns. They've been visitin' your fair city all week."

"How…" Morgaine paused. "You know what? I don't care how you know about them. I just need to find my crystal ball. It's in here somewhere." She looked at the ceiling. "Do you know exactly where it is?"

"Who are you talkin' to?" Finn asked.

"The ghost," Gwyneth answered before anyone could stop her.

"Spirits?" Finn cried. "The place is haunted?"

"He spends most of his time upstairs," Gwyneth said, trying to reassure Finn, but that clearly wasn't helping much.

Finn stared at the spot Morgaine was focusing on, so Chad stepped aside. Sure enough, Finn's eyes didn't follow, so the kid couldn't see him. *But now that he knows I'm here and looks scared out of his wits, I can have a little fun with him.*

"Chad…" Morgaine said in a warning tone. "I know what you're thinking. Leave the young man alone."

"Aww…you never let me have any fun…not that you can stop me either."

She huffed. "Please, just tell me where my crystal ball is."

"It's in an empty shoe box. Top shelf. Bedroom closet."

"Thank you."

As Morgaine marched to the bedroom, Finn followed, careful to skirt the spot where he thought the ghost was. It was all Chad could do not to blow a good chill down the human's neck.

———

Amber's phone rang. She was surprised to hear Rory's low voice when she answered, although she was happy to hear from him.

"How're you keepin'?" he asked.

"Oh, I'm keeping. Like I'm on ice." *Thin ice, with Mother Nature mad at me.*

"Ah. Whatever that means… I'm ready to come back to Boston. Is Finn still there?"

"As far as I know."

"Do you happen to have your powers back?"

She closed her eyes and thought of his cottage. Nothing happened. "Nope. I'm still grounded."

"I'm sorry to hear it."

His voice was muffled, as if he'd put his hand over the mouthpiece, but she heard him anyway. "Go fetch him, fellas. He'll be in the apartment directly above mine."

"So who are you sending for Finn?"

"Ah. I forget you can hear me. I guess you haven't lost all your muse abilities."

She was relieved that she still had her supernatural hearing. Maybe Gaia wasn't giving up on her completely.

"Speaking of which, I heard a bunch of people upstairs in your sisters' apartment. I think I recognized the managers' voices," she said.

"What were they sayin?"

"I wasn't really paying attention. I think I heard Finn say something about spirits. I don't know if he was out of whiskey or what."

"I'm not really thinkin' about Finn right now," Rory said in a low, sexy voice.

"Um, Rory?"

"That's me."

She wished he'd stop being charming for one minute so she could complete a thought… But that just reinforced what she had been considering.

"We need to have that talk, and I think it might be better to do that on the phone…now. When we're together, we keep getting—distracted."

He chuckled. "I know what you mean. But there's nothin' to talk about, really. Is there?"

Her heart sank. Would he be packing up his few

belongings and moving back to Ireland now that the leprechauns had lifted their ban on the dragons?

"I-I guess not."

He was quiet, but she didn't know what to say either. She should get off the phone before she choked up and he could hear it in her voice.

"On the other hand," he said, "I suppose there is one thing we need to settle."

She took a deep breath, figuring he wanted to give her the apartment—officially. Fortunately he forged on before she could interrupt.

"Do you want to live in Boston or Ballyhoo?"

"Ireland?" She was temporarily stunned.

"O' course we can make a home in both countries…"

A home? "Together?"

He laughed. "Sure'n you know we're meant to be together by now."

"Together, together?" she repeated, stupefied.

"We have a sayin' here in Ireland—not that we don't have many sayin's, but this one seems to fit. 'In our togetherness, castles are built.'"

Togetherness. "I—uh…"

"Do you need time to think on it?"

At last she recovered her composure. "No!"

"No? Do you mean you will not live with me, or you don't need time to think on it?"

"The second one. I don't need time. Of course I want to stay with you!" She finally let the tears fall. "Anywhere," she choked out.

"Ah, lass. You've made me a happy man."

"But what about that double standard? It's okay for you and me to 'live in sin'"—she used air quotes even though he couldn't see her—"but it's not okay for your sister? Shannon is apt to be furious."

"Marry me, then."

She couldn't speak around the lump in her throat.

"If you're worried about the paperwork, me cousins know a guy in Ulster who can make me a birth certificate, passport, the works. If there's no way to get there earlier, I'll see you in a few days and we can…" He lowered his voice. "Well, you know what we can do then."

"You betcha."

———

Chad watched the leprechauns from a safe distance, perched upon the large chandelier that graced the main entrance.

"You're a thief!" Lucky yelled. His voice carried up the stairwell of the Beacon Street brownstone.

Shamus scowled. "Keep your voice down. It's nuthin' you wouldn't have done yerself."

Lucky gasped. "What? Are you mad? We've never stolen from each other. And then you went and blamed it on the dragons!"

"I did not. You really must keep your voice down. Not everyone in the buildin' knows about dragons."

Lucky couldn't believe what he was hearing. "You did!"

Chad interjected. *"He's right about one thing. Finn is in the apartment right upstairs, and he doesn't know a thing about paranormals—well, except leprechauns."*

Lucky took a few deep breaths and tried to calm down. When he could finally speak in a quieter tone, he said, "You said the dragons' love of treasure must have led them to steal Clancy's gold."

Shamus straightened. "It could have. We all know they love their treasure and will do almost anythin' to protect their keep."

Lucky paced. "Fagan isn't goin' to like this."

"And you're not goin' to tell him."

Astounded, Lucky halted and stared at his brother. "And why wouldn't I?"

"Because if you do, I'll say you were complicit. O' course, if you are, I won't say a word and we can split it fifty-fifty."

Lucky shook his head. "I won't lie for you, Shamus." Then he withdrew a four-leaf clover from his pocket and tucked it into the buttonhole on Shamus's lapel.

"What's that for?"

"For luck. When Fagan and Clancy find out, you'll need it."

"But that's what I'm sayin'… They need never find out. All you have to do is keep your trap shut."

"There's one thing you're forgettin'," Lucky said. "Even if I were as crooked as you, and I'm *not,* there's a spirit who knows the truth."

"How? What did you see, spirit? You weren't in Ireland a few weeks ago, were you?"

"No. But I saw you plant Morgaine's crystal ball in a shoe box that belonged to either Chloe or Shannon, and you put Gwyneth's money under their sofa cushions."

"Ha! But you never saw me take any gold, did you?"

"I saw you produce a few gold coins from your pocket. By the way, Amber found them in her toilet, and you need to cop to it before she and Sly blame Rory for them."

"Show yerself, spirit. If you don't, I'll know you for a coward."

Chad's ghostly form floated down from the chandelier. On his way past, he gave the crystals a tug, which resulted in a tinkling sound. Shamus looked up at him and frowned.

Leaning over the little man, Chad said, *"Here I am. Boo!"*

The desperate leprechaun actually tried to punch him in the nose. His fist whizzed right through Chad's face and the ghost laughed.

"Sometimes I love not having a physical body."

Shamus's ruddy face turned bright red, and without warning he took a shot at Lucky. That effort met flesh with a smack. Stunned, Lucky staggered back a few feet.

When he recovered his balance, he yelled, "What the feck is the matter with you, Shamus? Have you lost your senses along with your pride?"

"I've lost nuthin'. And before I lose me gold too, I'm g—"

Lucky figured he was going to say he was going somewhere or already gone, so he grabbed on to his brother's coat. Shamus took another swing at him, and this time Lucky was ready. He ducked and while Shamus was off balance, Lucky sent a good uppercut to his chin.

"What's going on?" Morgaine called downstairs.

People poured out of the paranormal club, and Finn opened the door across the hall.

Before anyone could say "Whist," the two leprechauns were rolling and punching and grabbing and clawing. Lucky held on tight to Shamus's coat until the little fecker bit him.

"Ouch!"

The moment Lucky let go, Shamus disappeared.

"Feckers!" Lucky yelled.

"I don't know what y'all were fightin' about, but it sounds like someone needs to put a dollar in the swear jar," the redheaded witch said.

Morgaine hastily descended the stairs. "I'm sorry for the disturbance, everyone," she called out as she rounded the second floor. "You can go back to whatever you were doing. Sly and I will take care of this."

As if on cue, Sly emerged from the cellar door. "What's going on?"

Lucky pulled his throbbing hand out of his mouth. "Just a little brotherly spat."

Two other leprechauns appeared, seemingly out of thin air.

"Did you get all that?" Lucky asked.

"We did," the older one said.

Sly planted his hands on his hips and leaned over Lucky. "We don't like family fights in the hallway. We actively discourage any fights, and until now we haven't had a problem."

"Well, not since Morgaine and I made peace and got our own apartments," Gwyneth offered helpfully.

"None of you four even live here," Morgaine said.

"Before you blame the wrong dude, Morgaine, you should tell Sly that Lucky was trying to get his brother to fess up to stealing your shit."

"Oh." Morgaine glanced upstairs to where almost a dozen curious onlookers leaned over the railing. "You can all go back inside now. We've got this."

Most everyone mumbled some kind of assent and returned to the paranormal club. Gwyneth jogged down the stairs to join her cousin and Sly. She stopped when she got to Finn.

"Y'all need to pop back inside your sweetie's apartment too, hon. This don't involve ya."

He pointed to Lucky. "It sounds like me friend is in trouble. I'm not goin' to walk away while he's accused of disturbin' the peace."

"Tell him I saw the whole thing, Gwyneth," Chad said.

"Y'all don't think he'll be spooked? He looked a might scared when he learned you were in the buildin', Chad."

"He's a lot braver and more open-minded than you would think. Give him a little credit...and tell him I'll stick up for his friend."

Morgaine glanced at Gwyneth and nodded. While Gwyneth explained what Chad said to Finn, Morgaine whispered to Sly, who relaxed his menacing posture...slightly.

"We take care of our own," the older leprechaun said. "We'll find Shamus and bring him to justice."

Lucky hung his head. "He was given the right name long ago. He shamed us all."

"So, do you know where he went?" Chad asked.

"I've a fair idea where he might be," Clancy said. "We wondered why he wanted to go to Cambridge alone. I found his hideout."

"Did you now?" Lucky exclaimed. "Where is it?"

"In one of the boathouses on the river. There's an emblem in dark red on the door."

"Ah. That would be the Harvard Crimson," Sly said. "The college has rowing crews."

"Now it's just a matter of all three of us sneakin' up on him," Fagan said.

Lucky smiled. "That should not be difficult, considerin' we can come and go in the blink of an eye."

"When we have ahold of him, we'll take him back to Ireland for trial," Fagan said.

"He might never confess." Lucky turned to Clancy and placed a hand on his green coat. "Are you goin' to be all right if we never find your gold?"

Clancy nodded.

Fagan puffed out his chest. "Oh, Shamus will confess, all right. I have a nice dank place to hold him until he does." Then he tipped his hat to Morgaine and Gwyneth and bowed to Sly. "If you'll excuse us, we'll be on our way, and we should never have to bother you again."

The building residents just nodded and the three leprechauns disappeared.

"Well, most of them seemed pretty cool," Chad said.

Morgaine rolled her eyes and said, "One of these days I hope things get back to normal around here."

Gwyneth laughed. "When has this buildin' ever been normal?"

Chapter 16

IN THE APARTMENT'S KITCHEN, AMBER BEAT A chocolate cake mix by hand. Sure, she had a mixer, but taking her frustrations out on cake batter while wishing she had her powers back seemed like a good idea. She wanted to see Rory sooner rather than later, and waiting for him to get a passport so he could fly to Boston via airplane made her antsy as hell.

She turned around to grab the greased and floured cake pans and almost bumped into the white-robed figure of Mother Nature.

"Oh! I didn't see you there, Gaia."

The goddess smirked. "I like to keep my muses on their toes."

Amber lifted her brows hopefully. "Am I still your muse?"

"You are if you want to be."

"I want to be! I really do. I'm sorry about the stupid way I behaved before. Can you forgive me?"

Mother Nature offered a genuine smile. "Well, since you called your own behavior stupid and I didn't have to label it for you, it sounds like you've learned your lesson."

"I have. I swear it. I'm very sorry for bragging about meeting you."

"And you won't do it again?"

"Never."

The goddess didn't answer right away. Instead, she

strolled out of the kitchen and sat in the small dining area. "I've been thinking about your situation…"

"What situation is that?"

"I realize I may have forgotten to give you the incentive I've given other muses. With nothing at stake, you may not have had the proper motivation to stick to my simple rules. *Not* that you should need motivation to do what's right," Gaia amended quickly.

Amber just nodded. Until she knew what the goddess meant by incentive and motivation, she wasn't about to interrupt.

"For instance, Brandee was easy. She wanted a career in photography with her own gallery. I gave her the gallery on Newbury Street as a reward for her duties as one of my modern muses."

"I see…" Amber was only beginning to guess where Mother Nature was going with this.

The goddess picked up a lock of her own long hair and began curling it around her finger as if giving in to a nervous habit. "Bliss was more difficult to persuade. I thought losing all her belongings in a fire was her biggest problem, so I tried to solve that with a money tree." Gaia let her hair drop. "I still have a hard time believing she turned that down."

"What was it she really wanted?" Amber hadn't known the other modern muse that long and couldn't guess what she'd finally received.

"She wanted her husband to be made fireproof again. I had just gone to all the trouble of turning him mortal, but because he continued to work as a firefighter, she got all worried about him." Mother Nature tutted. "Talk about shortsighted!"

"Oh yeah. I heard about that. I guess Bliss realized her mistake too. But she got pregnant while he was human."

"Yes, it worked out for them, but don't get any ideas. The whole thing was a giant pain in the ass."

Amber's prospects were beginning to look up. She didn't want to get ahead of herself though. Maybe being forgiven was enough of a reward.

"You, I can't figure out at all," the goddess continued. "You wanted this apartment and a man to love who would love you in return. Well, you achieved that all on your own."

Amber couldn't help being relieved. If Mother Nature had given her those things, she'd have been worried.

Gaia rose and paced with her hands clasped behind her back. The vine that belted her gown trailed along the floor behind her. "I finally decided to stop over-taxing my brain and just come out and ask you." She halted and stared at her anxious muse. "What is it you want?"

Amber hadn't even thought about it. What did she really need? Not much. She had a great place to live— possibly two places. She had the man of her dreams and he'd recently proposed. Presumably, she'd have all her muse powers, including instant travel, so she didn't think that would count.

So she thought beyond herself. What could she do for someone else that would make her happy too?

"I, uh…I understand you have rules about humans and dragons committing to each other, but I would be eternally grateful if you'd make an exception to that rule."

Mother Nature reared back but didn't interrupt.

"I've never seen a love so happy and pure as Shannon

and Finn's. It just about killed Rory to think he'd have to tell his sister they couldn't marry—especially after he'd given them his blessing."

Gaia sighed. "I see where you're going with this, muse. It speaks well of your character that you want something for someone else. Something that wouldn't benefit you in the least. And yet, that's not good enough."

Amber's jaw dropped. *Not good enough?* Did that mean the goddess wouldn't grant that favor?

"That means I *can* grant your wish, but I have to do something for you too."

"Oh yeah. I forgot you can read my mind."

"Only when I want to. I thought you might give me an inkling as to what you really want, but I still don't see it."

"So, will you grant my only wish?"

The all-powerful one crossed her arms and scowled. "You're pushing your luck, you know. I *just* restored your powers, and you're asking me to make a huge exception to my number one rule." Then she pointed at Amber. "And what is that rule, Muse?"

"Never to reveal the paranormal world to humans," Amber said without hesitation.

Gaia's posture relaxed. "Very good. At least you know what an enormous favor you're asking."

"I wouldn't ask if I didn't believe the young man could handle it. By the way, does Shannon really have two hearts?"

Mother Nature laughed. "No, but she certainly has a big one."

"So does Finn. I think their love will win out over fear."

Gaia sat at the table again. "You believe—you

think… How can you be sure? He's going to learn he's in love with a fire-breathing dragon."

"As did I."

"I've looked into his soul, and he is indeed a trustworthy young man. I just worry about a human's initial reaction."

Amber thought hard. "What if the vampires were right there to wipe the information from his mind if he freaks out? He'll need a few minutes to absorb the information, of course."

Mother Nature rested her elbow on the table and cupped her cheek. "Again with the vampires… You're lucky the managers are the friendly sort. You realize there are less altruistic types. Right?"

Amber shrugged. "I'll take your word for it. The managers are the only vampires I know. Oh—and the wizard's wife. She seems less friendly, so I wouldn't ask her."

Mother Nature smiled, as if she knew a little more than Amber did about the situation—which, of course, she must.

"Ruxandra has her moments. It was touch and go for a while, but eventually she proved herself in a most unusual way."

"Dare I ask her about it?"

Mother Nature laughed. "Probably not."

Her laugh was a welcome change. She was still grinning when Amber realized she actually liked the Goddess of All… But using Gaia's own words, "It was touch and go for a while."

"Muse, I will grant your wish."

Amber didn't know whether to hug her or bow or kiss her hand.

"A simple 'thank you' will do," Gaia said.

"Thank you—*so* much." Amber realized the goddess must have read her mind again.

"No, I read your facial expression that time."

"Jeez, I wish I knew when you were in my mind instead of just in my apartment."

Gaia rose. "Well, I'll be neither place in a moment. Go gather your new friends. It sounds like you have a lot to do."

—∿—

Rory returned to the cottage from an evening at O'Malley's Pub. As soon as he walked in the door, he was nearly tackled by his ladylove and plied with kisses. He lifted her off her feet, welcoming her passion.

When they finally managed to tear their lips off each other, Rory grinned. "Ah, lass. It's glad I am to see you. But me sisters will be watchin' a porno unless we take this upstairs to me bedroom."

"Not to worry," Amber said breathlessly. "Your sisters are back in Boston."

"How? Does this mean you got your powers back?"

"Yes. Mother Nature forgave me, and I have more good news."

Rory scooped her up in his arms and headed for the stairs. "Tell me quick. By the time we reach me bed I won't be talkin' anymore."

Amber giggled. "I got Gaia's permission for Finn and Shannon to marry."

Rory almost dropped her. "Are you serious? You wouldn't be speakin' prematurely, would you?"

"Not at all. She said Finn will need to be told the truth

in the presence of the vampires, who can mesmerize him if he can't handle it. Then, if need be, they can erase all knowledge of paranormals from his mind."

Rory frowned. "So, there *is* a catch."

"Think about it, Rory. Finn has already accepted the existence of leprechauns. He loves Shannon so much he went after her and didn't give up until he found her. I really believe he'll decide to risk being married to a dragon—as long as that dragon is Shannon."

Rory began ascending the stairs while mulling it all over. He was certainly relieved that he didn't have to tell Shannon the engagement was off. He had no idea how he'd manage that without breaking both her hearts.

"How did you get Gaia to agree to that?"

Amber smiled. "Let's just say she grants one special wish when her modern muses agree to work for her. Think of it as a retention bonus."

He was surprised that Amber's special wish had been for Shannon and Finn—not herself.

"What made you waste your wish on me sister and her happiness instead of your own?"

Amber's eyes glowed softly. "It wasn't wasted. I already have everything I want, and making someone else so happy will just add to my own happiness."

"Oh, luv…" He didn't know what to say. They had reached the bed, so he laid her on it gently and followed her down. Cupping her cheek, he gazed at her. "You're a wonder. And I wonder what I ever did to deserve you."

"Well, for starters you protected and raised your sisters for… Oh man, it boggles my mind to think about how long you've done that."

He chuckled. "It's had its challenges and rewards."

She brushed the reddish strands of hair out of his eyes. "Maybe Shannon's happiness is one of your rewards."

"Ah, luv. You're my best reward."

He captured her lips in a passionate kiss. Their tongues sought each other and swirled as he heated up from the inside. She squirmed closer to him, so he cupped her buttocks and pulled her against his hard erection.

They were just beginning to sweat when he noticed a cool breeze across his skin. Glancing down, he saw their intertwined bare bodies and their clothing neatly folded at the foot of the bed.

"Now there's a grand power to have. When did you discover you could do that?"

She giggled. "Just now. I was wishing we didn't have to stop to get undressed, and well…"

He grinned. "Ah, luv. You amaze me, and not just because of your powers. The passion you have for—"

He didn't have a chance to finish his speech. Not only did she cut him off with a hard kiss, but she had also neatly rolled him onto his back and straddled him. He couldn't help the laugh that burst from his lungs.

She leaned away. "Are you all right with me on top?"

"On top, beneath, or on the side. I'm happy to have you anywhere on me, darlin'."

She grinned and backed down his body, kissing his neck, collarbone, and pecs along the way. She paused to suckle his flat nipple, and the pleasure that zinged through him made him gasp. She moved to the other one and did the same until her ministrations elicited an amorous groan.

She didn't stop there. She kissed her way down his ribs and laved his belly button. As soon as he chuckled, she took his member in her mouth, completely changing the sensation. A deep blissful pressure radiated through him, and his stiff cock grew even further. He hadn't thought it possible.

She had him arching and undulating until he was afraid he'd come too soon. He reached down and pulled her away, albeit reluctantly.

"Ah, lass. You're about to get a surprise if you keep goin' the way you're goin'."

"I like surprises," she said and tried to capture his staff with her mouth again.

"Let's be fair. You need some attention too, don't you?"

She smiled slyly. Instead of answering, she rose above him and sank down on his erection. "Ah… You're right. I needed this."

The sensation of her wet heat enveloping him like a velvet glove elicited another moan. They fell into a mutually pleasurable rhythm, and his fingers found her sensitive bundle of nerves.

Her reaction was instantaneous. She bucked and keened with each rub. Arching her back, she locked her elbows and braced her hands on the sheets behind her.

He reveled in her sensual ride. His own pleasure built to a shattering peak, and he climaxed as never before. Ecstasy shot through his body, over and over. When he gazed at her, she appeared to be screaming, but silently.

He briefly wondered if that was another power, but it didn't matter either way. He was simply happy that she was finding her release, which allowed him to ride his own pleasure right to the end.

Finally, when she seemed to have reached the last

aftershock, she stilled and collapsed on top of him. He wrapped his arms around her and held her gently, treating her like the precious treasure she was.

He didn't care if his castle's caves were full and his cousins wanted every bit of it. He'd have traded every golden chalice for this moment.

Now, back in Boston it was time to talk to Finn. First Amber and Rory had to warn the managers of a possible human overreaction, complete with screaming and an attempt to warn the world about the paranormals among them. The ulterior motive was enlisting Sly and Morgaine's help in case the information needed to be erased from the young man's mind.

With trepidation, Amber knocked on the door of apartment 3B. She'd barely knocked once when the door opened and Morgaine gave them a welcoming smile.

"I've been expecting you two," she said.

Rory and Amber glanced at each other.

"You have?"

"Come in." As Morgaine stepped to the side she chuckled. "I guess you don't know I'm psychic."

"Ah, that's it then," Rory said.

Sly stepped out of the kitchen with two glasses of red wine. Meanwhile, Amber was trying to put into words what she wanted to say.

"I'd ask if I could get you anything, but I'm sorry, Rory, we don't have any Guinness."

"I don't need a beverage, thank you."

"Have a seat." Morgaine gestured to the perpendicular love seat. "Sly, I think Amber would like a glass of wine."

"Thank you."

When he returned, Sly placed the glass of wine on the coffee table and sat beside Morgaine on the couch.

Amber took a fortifying sip. "Do you know what we want to talk to you about?" she asked Morgaine.

The psychic vampire-witch smiled. "No. I just got the sense that you were coming with some kind of request."

So much for having an ulterior motive. Amber cleared her throat, but before she could give her well-thought-out speech, Rory cut to the chase.

"We need to tell Shannon's human lover about her paranormal status before they enter into marriage. We're hopin' you'll be present in case he needs mesmerizin' to take the information out of his head."

Sly leaned back. "Are you expecting a negative reaction?"

"Not a' tall. He loves her so much that I believe he'll accept her and all her quirks."

Sly and Morgaine smiled at each other.

"We can relate to that," Sly said.

"Good. Then you'll help us?"

They stared at each other again, but this time the couple seemed to be having one of their telepathic conversations. At last Morgaine nodded. "We'll stay nearby. We don't want to intrude, so we won't be in the room—but that's because we know you can easily stop him from running down Beacon Street, screaming the truth."

Rory chuckled. "You can rest assured I won't let that happen."

"I can pop in and tell you if you're needed immediately," Amber added.

Morgaine nodded. "When are you thinking of doing this?"

"Right now, if you're able to stick around."

"Now is good," Sly said. "Morgaine has to go to Boston Uncommon to read tea leaves late this afternoon, but neither of us have anywhere to be before then."

"Perfect," Amber said. She turned toward Rory and took a deep breath. "Are you ready for this?"

"As ready as ever I'll be."

Amber took another big sip of the vampires' wine and hoped that's all it was. Just wine. She didn't detect a hint of anything else, so she tipped back her glass and finished it.

"Ah, lass. You drink like you're Irish already."

She smirked. "I *am* Irish already. Always have been."

He laughed. "You're right and not. But don't worry. I'll make a real Irish lass of you before long."

"That brings up a question of our own," Sly said. "Where are you two planning to live after your own wedding?"

Amber's brows shot up. "We haven't told anyone yet. How did you… Oh." Remembering in whose presence they sat, she said, "Never mind."

The other couple laughed. "We won't tell anyone unless you want us to."

"You're workin' at the tearoom?" Rory asked.

Morgaine nodded.

"I may see you. Bliss's friend Claudia has been wantin' me sisters and me to play a session there. We talked about tryin' to arrange it for tomorrow."

"You can be ready that soon?" Amber asked.

"Ah, luv. We're always ready to share our music."

"It sounds great," Sly said. "But we've gotten a bit sidetracked. We'd still like an answer to our question about where you two plan to live."

"Ah. We haven't quite finished discussin' that ourselves. Best I can gather is perhaps we'll keep a foot in both places."

Morgaine and Sly stared at each other again.

At last, Morgaine spoke. "I happen to know the building next door is going up for sale soon. I don't suppose you can afford it, but if you could, it might make a nice 'overflow hotel' for paranormal travelers."

Amber gasped. "What a cool idea!" Then her hope immediately faded. "But you're right, we probably can't afford it. These places go for millions."

Rory took her hand. "Mayhaps we can. If you want it, I'd be glad to look into the price and such."

She leaned away and stared at him. "Seriously?"

He shrugged. "I can't promise anythin'."

The only thing Amber could think of was, *How?* In what world was an Irish folksinger able to afford a down payment and mortgage for a million-dollar brownstone in Boston's Back Bay?

To the shock of everyone in the room, Mother Nature appeared and pointed straight at Amber. "Aha! I knew you'd want something."

Amber glanced at the others. Rory recovered quickly, having met the goddess once before. Morgaine's mouth was hanging open, and she grabbed Sly's hand.

Sly's expression quickly changed to a scowl. "And who might you be, besides an uninvited guest?"

Gaia rested her fist on her hip and sized him up. "You obviously don't have a clue who I am, *vampire,* so I'll forgive the unwelcome and introduce myself. I am Mother Nature." She focused on Morgaine and smiled. "*The* Goddess you worship."

Morgaine's hand flew to her chest as if holding her heart inside. She didn't speak or make a sound. Amber suspected she wouldn't be able to for a while.

"So, muse of air travel, it seems I've discovered the incentive you needed. But before I make all the arrangements—which I can do instantly of course—you and your dragon ought to see it. I'm afraid it's in need of a little attention."

"Oh? What kind of attention?"

"Mostly cosmetic. The decor is—let's say, 'taste specific.' The eccentric owner made his fortune from a few nightclubs in the seventies and eighties. Unless you *like* the idea of having a disco ball in your living room…"

Rory choked. Amber could tell he was trying not to say something that might insult the goddess's generous gift. Finally, he said, "I would enjoy remodeling it. Such a project would keep me occupied between sessions at the tearoom."

Morgaine finally found her voice. "And you could live here until the place is ready."

Amber chuckled. "We kind of have to. I signed a year's lease."

"And I paid for it—in cash." Rory grinned at her and she couldn't help grinning back. Suddenly, she remembered something.

"Wait! This doesn't mean you're taking back your permission for Finn to marry Shannon, does it?"

Gaia straightened. "Of course not. I'd never break a promise—well, unless I couldn't keep it."

Amber was both reassured and unsettled by that remark.

Rory stroked her back with reassuring caresses. "I guess it's time to tell Finn what he needs to know so he can marry me sister."

They both rose and bade the managers a good day.

—⁓—

Finn and Shannon sat on the sofa, holding hands. To the lad's credit, he hadn't run away, screaming, when Rory explained the special nature of his clan.

"So, you're tellin' me that Shannon will never age while we're together?"

"That's right, Finn," Rory said gravely.

"An' she'll outlive me by hundreds o' years."

"If not thousands. We're very hard to kill."

The young man hesitated only a second, then jumped up and pumped his fist. "Wahoo! I get to have a young wife until I die."

Rory was taken aback. *Is that the kind of man Finn is? Have I made a mistake by giving him permission to marry me precious sister?*

Gaia rose. "I know what you're thinking, dragon. And I know what the man you call Finn is thinking too. Before anyone jumps to the wrong conclusions, he's simply excited that he won't have to watch her grow infirm and die."

Finn looked confused as he sat down and took Shannon's hand again. "Well, o' course. What else would you think?"

Shannon stiffened. "Oh, I don't know. Mayhaps that your young, beautiful wife will make you look like some kind of hot man in your old age."

Shock registered on his face, and then he burst out laughing. "I hadn't thought of that, but you bring up a good point." Before Shannon could get angry, Finn cleared his throat and turned a serious face to Mother Nature. "I don't know how we'll explain it to the villagers. Have you any advice on that, Goddess?"

Gaia tipped her head and appeared to think. Finally she said, "You have two choices. I can make her appear to age, or you can move from place to place as people get suspicious. All I ask is that you never reveal the existence of paranormal beings to any human—without my permission."

"I won't. I swear it." Finn turned to Shannon. "Which do you wish to do, luv? After all, it's your body and your home."

Smiling, she said, "I think it might be fun to move about. We can see other parts of the country we love. But Ballyhoo is your village too. How do you feel about leavin' it for a few years, mayhaps only comin' home to be buried there?"

Finn kissed her knuckles. "As long as you're happy, luv, I'll follow you wherever you go."

Rory barked a laugh. "Truer words have never been spoken."

Epilogue

SO...THE WEDDING IN BALLYHOO WENT OFF WITHOUT a hitch. Well, no. That's not quite right. Shannon and Finn got hitched. Everything else went unhitched. I mean, unhitchy—oh, forget it. The wedding was awesome. Shannon and Finn are enjoying their honeymoon in their little caretaker's cottage by the sea.

The Arish cousins did split what was left of the family treasures—which *somehow* appeared to be more than anyone expected—with one notable exception. They gave a jewel-studded candelabra to the happy couple as a wedding present.

As it turned out, the leprechauns made up for their horrible mistake by finding more long lost Arish king's treasure that had been hidden in the bogs thousands of years earlier in case the castle fell. The Northern Irish cousins had followed the trail of the remaining stuff to Iceland and came back with much more than Rory had sold, so they were happy.

While in Ireland, Rory showed Amber his childhood home. As they were exploring the castle caves, a glint of something shiny caught her eye. It turned out to be Rory's grandmother's gift...his precious amber that he'd lost as a child. It was indeed the green variety and matched her eyes perfectly.

They discovered something else too. In what was once the dungeon they came across Clancy's pot of gold. Rory called out to Fagan immediately and explained that they *hadn't* taken it. Someone else was making it look as if they had. To Rory's surprise the leprechaun believed him instantly. Apparently Shamus had confessed and apologized for his greed only moments before.

As of this moment, Rory and Amber are shopping at Home Depot, picking out sophisticated finishes and fixtures to restore their new Beacon Street brownstone to its former glory.

Meanwhile, Chloe is in her walk-in closet, tossing her sister's clothing and shoes in a heap on the floor. At some point she'll stuff everything in a garbage bag and mail it to Shannon as a wedding present.

I want my readers to know that Chloe has been muttering to me all along about wanting her story to be told too. So I wrote it! Watch for book two in the Boston Dragons series, *My Wild Irish Dragon*!

Here's a sneak peek at book two in Ashlyn Chase's
sizzling Boston Dragons series

My Wild Irish Dragon

CHLOE ARISH SAT ON A HARD PLASTIC CHAIR OUTSIDE
the fire chief's office, tapping her foot while she awaited
her second interview for a job as a Boston firefighter.
She had already passed the Civil Service Exam and the
Candidate Physical Ability Test. The written test and
oral exam were more difficult for her than the physical stuff, but thanks to some coaching by her friend
and fellow dragon/firefighter Drake Cameron, she had
passed with flying colors.

Actually, the one thing she was most worried about
was her fake birth certificate. Now that she was a natu-
ralized U.S. citizen and had been a resident of Boston
for over a year, she met the most basic requirements. But
her life's history on paper was completely false, and this
job came with background checks.

Fortunately, her Ulster cousins knew "a bloke" who
could create a realistic forgery, picking a birthday that didn't
indicate her real age, which was well over a thousand years
old. She didn't look a day over twenty-three, so her phony
birth certificate was made to match. Just for kicks, they'd
picked July 4 as her birthday. America's birthday.

Just as she was checking her watch for the umpteenth
time, the door opened and out strolled a six-foot-tall
Adonis. Dark hair, chiseled features, and olive skin.

He was followed by the chief, who clasped him in a man-hug, and they pounded each other on their backs.

"Give my best to your family," the chief said. "I'm sure we'll see each other soon."

"I will. And say hello to yours for me."

Oh, feck. They know each other. Chloe had heard that nepotism was a regular thing among firefighters.

The chief nodded to her. "I'll be with you shortly," he said and returned to his office.

The Greek god gazed at her with intense dark eyes. "So, you're here for an interview too?"

She straightened in her chair. "I am."

"Let me guess. You're a secretary? Or, what is it called now? Administrative assistant?"

Her eyes widened. *What a chauvinist pig!* Did she want to give him the satisfaction of an outraged reaction? Hell yes.

"I'm here to interview for the firefighter position. Not that it's any of your business."

He had the audacity to laugh. "A little thing like you?"

She seethed inwardly and longed to shift into dragon form, to breathe a column of fire right into his face. Or not. That would be a crime—in more ways than one.

She tipped her chin up. "I passed the CPAT in record time."

"Really?" He said it as if he didn't believe her. "Record time, huh? I did too. I wonder who broke whose record?"

This arrogant fecker was getting to her. She had to tamp down her anger, and quickly, before she started snorting smoke out of her nose. Revealing her paranormal status to humans was strictly forbidden. She had never done it, but she knew someone who had. Mother Nature herself had punished the offender. The Goddess was *not* someone Chloe wanted to piss off—and Gaia seemed to have a temper as quick as her own.

Injure them with kindness was an American saying she was fond of. Or was it *Kill them with kindness*? She couldn't quite keep all the slang straight, but the meanings got through.

She smiled. "It looks like you may get the position. After all, they say it's *who* you know—not *what* you know." At least she hoped she'd quoted that one correctly.

His back stiffened and he frowned.

Yup. Got that one right.

Then he relaxed and smiled, as if he didn't care. "Or I could get it because of both. What do you have as an advantage—other than your sex?"

She gasped. "Excuse me? Are you accusing me of sleeping my way into the job?"

He coughed. "No, that's not what I meant. Not at all. I just meant that your sex is *female*. As in, your *gender*. There's only one woman in the whole department right now. They may want another one so they won't be accused of gender bias."

Oh, this ass is just digging himself in deeper and deeper.

"I don't need to use that to my advantage, but it's good to know." This time her smile probably looked somewhat evil as she pictured herself punching this guy in the gut. Messing with Chloe Arish was *not* a good idea.

The door opened and the chief said, "Come in, Miss Arish."

At last. It was her turn to prove she deserved and

wanted this job more than he did…probably more than *anyone* did. And her *sex* had nothing to do with it.

———

"So, you want to be a firefighter," the chief began as he took a seat in his comfortable-looking chair behind the desk.

"Yes, sir," she answered respectfully.

"Your scores are certainly impressive. You must be a lot stronger than you look."

You have no idea. Dragons were not only very strong, they were also fireproof and healed quickly. She couldn't be better suited for the job.

"Tell me why you wish to join our band of *brothers*," he said. It almost sounded like he was trying to provoke a response.

She wouldn't rise to the bait. "Well, sir, there was a fire back in my hometown. Our small volunteer fire department took too long getting from their homes to the station, and then to the scene. I heard children crying. The garda—policeman—wouldn't go in himself and wouldn't let me in. I could have helped. I'm fast and light on my feet. I could have made it to that bedroom before the whole place went up. One child died of smoke inhalation and the other was badly burned."

Leaning forward in his chair, the chief asked, "What about the parents?"

"They were at the pub, sir."

The chief waited, perhaps looking for some kind of judgmental reaction. She wouldn't voice her personal feelings about the adults involved in the incident. Her heart broke when she saw those children.

She needed to change the subject before the lump in her throat grew too large to speak. "I've been helpin' me brother and his wife rebuild an old brownstone on Beacon Street for the past year, so this would be perfect timin'," *Get yourself together, Chloe*. She tended to lapse back into her Irish dialect when something upset her. "It was gratifying work, but it's done. I would like, more than anything, to do something even more satisfying, such as protecting the neighborhood I've grown so fond of."

Chief O'Brian's eyes lit up. "Did I detect an Irish accent?"

Feck. She had been working so hard to rid herself of the telltale accent, hoping she could pass for an American. "You did, sir. I was born in Ireland."

He grinned. "My grandparents hailed from County Claire. Where did you come from?"

She almost slipped again and said County Kerry…but thank goodness she caught herself in time. Her cousins had given her a birth certificate that said she was born in Belfast. The Ulster address grated, but she couldn't exactly be choosy.

"I was born outside Belfast, sir. But we spent a lot of time in County Claire when I was a child." Best not to share that her father's family were the Kings of Ballyhoo, Ireland—further to the south—and she grew up in a castle built into the cliffs. If he checked the history books, he *might* find her name dating back a thousand years, so she left it at that.

His expression became serious. "Belfast… That might actually help. In this job, we don't *only* respond to fires. You may see some gruesome things. Did you grow up witnessing any victims of the bombings?"

She thought back to the Battle of Ballyhoo. Her father, the king, had had to slaughter his own brother and others involved in his attempted overthrow. They'd used boiling oil as well as crossbows, swords, and other weapons of the time. Such was the way of kingdoms and family feuds back then.

"I have seen many burn victims, dismembered bodies, and the like. It isn't pretty, but that's another reason I'm motivated to prevent such tragedies."

The chief leaned back in his chair, apparently impressed. He didn't say anything for several moments. And then, "Have you ever thought about becoming a nurse?"

Ah. There it was. That bias. But how should she answer that?

"Well, sir, by the time people get to the hospital, it's too late to *prevent* these tragedies. I'd really like to do all I can to stop the situations before anyone gets hurt."

He stared at her as if he had something specific in mind. "How are you at teaching?"

Shite. If not a nurse, he wants me to become a teacher. Can't women do anything else? She was just about to go off on a rant when he steepled his fingers and continued.

"I only bring it up because we're sometimes asked to present talks to elementary school kids. Most of the guys dread those things. You seem to like children."

"Ah." *Whew.* She was glad she'd managed to keep her famous temper under control. "I'd consider it an honor to teach fire prevention to such an impressionable population."

The chief smiled and seemed satisfied with her answer. Then he shifted uncomfortably in his chair. When he was settled again, he stared at her. "There's only one position, and to be completely honest, I had thought the last candidate was a shoo-in. Now I'm not so sure."

How should I respond to that? Thank you? She opted not to respond at all. She really did feel she was the right *woman* for the job, but saying so might sound like she was playing the gender card.

"Hmmm…" The chief stroked his clean-shaven chin. "I'm going to have to give this some serious thought. Keep your cell phone on. I want to talk with someone and get back to you as soon as possible."

Hallelujah! She had a chance.

Chloe walked out into the hall and was surprised to see the Greek god still standing there.

"Sorry, sweetheart. I hope you didn't have your heart set on the position."

He's still assuming I can't do the job. Well, I'll show both of them I can. She dipped low and grasped him under his delectable buttocks. Then she hoisted him over her shoulder and swung around to face the stunned chief.

"As you can see, lifting a grown man isn't a problem. In fact, I could carry him down the hall and deposit him on the sidewalk without breaking perspiration."

The chief burst out laughing, but her hostage let out a growl and said, "Put me down. Now!"

"Sure, *sweetheart.*"

As soon as she'd deposited him onto his feet, she turned to leave. She didn't miss the furious look on his face nor the flash in his dark eyes that would have skewered her, if he'd had such a power.

"I think you meant to say, 'without breaking a sweat,'" the chief called after her. He chuckled and murmured "adorable" under his breath. Fortunately he returned to his office before any more could be said.

Ryan Fiero stared after the retreating figure of an incredibly surprising woman. She'd embarrassed him in front of an old family friend, and if it got back to his large, legendary firefighting family, he'd never hear the end of it. Even with that, he couldn't help being impressed by the slender blond.

She didn't look back as she rounded the corner. Behind him, the chief's door clicked shut.

Oh no. He wasn't about to leave Chief O'Brian with *that* as his final impression. He pounded on the door.

As if the chief had been expecting a reaction, he opened it right away. He didn't stand aside, however. Apparently they were to have their parting words right there in the hallway.

"You can't… I mean…I hope you won't consider her based on that little stunt she just pulled."

Chief O'Brian folded his arms. "Not at all."

Ryan let out a relieved breath—until the chief spoke again.

"I was already considering her."

What? "But my family… If I lose out to a girl…" He scrubbed his hand over his face. He didn't know how to finish that sentence. *They'd never respect me. Never forgive me.*

Sure, his mother would. She was a saint. Her face should be in psychological textbooks next to the words "unconditional love." His father and six brothers, however, were another story. Their Sunday dinner conversations were unmatched when it came to fire-fighting bravado.

The chief clasped his shoulder. "Look, Ryan… I have to consider every candidate who makes it this far. I'm sure you understand that. It's nothing personal."

"Nothing personal? It sounds as if you've already decided."

"Not at all."

The chief took a good look at Ryan's face, which must have been etched with worry lines. At last he lowered his voice and said, conspiratorially, "I'm going to speak to the commissioner. Perhaps we can find the funds to hire both of you."

So it all comes down to money. What a surprise…not.

There wasn't a damn thing Ryan could do about a budget. He doubted the chief could influence the commissioner—and probably, the mayor—into allotting more money, even for the pricey Back Bay neighborhood. They had recently lost two firefighters in the line of duty. He'd heard one had already been replaced, but he assumed *he* would be replacing the other.

Ryan gazed at his feet and nodded. "I understand. Well, thank you for the opportunity."

"You're not out of the race yet, boy. Something could still come from the background checks, or any number of things. I want to be fair and thorough. Don't get discouraged if there's a bit of a wait."

"I won't, sir." The chief extended his hand and Ryan grasped it firmly. The handshake felt like a formal dismissal.

As the chief's door closed, Ryan thought that maybe

he should do a little background checking too. Just in case they missed something on the blond.

~~~

"How did it go?" Ryan's mother asked at the dinner table that night. "Do we have another firefighter in the family?"

His father laughed. "Of course we do! There's no way they could turn down our brightest son." He turned toward his wife and beamed. "It's a good thing the rest of them aren't here. Don't tell them I said he was the brightest."

"Of course I won't," she said. "All of our sons have their different strengths and talents, and we love them all equally."

"So, which one are you again?" his father asked jokingly.

Ryan felt his face heat. He tried to hide it by shoveling an extra-large bite of spaghetti into his mouth.

His mother folded her hands. "So, when do you start, dear?"

He shrugged and chewed slowly.

His father eyed him. "Something's not right. What aren't you telling us?"

They waited silently, until he couldn't pretend to chew anymore, and swallowed.

"Uh, there are background checks to finish and I guess some financial stuff has come up. The chief said to be patient."

His father leaned back in his chair at the head of the table. "Ah. That's just a formality. You've never been in any trouble with the law. You're a U.S. citizen…"

As his father droned on about the reasons an applicant could be denied, Ryan had a brainstorm. The blond had an accent. Granted it was faint, but he'd heard it. And the way she'd butchered American slang… She wasn't from the USA. With any luck, she'd turn out to be an illegal alien.

"So, how many applicants did you beat out?" Mr. Fiero was asking.

Shit. Lying wouldn't do any good. The chief was his father's oldest friend and the blond would come up in their conversation at some point.

"I only saw one other…*person* when I went for the interview. There were about a dozen names on the roster taking the CPAT, but we didn't all go on the same day. They said I broke the record that day, so I took that as a good sign."

His father looked at him askance. "You didn't do anything that would tip them off about our paranormal abilities, did you?"

Ryan stiffened, offended. "Of course not. I ran the course completely as a human. How can you think I'd do anything else?"

His father nodded slowly. "Just checking."

"You've always been so competitive," his mother added. "I don't blame your father for asking, even though we believe you know better."

As always, she was playing the diplomat.

"So…about the job…" his father continued.

Crap.

"You said you saw one other candidate who made it as far as the second interview. Was it anyone we know?"

He sighed. "No. It was some woman I've never

seen before." A woman hot enough to light his own personal fire.

His father's bushy brows rose. "A female? Ordinarily I'd say you have nothing to worry about, but with only one female firefighter in the whole city—well, you know how it looks."

His mother tilted her head. "No, dear. How does it look?"

He growled. "Don't get all feminist with me. You know darn well a woman can't physically equal a man, but if it looks like the department might be accused of bias… If certain groups obsessed with equality get hold of the information, it could unfairly disqualify our son."

His mother batted her eyelashes. "Oh dear. I wonder if Gloria Steinem has heard about this yet."

"Mom. Dad. Don't worry about it. Seriously. I've got this."

His father's frown said it all. "You'd better."

COMING SEPTEMBER 2016

Acknowledgments

A huge thank-you to the people of Ireland (Dublin to Galway and the entire southern coast) who welcomed us and treated us so well. *Us* meaning my darling daughter and me. This was a mother-daughter trip. Ireland was next on her bucket list, and I told her I needed to go for research purposes. She did all of the driving in Ireland and kept us on the right side of the road. I mean the left! See? I would have gotten us killed.

About the Author

Ashlyn Chase describes herself as an Almond Joy bar. A little nutty, a little flaky, but basically sweet, wanting only to give her readers a satisfying experience.

She holds a degree in behavioral sciences, worked as a psychiatric RN for fifteen years, and spent a few more years working for the American Red Cross. She credits her sense of humor to her former careers, since comedy helped preserve whatever was left of her sanity. She is a multi-published, award-winning author of humorous erotic and paranormal romances represented by the Seymour Agency.

Ashlyn lives in beautiful New Hampshire with her true-life hero husband, who looks like Hugh Jackman with a salt-and-pepper dye job, and they're owned by a spoiled brat cat.

Ashlyn loves to hear from readers! Visit www.ashlyn chase.com to sign up for her newsletter. She's also on Facebook (AuthorAshlynChase), Twitter (@GoddessAsh), Yahoo groups (ashlynsnewbestfriends), and you can ask her to sign your ebook at www.authorgraph.com.

Strange Neighbors

by Ashlyn Chase

—◦◦◦—

He's looking for peace, quiet, and a little romance...

There's never a dull moment when hunky all-star pitcher and shapeshifter Jason Falco invests in an old Boston brownstone apartment building full of supernatural creatures. But when Merry MacKenzie moves into the ground floor apartment, the playboy pitcher decides he might just be done playing the field...

A girl just wants to have fun...

Sexy Jason seems like the perfect fling, but newly independent nurse Merry's not sure she's ready to trust him with her heart... especially when the tabloids start trumpeting his playboy lifestyle.

Then pandemonium breaks loose and Merry and Jason will never get it together without a little help from the vampire who lives in the basement and the werewolf from upstairs...

—◦◦◦—

"The good-natured fun never stops. Chase brings on plenty of laughs along with steamy sex scenes." —*Publishers Weekly*

For more Ashlyn Chase, visit:

www.sourcebooks.com

Flirting Under a Full Moon

by Ashlyn Chase

—~~—

Never Cry Werewolf

Brandee has been dumped in every way possible, but by text is the last straw. That's it—she's officially done with men. Unfortunately, she's just been told her "soul mate" is the drool-worthy hottie all her friends call One-Night Nick.

Nick has been searching for true love for one hundred years. After all, werewolves mate for life, and he does not want to mess this up. As soon as he kisses Brandee, he knows she's the one. But how will he convince a woman who knows nothing of paranormals that she's about to be bound to a werewolf forever?

—~~—

"Hot sex scenes and a breezy tone with a nice, happily-ever-after ending makes Chase's story a fun read." —*Booklist*

"It made me laugh, crafted a mystery that had me guessing, and the romance was sweet, steamy, and paranormal." —*The Romance Reviews*

For more Ashlyn Chase, visit:

www.sourcebooks.com

How to Date a Dragon

Flirting with Fangs

by Ashlyn Chase

—◆—

Let the sparks fly

Bliss Russo thought nothing exciting ever happened in her life. Until her building caught on fire and she had to be carried out of the flames in the arms of a gorgeous fireman. Sure, her apartment is now in shambles and she'll have to start her huge work project completely from scratch. But at least her love life is finally looking up…if only she can find her red-hot rescuer again.

Dragon shapeshifter Drake Cameron is the last in his clan, and the loneliness is starting to claw at him. He's met only one woman who might be able to stand the shock of his true nature. After all, she barely batted an eyelash when her home burned down. And feeling her curves against him was as hot as any inferno. Just when he thinks he'll never track her down, she walks into his firehouse—with no idea what she's about to get herself into…

—◆—

"Zany characters, sarcasm, sizzling sensuality, humor, originality, arson, dragons, passion, romance, and true love abound in this delightfully entertaining story." —*Romance Junkies*

For more Ashlyn Chase, visit:

www.sourcebooks.com

Kissing with Fangs

Flirting with Fangs

by Ashlyn Chase

———

There's something he's never told her...

When her workplace burned down, Claudia should've taken it as a sign to move on—and not just professionally. She's been secretly lusting after her mysterious boss, Anthony Cross, for years. There's no way she should agree to help him rebuild if she wants to keep her heart intact, and yet it's impossible to stay away...

The flames that destroyed Anthony Cross's beloved bar are nothing compared to the heat he feels every time he lays eyes on Claudia. But he can't have her—it's against paranormal law for a vampire to date a human. Besides, he has some dangerous enemies, and one in particular already has her sights on Claudia. He owes her the truth—both about his feelings and his vampire nature—which means their lives are about to get hotter than ever...

———

For more Ashlyn Chase, visit:

www.sourcebooks.com

My Wild Irish Dragon

Boston Dragons

by Ashlyn Chase

Dragon shifter Chloe Arish uses her wits and Irish charm to get her way in life. She is hell-bent on becoming a Boston firefighter, knowing she can work every bit as hard as a man—harder if she wants his respect.

Ryan Fiero—of a legendary Boston firefighting family—can't possibly let a woman best him on the job. He'd never hear the end of it from his father and older brothers.

But when they discover each other's deepest secret—she's a dragon and he's a phoenix—can they get themselves out of the trouble they've found in each other's arms?

Praise for *How to Date a Dragon*:

"Pure pleasure. It's like spending time with your favorite friends." —*Night Owl Reviews, Reviewer Top Pick*

"Zany characters, sarcasm, sizzling sensuality, humor, originality, arson, dragons, passion, romance, and true love abound in this delightfully entertaining story." —*Romance Junkies*

For more Ashlyn Chase, visit:

www.sourcebooks.com